Consolidation

Worlds Beyond
Book 2

Peter Apps

Published in the United Kingdom

TAUP UK
Sheerness
Kent

enquiries@taup.uk

Chapter 1

Chief Petty Officer Hammond snapped to attention as Admiral Smythe stepped into the flight cabin.

"Relax, Chief." the admiral said then grinned, "I know that was a stupid order but I really do want a quiet chat with you so do your best to comply, please."

CPO Hammond also grinned managing to stand not quite at attention.

"Your reconnaissance reports have improved remarkably while Lieutenant Barclay has been your skipper."

"Sir?"

"Lt. Barclay would be a good officer if he wasn't so damned lazy. Do I need to ask for a copy of your handwriting to confirm that you write the reports?"

"No sir."

"It's your job to fly this gasbag and his job to direct you and make the sighting reports. He gained his lieutenancy because his father has influential friends and so far he's just a dead-weight. Am I going to be the only one to breach discipline or are you going to reply honestly?"

"If you insist, sir." CPO Hammond replied, "He was keen enough to start with but he got bored. He's happy enough doing the rounds of your parties, entertaining the ladies but he won't settle to the routine."

"He will in his next appointment. Captain Harvey is ambitious and won't tolerate passengers. I came aboard to discuss your next skipper, you see he also has influential friends including the king and the Duke of Barabourne. He's fifteen, was expecting to complete another year at Dartmouth and was promoted at the king's request. He's currently attached to the Duke of Barabourne who's fourteen and is also the king's favourite."

Admiral Smythe could not help grinning at the CPO's pained look.

"It's not so bad." the admiral continued, "I thoroughly approve the appointment because they're developing a revolutionary new form of communications. It's called radio and I want my ships equipped as soon as possible."

"Ah yes sir. You mean their fathers are developing radio. You want them kept happy and their boys kept out of the way."

"No, I mean that the boys are closely involved with development and this airship will be used for the next set of experiments. Neither David nor Jimmy are the spoilt brats that you're expecting.

"There's something you need to know about His Grace. He has taken on responsibilities way beyond his age. His guardian would normally be in charge for a few more years but there are parts to His Grace's life that only the king understands. He doesn't need bed rest but he needs to escape at times. Not crashing the ship will be a challenge, it's physical, immediate, and burns off his nervous energy. He'll feel better for it when we land at Barabourne. Jimmy is a naval officer and responds well to pressure so Jimmy will respond to the demands of being a skipper while David relaxes without responsibility. You have a question?"

"Yes sir. You're calling them David and Jimmy."

I've spent time at Barabourne, it's very informal but don't be fooled, there's still order there. There's a number of boys, including His Grace who are studying under various tutors and the youngsters take their education very seriously. Surprised?"

"A little, sir."

"My orders are that, you make the safety of the airship your first priority. You will override any command that you consider unsafe. You will train Lt. Clark to command an airship which means ensuring he understands every job that needs to be done. You will also train any civilian that wishes to learn. Finally, you will treat orders from Lt. Clark concerning the experiments as requests to be carried out if you consider them safe. To be clear, once you are in the air, you will command any flight."

"Aye, aye, sir. It's a bit unusual though, sir"

"I'm ordering you to disobey your skipper. That's not unusual; it's unique."

"And it's just for a new signalling system, sir?"

"You'll understand when you see it in action."

"Yes sir." It was all that CPO Hammond could say.

"Very well. I'm reassigning your flight cabin crew. Thanks to your efforts they're ready for promotion and your present assignment will hold them back. I'm afraid that you're to train up lads from

Barabourne and two are waiting outside. To add to your problems you're to fly me there. I wish to speak to the duke's uncle before carrying on to Windsor."

"Aye, aye, sir." CPO Hammond replied though with very little enthusiasm, "May I call them aboard?"

"Chief, I'm not here to catch you out. I'd run naked through Portsmouth if it helped me get radio quicker. You're the skipper of this airship for this trip, I'm a passenger. Do what you need to do."

CPO Hammond looked through the cabin door, saw two boys waiting in the at-ease position and yelled, "You two, on board now."

As they scrambled up the ladder into the cabin he yelled again, "Against that bulkhead; at ease. You don't move or talk unless I say."

He glowered at them though he approved of their obedience but obvious interest so he continued in a lighter voice, "Airships like these can be flown by a single person in the flight cabin. There's usually a crew of three because it's far less tiring and all three can act as observers. Names."

"Clark, chief."

"Pevensey, sir."

"How come you know to call me Chief and not sir?"

"Cadet training, chief."

"Very well. Our new skipper is a Lt. Clark. A coincidence?"

"Not really, Chief." Jimmy Clark replied, "It's complicated though."

"I suggest that you leave it that, Chief." Admiral Smythe said, "I'd like to get under way."

"Aye, aye sir." CPO Hammond replied, "Can either of you navigate."

"I can, Chief." Jimmy replied, "At least a little."

"Very well. Plot a course for Barabourne. The latest weather reports are on the map table. You're the helmsman and Pevensey will be flight control. Now both positions are close together and nothing happens quickly on an airship. Just follow my directions and we'll be fine."

CPO Hammond explained the controls to David while Jimmy plotted the course as ordered.

"That lever locks the wheel while you adjust the trim or drop ballast." he was finishing as Jimmy showed him the chart, "The helmsman can steer with one hand while he works the elevators with the other. Let's see what you've got, Clark."

He studied the chart.

"You allowed for wind which is good but I'd say it would be a bit stronger at 1500ft. I wouldn't be surprised if it was a bit more southerly at that altitude as well. Pevensey, do you remember what I just told you?"

"Yes sir, er Chief. Ring for engine readiness. Raise the indicator to tell the ground crew to release us from the mast and pull the lever marked *docking ballast*. Ring down for 100rpm."

"Very well. Pevensey, release ship."

As the chief predicted, nothing seemed to happen. The airship drifted back from the mast and then the top came into view sinking down the cabin window.

"It's easy to be impatient." CPO Hammond explained, "When you're a bit more experienced, you'll want to show off, order elevators to 70° and full ahead. Just remember that it's this cabin that will be smashed when we hit the mast."

"Aren't we above the mast now, Chief?" Jimmy asked.

"Ring for 850rpm. Helm 40°. Steer 060°."

Both boys were excited, struggling to concentrate on their duties. There was no doubt that the airship was climbing and as they gained in confidence so they peered out at the expanding landscape. The CPO watched them approvingly. They were obviously more than just village boys but they were eager and were responsive. The ship turned, slowly drifting up to its cruising height and as the engine revolutions increased to maximum so the ship settled on its course.

Admiral Smythe strolled to the front of the cabin then beckoned CPO Hammond to join him.

"What do you make of them?" he asked.

"They'll do. I've had worse hands who should have been experienced."

"Very well. So do you think that you can handle Lt. Clark and the duke?"

"So it is them." CPO Hammond exclaimed, "I still don't understand why."

"About a year ago David went riding and vanished. They found his horse but there was no sign of him. You may have even been involved in the search. A few weeks later he reappeared in just as mysterious circumstances walking across a field. Now the really strange part is that he returned with an incredible amount of scientific knowledge and extremely liberal views. Surprisingly, all of his ideas seem to work. He's fourteen, needs companions his own age and the result is that those two boys are developing a communication's system that works in all weather and at night. Yes, there are engineers and scientists that understand the theory better and who are developing it even further but they are the real experts in putting it to practical use."

CPO Hammond nodded, "Yes sir. I can see that they're bright; they didn't resent me snarling at them when I ordered them aboard, either."

"They won't." Admiral Smythe said, "Remember what I said about liberal views. David should be away at school but he goes to the village school with a group of the brighter estate boys. He'll play games with any of the village children who aren't supposed to be working and everyone calls him David. However on a Sunday, he's very much the duke, everyone calls him Your Grace and everything is in its proper place."

Admiral Smythe paused, "Lt. Clark should be your skipper but he knows that he was promoted far too soon to take up his proper duties. They've both agreed to add you to their list of tutors. Again there's an exception. You must ensure that the experiments they need are carried out."

"And Lt. Clark needs a bit of rank to get his ideas across."

"That's the idea."

"It's the first time that I've had an admiral explaining things to me so I'll support them in any way I can, and that includes bawling them out if I have to."

"Good man! Do you want to see what they're up to?"

"That looks more like Winchester than Southampton down there. Let's see what the lieutenant does with navigation, sir."

As if on cue, Lt. Clark called out, "We're a bit north of our track, chief. Permission to alter course."

"Carry on. Pevensey should have been watching. Let him take the helm while you plot a new course."

"Aye, aye, Chief."

"Are you sure, Chief?" Admiral Smythe murmured.

"It's a clear day, not too much wind and no thermals. How about putting them under a bit of pressure, sir?"

"Very well. Go ahead!"

"Mr. Clark, steer a zigzag course. 20° either side of the planned course, 10 minutes each leg. Inform me when we're 10 miles from Barabourne."

Jimmy swallowed nervously as he turned back to the chart.

"Mr. Clark, we're losing height. How soon before you turn onto your new heading?"

Jimmy looked desperately around but David was already back to the flight controls and heaving on the lever. Without electricity, everything was mechanical and cables ran from the control cabin to the elevators so it took strength to operate them. A grown man could hold a steady course and maintain height but it was too much for David.

Jimmy hurried around.

"I'll do the flight desk." he said, "You get a feel for her when she turns. Turn to course 055°. In ten minutes we'll turn to course 095°. We can afford some height change while I check our position."

"Mr. Clark, I'd appreciate an answer to my question."

"Question?" Jimmy hesitated, glancing at David who nodded, "Sorry Chief, we're turning now. We're also climbing to the correct altitude."

The flight cabin was designed to be an airborne lookout post and the sides were mainly windows. The controls were grouped on desks towards the rear centre of the cabins with pillars taking the control cables and speaking tube up to an access way that ran the length of the ship. The airship design had been in use for nearly sixty years. Its main purpose was observation, able to stay in the air for two or three days so there were seats around the cabin walls which could act as bunks. There were toilet facilities which were so basic that it was unwise to use them over land. Airships had pushed development into lightweight materials and the navy used plastics that, on this world, were too expensive for general use.

There was a second stern cabin which had its own crew of three. It housed the engines driving the propellers and acted as a stern lookout. It was possible to reach the stern cabin via an access way but it was small and cramped. There was a speaking tube but it was difficult to use above the noise of the engines. During the day it was often easier to use semaphore signalling instead.

With a cruising speed of sixty miles an hour, they had been in the air for nearly three hours and both boys were becoming tired. The novelty of seeing Southern England laid out beneath them was wearing off as they tried to get used to the controls. Despite seeming to be unconcerned, CPO Hammond watched them carefully, feeling the ship's uncomfortable corkscrew movement. It was caused because they were over-compensating for the up and down movements and the simultaneous turns to port and starboard. As the voyage progressed, so it gradually eased.

"We're ten miles out, Chief." Jimmy called out.

"Reduce revolutions to half. Adjust heading to compensate. Vent the central air-bag for twenty seconds."

"Aye, aye, Chief." Again the CPO noticed how David indicated which lever to operate.

"Twenty seconds, Chief?" Admiral Smythe queried.

"I'll order a ballast drop and we can level out at 750 feet but let's just wait for now." CPO Hammond replied.

"1000 feet, Chief." Jimmy called out, "Aren't we dropping a bit fast?"

"What do you suggest?"

"Gas vents and water drops are balanced aren't they? A ten-second ballast drop?"

"How high is Barabourne above sea level?"

"I forgot. Twelve seconds?"

"Carry on."

The airship sailed serenely on, oblivious to the increasing tension that its young skipper was feeling. He was waiting for CPO Hammond to take over, unaware that the chief petty officer was watching him closely and liking what he saw.

"Adjust course so that you're flying into the wind. Fly over at one hundred feet above ground level. Don't forget to adjust to sea level. Keep the airspeed to 10 knots. We'll fly over once, circle round and land. Be ready to respond to my orders. Call out any ballast drops or gas vents."

"Aye, aye, chief." Jimmy snapped back but still wanting the chief to take over.

He was sweating profusely as he gave his orders, and followed his own.

At one point he called out "Port 20."

"Allow for the slower speed, Port 30." CPO Hammond said quietly and Jimmy nodded.

A few minutes later the chief called out, "Vent five seconds gas. Drop the anchor."

Jimmy looked startled but obeyed.

"Ground crew are signalling, 'Cable attached'. Reduce engine revolutions. See if you can hold it stationary relative to the ground."

The anchor was simply a long cable with a loop on the end. They would not have made the flight if the ground crew had not been in place. It comprised of a crew with equipment on trailers hauled by traction engines. A platform could be set up and a mast erected to dock an airship. The ground crew had run out their own cable to connect to the anchor.

The airship hovered as the ground crew wound in the cable, taking in the slack.

"Stop engines." CPO Hammond commanded, "The flight crew is relieved. Line up. Atten SHUN."

Startled again, both boys obeyed.

"A competent officer could have made this flight single handed and kept station with other ships. You, Pevensey! Why do we have such large windows for this cabin?"

"So that we can have lookouts looking for the enemy, Chief."

"Many officers think it's so that they can strut around, telescope under their arm impressing the girls or a passing admiral."

CPO Hammond allowed them a moment to giggle before calling them back to attention then continued, "You are not experienced, you have a lot to learn and you, Mr. Clark, do not kid yourself that you can navigate. Don't worry, that can all be learned and you're already better officers and crewmen than many I've seen. You cooperated and helped each other, you listened to what I said, and you learned quickly."

He glanced towards Admiral Smythe before continuing, "If you want to learn to fly one of these then I'd be pleased to be your instructor. However, I do mean *your instructor* and you will obey orders. From now on, I expect you on parade at 6am for an hour's physical training. We'll try for training flights for at least six hours a week. I'll inform Petty Officer Thwaites that he's got two volunteers to clean the burners. Tomorrow will do, immediately after PT. Then you'll have the rest of the day for your other work. Questions?"

"Yes Chief." David said, "I've got friends that want to join in the training but some can only visit at weekends."

"I take it that they're at school or something."

"Or something, Chief. I'm sorry but I can't explain everything yet."

"Understood. Anything else?"

"Darren's only eleven."

CPO Hammond smiled, "Midshipmen don't start until they're twelve and even then, it's college. You struggle with the controls at fifteen. We'll see what we can do, though."

The ground crew's indicating that we're secured so you're dismissed. Go before I change my mind."

"I believe that they're preparing accommodation for you." Admiral Smythe said, "Is there anything that you need?"

"No sir. They know what to expect and they're keen enough. Let's just see how it goes."

"Very well. Is PT at 6am really necessary?"

"For a couple of weeks then we'll fit it in with their usual schedule. Today they were on their best behaviour. It won't last so let's get them used to a bit of discipline. I was also thinking about that physical release."

"It sounds reasonable. Carry on!"

CPO Hammond strolled round to find the Petty Officer in charge of the rear gondola.

"Having fun hobnobbing with admirals, are we, Chief." PO Thwaites grinned, "I saw your new crew, they're a bit young, aren't they."

"And they're reporting to you, tomorrow to learn a bit about the engines. I've told them that they're on burner cleaning but you can give them any dirty job that you can find."

PO Thwaites looked surprised, "I didn't think that you'd want your crew with dirty hands before handling all those maps."

"One of them's our new skipper. The other is a duke who's all pally with king, but they don't seem so bad. I've known worse and they want to learn, so on board, they're just ordinary seamen."

"If you say so, Chief. Five quid says they'll run at the first bit of hard work."

"You're on. They've got PT at 6am tomorrow with orders to

9

report to you immediately after. Let's see if you can put them off."

"You sure? You say one of them's our new skipper."

"Remember their ages but don't make any other allowance for them."

He might have said more but PO Smith, the petty officer in charge of the ground crew was waiting for him. A boy of about thirteen was standing beside him.

"This is Billy, Chief. He'll show you to our cottage and then explain what they're doing here." PO Smith saw CPO Hammond's look and grinned, "I know. They're all kids but they know what they're doing with the practical side and there are adults around, but most are scientists or engineers."

Meanwhile, David and Jimmy had greeted their friends who had excitedly watched the airship's arrival. David noticed his uncle Jethro, who was standing with Admiral Smythe, also watching but from a discreet distance and hurried over.

"I'm beginning to see a disadvantage in radio." Admiral Smythe grinned after David had greeted his uncle, "It seems that I'm no longer required at Windsor but I'm to organise trials as soon as possible and I'm to send daily reports."

"We've got mobile equipment which we can use. The problem is, it's going to be harder if we're modifying the airship while using it for tests."

"Let's start with the trials. Can you handle another ship and crew here?"

"I don't see why not. Jimmy might have some problems though." David replied.

"Explain."

"Jimmy understands what we're doing. How will a fully experienced officer feel about treating him as senior?"

"Airships are not the most popular assignments for young officers. Even if there's a battle, airships can do little more than observe so there's little chance of glory, even in war. I'll make sure that he understands and you might benefit from an experienced officer. In return, he should be happy to realise that he is being noticed."

"David, I'd like a quiet word in the library, please." Jethro said.

Once they were settled, Jethro continued, "I don't pretend to understand your other tasks but aren't you neglecting them for a new fad. I know that airships are exciting but you mustn't forget your other responsibilities."

"I'm not Uncle." David replied, "We're waiting for the spring equinox on the stone circle world and Billy visits regularly, Danny and Darren have problems but they're coping."

"Very well but you're putting Billy in moral danger from what I hear." Jethro continued, "Just what is it between him and Cradawg?"

"It's nothing unusual on their world." David replied, "He looks forward to his visits so I just don't know about stopping him."

"Just remember that you have a responsibility to your people. Look out for him."

"I'm more concerned about his brother. Billy gets him to help in my offices but he just freezes if he sees me. I thought that we got on all right the night he arrived, but apparently he was confused by being rescued. Now he thinks that if he steps out of line, Billy will be sent away as well as him."

"Very well. I'm a little concerned that Godfrey and Isabella may not be waiting for the marriage bed but your mother seems to be encouraging them. What about you and Olivia?"

"Are you looking for something to worry about?" David asked.

"No, not really. The dukedom is in good hands but it would be embarrassing if you gave the rector ammunition for one of his sermons so be discreet. You say your other-world friends are having problems remaining in the background at home. It's a different sort of discretion but it is a problem."

"Yes I see." David said, "First, Billy is not your usual servant. I could feel very sorry for Cradawg if he upset him. I'm still following Wilson's advice over Godfrey and Isabella. I'm keeping my mouth shut, my wallet open and I'm leaving it to Mother. If Isabella did get pregnant, then it would be harder for her father to withdraw his consent. I did buy condoms from Danny's world but I haven't used one yet. Olivia and I both want to, but Olivia's parents are pushing her to catch me and it puts us both off."

David paused, "Darren is suddenly more interested in airships than cars or computer games, and is studying our hot air engines rather than their petrol engines. Danny and Darren are tending to do more by hand rather than with computers. As you can guess, they would be laughed at if they tried to explain why. It's not so much being discreet but hiding a large part of their lives."

"I think that you've given me too much information about your private life." Jethro laughed, "I needed to do the guardian talk and I am reassured so I won't even bother warning you to be careful. Go and play with your airship."

David found his friends being shown over the airship as Darren struggled to move the elevator lever but it was Danny who took David to one side.

"Social workers are nosing around." he said, "They're usually desperate for Mum to take in a kid but now they don't even ask. Mr. Barton reckons it's because we've all changed. There's a mystery about where Todd is and I fouled up.

"Don't get annoyed, Craig Williams has been learning Morse code and we practice together. He's into spy-stuff so he loves knowing a secret code. I told him it's to do with our steam-punk and he wants to know more. I told him no chance and that Mr. Barton and my Dad wouldn't let him anywhere near you all the time you both want to take a pop at each other."

David nodded, "It leaves us covered so I've got no problems with that. What did he say?"

"The steam punk sounds like fun but I just don't like the way that he, meaning you, thinks that he's so much better than us." Danny repeated, "I just said that you're not like that but I couldn't explain why, could I, so it sounded a bit lame."

"Anyway, he's good at Morse code and you know how boring Mr. Fraser's lessons are. Well we started tapping Morse code to each other. Would you believe it, he could read it. Luckily we were talking about football and not about him but we got a lunchtime detention and he wanted to know what we were talking about."

"How come he could read it?" David asked.

"Apparently he was in the Navy and was one of the last to be trained in wireless telegraphy. I said that we were into steam-punk and would be trying out some new gadgets over the holiday but I don't think that he believed us."

"Do you know anything about him?"

"Not really." Danny replied, "He did say that he regrets not signing up for longer though."

"I remember him and I didn't like him much." David said, "He could be useful but even if we got him a commission over here he'd regret moving or that he was in the navy instead of the army this time, or something."

"Yeah, you could be right. Sorry though."

David shrugged, "Don't be. Ken Rogers at the forge can't keep up with your Dad's orders from Ebay. Godfrey takes a load by steam tractor and trailer to the lane on this world, your dad drives up on yours and the portal makes a vehicle to vehicle transfer. It's amazing and I don't understand how it's done but it happens. You visit every weekend and nothing else has gone wrong."

"I still can't get used it though. You a duke for real, visiting a place like this, it's unreal and me travelling to other worlds. I thought that Darren was going to wet himself when the airship arrived. Mum and Dad are weird though."

"How so?" David asked.

"She won't let us cycle to the portal, Dad or Mr. Barton has to drive us. She reckons these lanes are too dangerous to cycle along but doesn't say anything about portals or airships being dangerous."

David laughed, "Maybe it's as well. I want to go up to town for a few days. I need to speak to the Electrical Committee. If you're on half-term, do you want to come? Godfrey is even more involved in his road vehicles and Todd still seems to be teaching our experts about electricity."

"Cool!" Danny exclaimed, "Are we flying there?"

David glanced towards the corner of the house.

"It's a thought. There's Todd and a couple of footmen with the radio." David replied, "That part is easy if we use batteries from your world but we need to install one of Godfrey's generators and run the cables. It's safe enough inside the gondolas but we're a bit worried about sparks. Anyway, I'll speak to Jimmy."

Jimmy was talking to CPO Hammond when they found him.

"How are you coping with us all, Chief?" David asked.

"You're all keen enough but it's young Darren, sir." the petty officer said, "What's this helium, he keeps talking about?"

"You're officially one of my tutors so call me David. Danny, what do you know about helium?"

"It's a gas, the second lightest gas after hydrogen but it's completely stable, it doesn't combine with anything. You can get hydrogen from water and all sorts of rocks but helium just drifts upwards into space so it's difficult to find."

"Yet Darren thinks that you can."

"He's been bending my ear about it, too. Apparently it's created deep down towards the centre of the Earth then it seeps upwards and gets trapped in pockets. It might be another project to find it unless you're going to develop aircraft with wings."

"Not yet." David replied, "Jimmy, I need to go up to town for a few days. Could you fly us there? Chief, I know you wanted to get started on our training but it is important."

"You can still report at 6am tomorrow. With the skipper's permission, we'll leave at 09:45hrs. We're due to start testing this new wonder signalling system at 10:00hrs so we're due to fly anyway."

CPO Hammond paused, "If I'm a tutor then I should remind Lt. Clarke that it's the skipper's job to vacuum the landing crew at St. James park to be ready for us. You need to work out our estimated time of arrival and include it in the message."

"If the King is at Buckingham Palace, I can radio Lt. Worthington to warn the crew." Jimmy replied, "It'll be a ground test for the airship equipment. I'll plot the course."

CPO Hammond looked puzzled but did not respond. He remained puzzled as the equipment was set up and Jimmy tapped out his message. Puzzlement became bewilderment when he started writing in response to a series of clicks from the apparatus.

"Good, he is there." Jimmy exclaimed, "I'm sending the details now."

The clicking and tapping continued until Jimmy turned to CPO Hammond and said, "We can expect the latest weather report from them at 10:15hrs, Chief."

"From London, when we're airborne." CPO Hammond said seeking confirmation."

"That's right, Chief."

"Very well, Skipper. This time Mr. Pevensey will be a passenger so we need a crew member. Could I suggest young Darren? They'll only be short hops and between us we could supply the muscle power if he needs it."

The following morning proceeded as planned. He watched, impressed as the boys duly reported for their PT session and then

David and Jimmy reported to the engine gondola for cleaning duties. He summoned Darren, to have radio explained; one advantage of so many youngsters being involved was that they could speak at a level that he understood. As the airship took off, it quickly became obvious that Darren was not big enough to handle the controls and he was almost in tears with disappointment.

"Skipper, you take over and I'll handle both stations." CPO Hammond said, "Start teaching Darren navigation."

Darren looked much happier and after that, the flight was uneventful. The first thing that Danny noticed when they disembarked was a slight smoky, sulphurous taste to the air. It was not severe and he quickly got used to it as he also got used to the dirty, sooty façades of the buildings.

"Are you sure that you want to walk?" David asked and Danny nodded though when a horse drawn Hansom cab trotted past he nearly changed his mind.

"I keep forgetting how different your world is." he said, "Steam lorries and horse drawn cabs are so cool. I'd like to ride in them all. "

"I'm glad that you could come with me." David said, "I did have a reason for asking you. I've never forgotten how your mum helped me and how the government helped her. We've got nothing like it and we're supposed to be the richest country in the world. If someone were to get lost here then the assumption would be that it's because he's too lazy or too stupid to help himself."

Danny nodded, "Go on."

"I suppose that we would call them alms but you know Jamie's story. Most donate a few pounds and think that it's enough but it isn't. There's none of the checks and backup that exist on your world."

"I think you're great." Danny said, "You're paying for those warehouse conversions for the homeless and you're paying for tools so that they can earn a living. Can you do much more?"

"Not really. I'm getting more opposition than support from my fellow peers. Lord Carlton and his cronies are stirring them up a bit but the general attitude is I'm just encouraging more people to live on handouts."

"I've heard it on my world." Danny replied, "How can I help?"

"Sir Douglas Mayhew is a good man." David explained, "Father liked him as well and his firm has been our family solicitors for years. However, he's a bit old-fashioned and doesn't understand what it's like to be poor or homeless. He'll do his best to appoint a good man to run the warehouse schemes but he'll appoint a businessman not a care worker. I want to look around to make sure that there're no problems and I'm hoping that some of your mum's knowledge has rubbed off on you."

"I'll do my best but you should have brought Billy or his brother."

"You know what's possible. I know that this sounds so snobby and I like Billy but everyone will assume that he's just a servant and it gets wearing explaining the situation."

Danny laughed, "I know what you mean but am I so much better?"

Before David could reply, another voice called out, "Hey Pebbles, how are you doing, old sport?"

"Oh God, I'm sorry I said that about Billy." David muttered as he turned to greet the stranger, then in a louder voice he replied, "Hello Markham. How are you?"

"Absolutely tops. And you? How come you didn't join us at school as you planned?"

"One or two things happened and I have tutors."

"Do you know? Ginger said that you go to the village school with the oiks."

"It's true I do go there for some subjects but I have tutors for others. It's working out quite well." David replied

"Bloody hell, what makes you go slumming like that? I tell you what, send your man on, we'll find a café and you can tell me all about it."

"Thank you." Danny interjected, "I can't believe that I look grown up enough to be called a man but it was nice of you to say so."

Markham stared, shocked and confused.

"I'm sorry but I haven't seen you before." he said eventually, "We should have been introduced before I spoke."

"Danny, May I present the Honourable Miles Markham. Miles, may I present Mr. Daniel Lambert." David said.

Miles recovered fast, "One of your less reputable friends,

16

Pebbles? Well never mind. We can still find that café and you can tell me all about it. I don't suppose you're keeping up with events so have you heard about this new electric light. Everyone's trying to get it installed but the list's so long. Father's speaking to a couple of friends on the commission."

"I think that they're giving priority to the worst smog producing areas." David said.

"Pandering to the masses. If they spent less on gin and more on looking after themselves, they'd be able to afford decent coal. Did you know, some do-gooder's giving them free accommodation. Shall we go?"

"I really don't have time." David replied, "We've just arrived by airship and we need to change. We're visiting the Electrical Commission ourselves this afternoon and times getting on."

"Surely your uncle knows people there. I know you're the duke but they won't listen to a boy like you."

"We'll see but it would be bad form to be late. I'll present my card soon."

"Very well. Please call soon." Miles replied as he took his leave.

Danny looked quizzically at David, "You didn't tell him anything. Why not?"

"I think that I learnt more, just by listening."

Danny nodded, "OK, how does presenting a card work?"

"I'll call and leave a card. If he wants to talk, then he'll be at home. If he doesn't want to talk to me, or he really is out then I'll bend the top left corner to say that it was just a social call. Between you and me, I'll do my best to call when he's out."

"Gotcha. Now why does he call you Pebbles."

"*Pevensey* Bay, there's a beach and on the beach ..."

"Gotcha again. It's a bit feeble isn't it?"

"Well you've just seen him."

"Gotcha."

David grinned, Danny was good company and just playing with the word 'Gotcha' had cheered him up.

They reached the town house and enjoyed the meal waiting for them before changing. This time they did hail a cab to take them to the commission. There was a small crowd waiting in the foyer but they strode past and into the conference room. Danny almost felt the angry or jealous eyes boring into his skull but inside, they were greeted cordially.

The chairman, Sir Gerald Bartlett greeted them.

"You've no idea how popular electric light is." he said, "We could all get rich on the bribes we're being offered. His Majesty is insisting that the worst polluting areas are equipped first and insists that we are guided by expert opinion. What you call the pilot schemes have been working for a month now and the initial results are promising.

"Our main problem is resistance in installing it all. I'm coming to appreciate just how difficult some people's lives are and can see why they resent us disturbing what little they have."

"But you do see that we have to reduce coal consumption amongst the biggest users of sea coal?" David said.

"Yes of course. Our brief is still to prevent smogs. His Majesty would be most displeased if we allowed electricity to become a toy for the rich as you once, so charmingly put it."

David grinned before becoming serious, "Very well. Another of my schemes involves tackling homelessness in London. Some have all sorts of problems but there are plenty who would respond to help. I think we might consider courses in maintenance and installation. I'm thinking that they might explain it all to their own class better than you or me."

"That is what I wanted to discuss with you." Sir Gerald exclaimed, "We're hampered by lack of equipment and by lack of electrical artisans. The Treasury is offering start-up loans to as many firms as possible to start producing what we need and if you approve training schemes which could eventually become apprenticeship schemes then that is our second problem tackled. It must all be a drain on your resources though."

"It is in the short term." David replied, "However, we hold the licences and the patents and we have years of new projects to develop so we should do very well in the long term."

"Even so, I'll see if I can convince the Treasury on the need for training and see if they can't help to bear the load." Sir Gerald replied.

"It would help." David agreed, "I get accused of being too egalitarian but I am aware of the differences between the classes. I'm also aware of how we all mistrust each other. Solving that problem might break down a lot of resistance."

"Indeed it might, Your Grace." Sir Gerald replied, "Let me know if I can help."

Chapter 2

To Danny's relief, a messenger arrived, summoning them to the king. He was never bored on this world but he had nothing to contribute to the discussions and he was restless. Once again though, he was aware of the anger and jealousy as two mere schoolboys were escorted to an ante-chamber. He was also a little nervous as he tried to follow David's example and kneel for the monarch.

"Relax, Danny." Charles VII exclaimed, "It's good to know that His Grace still remembers how to behave though."

Danny grinned, "Back home, I've stood outside the gates but that's the closest I've got to royalty before."

"We do understand and it's David who must remember that he's a mere duke and so, low down in the order of precedence."

"Yes sir." David laughed.

"Very well. Enough teasing. David you may relax too. That was an impressive use of radio in arranging your trip. What's Todd's phrase? Ah yes, is everything still AOK?"

"Yes sir." David replied, "The commission now fully supports us and we're well ahead of schedule. I'm more concerned with some of my other projects."

"Ah yes, preventing the great decline," the king replied. "We must admit, we can see how much effort is wasted in maintaining our ranks at the expense of everything else but it's making it apparent to others that is so extraordinarily difficult."

"Yes sir, but you deal with those who have most to lose." Danny piped up.

"An extremely good point. How long can you remain in London?"

"I'm on half-term. I need to get to school on time next Monday. I wish you could command it to let me stay longer."

"We have to accept that our divine right is limited to one world." Charles VII laughed, "However, what do you know of helium?"

"Darren is the real expert." Danny replied, "You should speak to him."

"We are speaking with you at present." King Charles paused, "Our apologies. You simply meant that Darren is a greater expert.

Can you explain why?"

"He's got a real thing for airships. You should have seen him struggling with the controls but he wanted to fly it so much. He's learning as much as he can about them."

"Very well. What you call aeroplanes will eventually replace airships but it is in the hands of a stable hand who is far more concerned with marrying way above his station. Godfrey is responsible for developing engines is he not?"

"He's focussing on carriages and tractors, sir." David explained, "None of us have really thought about aeroplanes. Godfrey needs projects that will be immediately profitable to provide an income suitable for Isabella's rank, though."

"You've interrupted our conversation with Danny and you have contradicted us. Never mind that you've contributed useful information, you have breached court protocol."

"Yes sir. I'm sorry." David replied.

"We were not censoring you but explaining the problems we have at court. Helium was mentioned during our visit to Barabourne and we did ask for a report. Send for Darren please, is he on this world?"

"Somewhere above it." Danny laughed, "He's in the airship being taught to navigate."

"Instruct it to leave him here on its way home." The king paused, "It's thanks to you boys that I can give such an order. You Danny, probably don't realise how incredible it is to be able to divert a ship that is nowhere in sight."

The king paused, "David, I wish to induce a few heart attacks among my stuffier courtiers so it would be better if you weren't here. Your friends have a natural politeness which I enjoy and you all have a knack of getting things done. I hope you don't feel too insulted."

"The portal reminds me that I can't do everything, sir." David replied, "I wonder if you could do something for me though. Could you ask the Honourable Miles Markham and Lord Markham to assist me."

"Certainly but I wouldn't have thought that you would have wanted them involved in your schemes."

"I don't but I want to check a few things out and I'd like to be discreet. I don't think that anyone would like a duke snooping around, I'd never pass myself as homeless but a downtrodden servant might work."

"You could send one of your friends."

"I'd like to see for myself." David replied, "Lord Markham will deal with the immediate problems and it leaves me free to play. At least that's how the portal described my time as Jimmy's servant."

"He shall have it by special messenger this afternoon. We will make it clear that you are acting on our instructions and that we expect absolute discretion."

"Thank you, sir."

It was the following day that David called on the Markhams who were unusually excited by his visit as David was hustled into the library as quickly as was polite.

"It'll be an honour, Your Grace. How can we help you?"

"I need to visit places around London quietly. I need you to appear to be the one actually making the visits with a young servant in attendance who you don't treat well. I will be that servant."

"You sir. Why would you need to forget your station in such a humiliating way?"

"I'm afraid it's confidential except, if I don't go incognito, I won't get the information I'm looking for and I'd have to let myself go for a month before I could fit in."

"I see." Lord Markham said, "You wish to be in disguise as a spy for His Majesty."

It was close enough for David so he nodded.

"Very well but I do not normally have a servant in tow."

"No, it's not usual which is why you get so annoyed." David explained, "You've brought me along to carry some packages and I'm anxious to help and keep getting in the way. You tell me to get out of your sight or something which gives me a chance to look around."

"If I may say so, it is a little contrived." Lord Markham said, "Do not offer explanations. The background story would fit if I told you to wait somewhere and you just wandered off. Now why am I in this place, where ever it is?"

"You're interested in electric light and you're determined to get it. You're going to see what's so difficult about installation, you also want to bully the firms involved into supplying you."

"I'm not sure that I like the word *bully*." Lord Markham

remarked.

"Those who don't like you, call you pompous and overbearing." David said, "Those traits could prove useful, especially if they were emphasised. I apologise if I've annoyed you but I shudder to think what people say about me behind my back."

It was the first time that David had seen Lord Markham laugh or see any warmth in him.

"I understand and I do know what people think of me. We're going down towards the river in the East End. It can be pretty dire in those parts." Lord Markham said.

"We're installing electricity in areas that use the most sea-coal." David explained, "They tend to be poor but not the poorest."

"Ah yes. Smog." Lord Markham exclaimed, "It does disrupt business. I shall be at my most pompous and overbearing best."

David grinned, "Tomorrow morning then? I'll report to you at 10 o'clock as you ordered."

"Don't be late, boy." Lord Markham grinned back.

David was surprised. He would also have described Lord Markham as pompous and overbearing who would struggle to be sociable with any commoner but instead he found a warmth in the man which made him seem a completely different person. Miles had listened intently but had contributed nothing and David guessed that he was just not interested. Little did interest him unless it was the next social event.

The next morning David arrived dressed in boots, heavy serge trousers, worn and torn at the knees, a thick woollen jacket and a peaked but otherwise shapeless cap. He stood waiting beside a steam car as Lord Markham hurried down the steps to pause, apparently glaring at David. The effect was spoilt though only David saw him wink then glance down at the door handle. David got the idea and opened the door for him before climbing in beside the driver.

"Watch that dial and feed the coal." the chauffeur rasped, "Can you do that?"

"I've done it before." David said, "This car's enormous, though."

As the car pulled away, the chauffeur saw that David knew how to spread the coal evenly and relaxed.

"It's too big for London." he said, "I may as well be driving an omnibus but His Lordship likes to be noticed."

David grinned. While the back seats were enclosed in a comfortable carriage style compartment, the front seat was only protected by a windscreen and the seat itself was little more than a hard wooden bench. It was still February and the weather was changing for the worse. Sleet turned into snow and David was pleased for the heat from the boiler.

They drove steadily on until the chauffeur pulled up and leapt out to open the compartment door.

"As I said, My Lord, the roads are too narrow from here on for this thing."

"No matter." Lord Markham replied, "I'll take the boy in case I need any errands."

"Yes My Lord." the chauffeur replied.

"Walk beside me boy." Lord Markham commanded and David dutifully obeyed.

"I don't use that old steamer much but I thought that it was suitably pompous and overbearing for today." Lord Markham explained.

As David grinned, Lord Markham snapped, "Don't grin, I don't share jokes with errand boys. You didn't consider transport or why we should be walking here and this weather works to our advantage. You can sneak off somewhere to get warm.

"Now, you've set up temporary generating stations on barges while the main generators are being built. The barges can then be moved to new locations as required. I am interested in electricity so I will allow myself to be shown around and then I will also visit a factory of mine that is nearby. I shall return to collect you because I have some boxes that need carrying from my next port of call. Does that suit?"

"Yes it does." David replied, "I should seem unprivileged enough."

"Quite. We're nearly at the place you mentioned so drop back, and walk about three paces behind me."

Lord Markham was enjoying his part in events though David was less happy as the cold and the wet snow seemed to seep through his clothes. They arrived at the junction of several roads. In other places a roundabout would grace the centre but here it was just an empty space ringed by market stalls, known as St. Justin's Circus.

"Wait here." Lord Markham commanded and strode off. In his

expensive clothes he was conspicuous as he strode through the crowd and enough had heard his order to David who was getting colder by the minute. He did not have any money and he looked longingly at a stall selling hot food.

"That sort just don't care." a voice said, "Come and stand by the brazier."

David turned to the voice, a stall holder who beckoned him over.

"I bet 'e's snug and warm by now." the stallholder said holding out his hand, "I'm Jeremiah."

"David."

Jeremiah looked at him suspiciously, "You don't do 'ard work. Your 'ands are too soft."

"I usually work in the house." David replied, "It's a long story but suddenly I'm an errand boy."

"Lindsay, are you staying open?" Jeremiah asked.

"Course I fucking am." the stall holder exclaimed, "This fucking cold snap and me selling kindling and lucifers. Course I fucking am."

Jeremiah grinned, "Don't be shocked by 'er language. She's got an 'eart of gold. No one's going to be buying knives in this weather so 'elp me with this tarpaulin. I'll buy you an ale and you can entertain me with your long story. Lindsay, look out for David's toff, will you?"

Soon a small group were seated around a table and a tankard was set down in front of David.

"It's only small beer so it's not very strong. Now let's hear what you're up to."

"OK!" David said, "It's true I live in a big house and it's true that suddenly I'm an errand boy. I think you've guessed though, it was a set up and it turns out that Lord Markham is a better actor than I am. You see, I really want to talk to you and I find people talk to me better if they don't know who I am."

"So you want to spy on us and I've just bought you a drink."

"No, I want to talk to you. It is important that I hear what you have to say."

"Then you'll say we've got it wrong and tell us what to do."

"It's to do with smog." David said, "It kills thousands, especially in districts like this and it brings everything to a standstill.

It's caused by all the cheap coal that's being burnt and smoke getting trapped in the atmosphere."

"Go on." Jeremiah said, "I'm listening and I want to see where you're 'eading."

"The plan is to confine coal burning to places where they can build chimneys high enough for the smoke to get carried away. We want to start by replacing your gas and oil lamps with electric light and later by electric heating as well. I want to know why you don't want it."

"You want us to be honest. You be honest with us. Who are you?"

"David Pevensey, Duke of Barabourne." David replied.

There was a startled silence which was interrupted by a big man, with a scar down his cheek and a broken nose who approached to hover over David. He was carrying a heavy stick with a solid brass handle and holding it more as a weapon more than a walking stick. The other customers looked on, some nervous and some expectant.

"The Duke of Barabourne?" he asked in a surprisingly gentle voice, "I'd be right honoured if you'd shake my hand."

As David stood up he added, "May I buy you another drink?"

"I'd be delighted." David replied, "Have we met before?"

"No sir, but you saved my older son from Dartmoor though you don't realise it."

"No. I'm sorry."

"It was last Christmas. Chris had gone up West. He had spent all his money on booze and was trying to walk home. The cold and the booze got to him so he passed out and was picked up by the bobbies. You rescued your boy and looked after the rest."

"I see. Please will you join us?" David said, "Again there's something that I want to understand. May I ask some questions?"

"Go on." the stranger said cautiously.

"You say he faced Dartmoor. Had he been in trouble before?"

"I'm not giving you no details."

"I think you've answered yes and that's all I need. Now they were held for a few days. Why didn't he explain what happened."

"He was beaten for speaking without permission and didn't try again. My turn. Why did you go to so much trouble for them?"

"Jamie and Billy were brothers and orphans. Billy came to me

26

as a boot boy but we became friends and now he helps with my work. He wanted to find Jamie so I helped."

"You're a duke, this Billy was a boot boy and you became friends. Why?"

"Last year I hit my head, lost my memory and wandered off. I spent time in an orphanage then a nice family looked after me until I remembered enough to get home. I think I see people differently now."

"I've heard parts of the story." the man said, "I'm Cooper Tamzon. Now tell me why we should let you set us up to pay more to be warm."

"Smog interferes with everything and it's getting worse. Imagine if it got so bad that everyone tried to clear out of London. Electricity will be free for a while but when it has to be charged, it has to be priced better than sea coal to do any good."

"Fair point. Does that justify your men breaking into homes and doing what they like?"

"That shouldn't happen." David exclaimed, "Tell me."

"Some of your men don't like it but they're on piecework." Cooper admitted, "They tell me that they get paid by the house and the law isn't interested."

"You understand that I don't have a magic wand, don't you." David said, "I suppose everyone promises to do something so it won't mean anything if I said I would try."

Cooper nodded slowly, taking in what David said.

Just then a girl rushed into the bar and yelled, "The nob's back."

"Will you give him a message, please. Will you ask him to come over and join the Duke of Barabourne and his friends."

She mouthed the invitation then satisfied that she had got it right, curtseyed and hurried off. She curtseyed again and delivered it, obviously accurately enough for Lord Markham to hurry over.

"They know who you are." he gasped.

"They do." David replied, "It seems that the electrical workers have been breaking into homes. You look like someone that people should listen to. Could you go and explain that from now on victims will have Sir Douglas Mayhew representing them and action will be taken against their firms and themselves individually. I don't know if any of these men will accompany you but you could also explain that anyone who prevents a breaking-and-entering will also have my support."

"You wish me to be as pompous and as overbearing as possible, I take it." Lord Markham replied, "Am I still acting under His Majesty's instructions?"

"I think so." David replied, "It's still to do with introducing electricity but this is not a problem we expected."

"You may be surprised to learn that despite my reputation, I disapprove of bullying or intimidation so I'll be happy help. Would anyone care to join me?"

Cooper stood yelling, "Skevi, get over here. You look after His Grace. He doesn't need trouble, get it?"

A young, well-built man of about twenty hurried across, answering, "Yes Dad."

To David, it seemed as if Lord Markham marched off like a general leading his troops into battle but David was satisfied. Even Lord Markham looked as if he was enjoying himself when they returned.

"They got the message and you're right. The message is going up the ranks far faster than it would have come down. We should go. Your work is done for now."

"Yes, you can go, but I might find rooms and stay the night. I really do appreciate your help so perhaps you'd dine with me one evening."

"It would be my pleasure but I'm not sure about leaving you though."

"He'll be safe enough, sir." Cooper replied, "I owe him for saving Chris."

"I'll be all right." David said, "There are things that I need to do, though."

"In that case, good day to you all."

"'e's not bad for a toff." Jeremiah said then paused, "You want us to forget that you're a toff so you don't count."

David grinned, "You're learning. I'm converting warehouses into cheap accommodation for the homeless. I want to see how they're working."

"Skevi. Go and find Tommy Dawson." Cooper commanded, "What's this about rooms?"

"I'd like to spend a night in one of the warehouses to see if they work."

The crowd around him was even more friendly than before, impressed that David had tackled a problem so quickly and Tommy had no idea who he was talking to when he arrived.

"It's OK lad, we're not going to eat you." Cooper said, "We want to know about the warehouses. Can we put up our young friend here up in one?"

"Go for the Stable Row one but try to avoid Mrs Hawkes. Don't go to Dorrit Street."

"How long were you out of work?" Cooper asked.

"Nearly a month." Tommy replied, "They'd just opened so no one really knew what was going on. They set me to doing the alterations, the food was good and the bed was clean. Mr. Jones let me stay when I got another job but charged me full rent. When he reckoned it was enough to find rooms, he gave me back half. I like him."

"What about Mrs Hawkes?" Cooper asked.

"She reckoned that he wasn't keeping the books properly. Not fiddling them but like with my rent, it didn't show up or something. He fed folk that showed up at the door but they weren't booked in so food was unaccounted for and it worried her."

"That's the problem." David said, "I like the sound of Mr. Jones but what about the next guy who really is fiddling? I should visit."

"No." Cooper said, "You did right getting the adults to sort out the trouble. I reckon you'd do more good as the duke at Stable Row. Now Tommy, what about Dorrit Road."

"I don't know." Tommy replied, "What's going on?"

"We're giving David here a lesson in the real world and we don't want him getting into trouble."

"It depends what sort of trouble he wants." Tommy replied, "He could become one of Mr. Dobson's favourites. There's a rumour that he fences stuff as well."

"Sit." Cooper snapped, placing his hand on David's shoulder and pressing him down as David tried to leap up, "You're our responsibility now and you're not going to go charging into trouble. Tommy, how sure are you?"

"Like I said, it was all starting off. I reckon the bosses are trying but they've got a wrong 'un in Dobson."

"Why do I hear so much about boys being attacked?" David asked, "Surely girls are more at risk."

"Like your maids in your fancy houses?" Cooper asked quietly, "I know, they're all safe with you but look at that couple over there, they'll be off finding a quiet alley soon. That's normal so why talk about it. Now imagine if it was two blokes."

David nodded, "It simply attracts more attention. I also happen to know more boys than girls."

"Is it really safe to talk in front of him?" Tommy asked.

"Go on." Cooper said, "Let's get it all out in the open."

"There's this magistrate. They say girls get lighter sentences if they agree to go to his *special* school. Blackie helps, providing he gets the boys."

"PC Blackman." Cooper snarled, "I'd kill him myself, if I wasn't sitting with a magistrate that is. I take it that you sit on the bench."

"I was nominated to replace my father but I never sit."

"So David, are you ready to run or are you going to have a shot at sorting some of this out?"

"Is the magistrate Sir Cloudsley Pomfret-Smythe?" David asked.

"Do you know him?" Tommy asked suspiciously.

"Only from when we reported him to the Lord Chancellor's office but we didn't know about this. I guess I'm hoping that there's only one of them."

Cooper handed Skevi some money.

"Take David up to the main road, hail a cab and stay with him until he's home." Cooper said, "If we've got your backing we'll speak to Mr. Dobson. Don't worry, we won't harm a hair on his head - if he listens to us."

"Fair enough. I'll see what we can do about that policeman and Sir Cloudsley."

"Yes I think you will. One more thing, if you try to come here alone then I'll tan your hide. It's not that safe around here."

David grinned, "I understand. Thank you."

"You've got guts, kid." Cooper added, "We'll make this electricity thing work. Don't you worry about that."

David was always concerned that he was being manipulated, unsure what the portal could contrive and what was a real coincidence. Later it would seem like a remarkable coincidence that as they trudged through the narrow streets so they heard a police whistle getting closer. Suddenly a youth of about seventeen dashed past them, stumbling against David in his frantic haste to get past. The policeman wheezed into sight, losing the struggle to catch the boy. He stopped, gasping for breath but suddenly grabbed David's wrists. Before he understood what was happening, David found himself handcuffed.

"You'll do." he said, "Let's see. Obstructing a police officer in the course of his duties and letting a felon abscond will do for a start."

David felt uncomfortable as the policeman felt around in his pockets but was more shocked when he pulled out a necklace.

"Thieving as well are we? That'll do nicely." PC Blackman said before turning to Skevi, "You tell your dad that I'll settle for 6 strokes of the birch if you're at the station tomorrow for 10am. That should do for accessory after the fact. If you don't turn up, I'll come looking and who knows what I'll find on his stall."

Skevi looked helplessly at David who gave a quick nod. Skevi turned and hurried off. PC Blackman pushed David in the direction of the police station. He was scared, but he trusted Cooper Tamzon. PC Blackman led him to a bare windowless room with just a table and two chairs locking the door behind them before removing the handcuffs.

"Strip." he commanded.

"I demand to see a solicit ..." David began but was interrupted as a blow to the head made him stumble. PC Blackman pulled the belt from around his waist

"Disobeying a police officer in the course of his duties – six strokes. Strip or I'll make it twelve."

David reluctantly obeyed. It occurred to David that PC Blackman was enjoying his reluctance and nervousness so he undressed slowly, calmly folding his clothes over one of the chairs before turning to face PC Blackman, hands unconcernedly by his side. He gulped as he was told to bend over the table and his legs were kicked apart.

It was worse when he felt the policeman's hands on his buttocks before they slid between his legs.

"Nice." Pc Blackman murmured as he straightened up, "Let's

31

get business sorted out and then we'll have some fun. At least, I'll have fun. It's up to you whether you enjoy it or not."

David heard a whistle, a slap on his backside then a fiery pain streaking across him. He endured two more before he screamed and burst into tears. He tried to straighten up but PC Blackman pushed him back down.

"You stay there and you don't move." he snarled, "I'm going to write out your statement for you. Don't worry, you won't have to read it or sign it. I'll do it all for you. Shouldn't you thank me for saving you all that work?"

David remained silent and PC Blackman slapped him hard on the bruises that were forming.

"Thank you for saving me all that work. Constable." David whispered, "I appreciate it."

"What a nice polite boy you are." Constable Blackman smirked, "If I remember, I'll bring some water as a reward."

"Thank you, Constable." David whispered.

David was scared now as well as in pain. He was sure that Cooper would do something to help but he was not sure if he would be in time for it was obvious that PC Blackman was planning on raping him and the thought terrified him. He thought of hiding beside the door and bringing a chair on the policeman's head when he entered. The problem was the table was in full view of the inspection hatch in the door and if he was not sprawled over the table PC Blackman would know that he was up to something. It seemed like days and it was a few hours before the door opened. He tensed, almost losing control of his bladder.

"David!" Danny shrieked, "Are you all right? It's OK! You can stand up."

David flinched, pushing Danny away when he tried to help but it was enough to stir him. He pulled himself up and looked around before pushing Danny back again as he sat back on the table. It was only then that he realised that Cooper Tamzon, Lord Markham, Skevi, and Miles Markham were also in the room. Sitting on the table should have been painful but all he could feel was relief.

"Come on, David. Let's get you dressed." Danny exclaimed.

"It's too late for me to feel modest. I want a bath and fresh clothes." David replied then pointed to his old clothes, "I want them burnt."

David shuddered, "But not yet. I need them for court tomorrow."

"Don't worry, my boy." Lord Markham said, "There's no question of you facing court on these trumped-up charges."

"Yes, I must. It's a chance to get Sir Cloudsley."

"Forget it." Cooper snapped, "You've done more than enough. Let someone else deal with it."

"You thought I'd run. Now I'll see it through. Let's see what happens."

"Hang on, Pebbles." Miles suddenly interjected, "Why does it have to be you? Father said the name on the statement was Robin Cashman and this Robin had committed dozens of other crimes."

"Go on." Lord Markham said.

"Well unless Pebbles and this Robin bod are twins then it could be anyone being dragged into court tomorrow. I'll do it."

"No way." Danny exclaimed, "Where I come from that would be so wrong."

"He's right." David exclaimed, "Look what happened to me."

"I don't know where you came from young Daniel but here, in time of war, you could all find yourselves commissioned and leading troops into battle. It won't do Miles any harm to suffer a little hardship and danger." Lord Markham turned to Miles, "You do realise that it's not going to be a game?"

"Pebbles' arse told me that, Father." Miles replied, "I was supposed to be measured for a new evening suit ready for Lady Stanton's ball but this is a teeny bit more important isn't it?"

"A very teeny bit, lad." Cooper smiled, "Your dad should be proud of you."

Miles smiled but looked decidedly nervous now that he was committed.

Cooper turned to his son, "Skevi, Danny is about David's size. Take him down to Silverstein's. Go round the back and knock on his private entrance. Tell him that we need a complete set of clothes for a gentleman, urgently. Also tell him that I'll settle on Friday and that there'll be something extra for his trouble."

Lord Markham opened his wallet and took out five £20 notes.

"Will this be enough?" he asked.

Skevi took two of the notes.

"You're not in Harrod's now sir. Come on, Danny."

33

"Another son to be proud of." Lord Markham said to Cooper, "It was clever arranging those diversions to keep Blackman busy. You must tell me the full story sometime but perhaps not in a police station."

Cooper grinned and left the room returning moments later with a terrified, young constable in handcuffs.

"We hear good things about you, Constable Pritchard, so you're safe with us however you answer." Cooper said, "Which laws are you going to defend? The ones that say we're assaulting police officers or the ones concerning perverting the course of justice?"

"If you're going after Blackman then I'll help you. The bastard should hang."

"This is a sub-station manned by you, Blackman and PC Croft." Cooper said, "You've got rooms upstairs."

PC Pritchard nodded but as he began to speak, Cooper said, "Don't tell us. If you crossed Blackman too much, then you'd lose your job and your home."

PC Pritchard smiled but stayed quiet.

"What about PC Croft?"

"He replaced Ian Jarvis and only been here a month. I think he's OK but he doesn't want to be found in an alley like Jarvis."

Cooper removed the handcuffs and handed PC Pritchard some keys.

"Make it business as usual but no-one is to come back here. Understood."

PC Pritchard nodded, "What about PC Croft?"

"That's your first decision, son." Cooper chuckled.

"I'll put him on the front desk." PC Pritchard said, "My second decision is that I'm coming back here. At the moment you're all vigilantes but if you assist me with my enquiries …"

"Good man." Lord Markham exclaimed.

David was still sitting naked as everyone returned.

"I'm not dressing until I've had a bath." David snapped, "Stop fussing around me."

"We've got a bathroom upstairs." PC Pritchard said, "I'll send Croft up to light the boiler and show you to my room. You can rest there."

"He'll be all right." Cooper said, "He's just got to deal with what happened to him."

"Very well. This young man is going to stand in for David and face court tomorrow. Now how come, he's not going to identify himself?"

"Normally, PC Blackman has him for the night so he'll be in no mood to argue tomorrow. Tomorrow he'll be sized up by the court jailers and if anyone wants a piece of him he'll be brought back here for *further questioning*. The court's a bit too public even for them. When everyone's finished with him, he'll be sent onto Dartmoor. By the time he's released no-one will be interested in his stories."

"What can Miles expect tomorrow?" Cooper asked.

"He'll be stripped and groped a few times. They won't be searching him but deciding on how much they're willing to offer Blackman. Highest bid goes first, lowest bid gets what's left, you see. If he looks at them wrong, he'll be beaten. If he tries to speak, he'll be beaten. Let's face, if they're bored, he'll be beaten. It would have to be pretty important before I volunteered."

"I agree." Cooper said, "There has to be a better way."

"Miles, it's your decision." Lord Markham said, "You didn't know how far this corruption went when you first volunteered. You may withdraw without any shame."

"Noblesse oblige, Father." Miles replied, "We expect the masses to respect our position, this goes well beyond pampering them and expecting them to stand on their own two feet."

"Very well. PC Pritchard, I suggest that you take Robin Cashman into custody and do what you have to. Erm, obviously you are no PC Blackman but he needs to learn his place. I mean ..."

"Father's worried that if you don't rough me up a little, I'll cosy up to Sir Cloudsley and invite him for drinks at the club." Miles laughed.

"Blackman likes hurting people but he reckons humiliating them controls them better." PC Pritchard said, "If prisoners cause trouble, we can strip them, turn the hose on them and keep them there while they wash themselves with strong lye soap. It's meant for delousing, and it stings, I mean really stings especially when you're soaping your more private parts."

PC Pritchard paused, "We warn them that they'll go into court in prison clothes, smelling of the lye and probably in chains if we still don't trust them. They look like hardened criminals which doesn't help. Now, if someone was really protesting about mistaken identity and we didn't want to believe him ..."

Miles removed his jacket and tie, then started unbuttoning his shirt while PC Pritchard tried ushering the others out.

"No." Miles called out, "David wasn't allowed his dignity. Let's do it properly."

When David came down later he looked a lot better as he stared at Miles who was wearing thin cotton trousers and shirt, both of which had black and white hoops around them. He was handcuffed with his ankles chained as well, together with a chain linking the two sets of manacles. The smell of lye filled the room.

"Miles?" David asked.

"Don't speak to the prisoner, please sir." PC Pritchard said, "He's ready for court tomorrow."

David looked at Lord Markham who said, "It's his way of helping. Let him follow it through. Now that you're here, we can put him in his cell and interrogate Blackman."

Soon, PC Blackman was standing in the room, he wore his uniform trousers and a white shirt with his hands cuffed behind his back. He turned to Lord Markham.

"I don't know how you've become involved, sir but these low-lifes are in a lot of trouble. I assume that they burst in here to rescue Cashman. Did you arrive on other business?"

Lord Markham called David over, "Do you know this boy?"

"Yes sir. He's Robin Cashman. He's a well-known thief and pickpocket in these parts. I'm sorry that he's caused you so much inconvenience."

"I say that he's David Pevensey, Duke of Barabourne and that we visited Mr. Tamzon today to discuss problems with the installation of electrical supplies."

Blackman visibly paled as the implications sank in.

"His Grace, understands that there is no shame in his behaviour. Indeed, he volunteered to continue the charade to ensnare others. He will testify to your shameful and disgusting acts towards him. My son is standing in as Robin Cashman now and in due course he will testify against those who abuse him. You all face sharing prison with others who you've abused and I'm sure you'll be confessing all in the hopes of easier sentences."

"Could I just escape?" Blackman asked, "I've got money to

cover expenses."

"It's a funny thing." Lord Markham laughed, "You been caught by smogs. His Grace has been commissioned by the king to end them, and you are one of the obstacles to the local people trusting the authorities. I doubt whether you have enough for us to defy the king so blatantly. It can be a funny old world at times, can't it."

As Blackman was taken away, David said, "I am ashamed. I was too scared to argue or even move from that table. I just left my arse on offer."

"I watched Miles as he was treated like a troublesome prisoner. He stopped being the silly boy he pretends to be and became meek and obedient. He said that he was not going to be ashamed but as control slipped away so did his confidence."

In a world without telephones or the Internet, no-one outside the police station knew what was going on. The real Robin Cashman was shocked when he was arrested just before midnight as he was setting out on that night's burglary. His protests that his dues to PC Blackman were up to date, did not help. He did not calm down until the icy cold water sapped his will to continue and he found himself in a cell, dressed and manacled like his alter ego.

Chapter 3

For Miles the experience was every bit as bad as PC Pritchard suggested it would be. Later he would describe how he heard a young girl begging and crying before hearing a very loud slap and a scream. He also explained the bruise on his cheek.

"They asked my name when I arrived and I tried telling them the truth. They didn't hit me when I said Robin Cashman."

Miles described his court appearance so well that David could imagine being there. He was led up into the dock and left standing until the clerk of the court asked his name. As ever, Sir Cloudsley showed scant regard for proper procedures.

"The Honourable Miles Markham." he replied.

Sir Cloudsley glared at him. "A gentleman would not need delousing or be wearing prison clothes and he would certainly not need manacles to appear before this court. The clerk of the court will ask one more time and if you lie again you will be taken down for six strokes of the birch."

Miles looked at David, "I lost my nerve. I forgot about Father and the rest of you being nearby and could only think about David's arse, the bruises I mean and how it must have hurt. I told them Robin Cashman."

"That's better." Cloudsley said more calmly, "Are you going to waste the court's time further by pleading not guilty?"

Miles just shook his head.

"Very well. For lying in this court, 6 strokes of the birch. It can be administered while waiting for transport." Sir Cloudsley looked at his papers, "Ah yes, there's a request that you be kept for further questioning into the murder of PC Jarvis. You will be kept in police custody for a week before being transferred to Dartmoor to serve twenty years hard labour."

Miles shuddered, "I was down the stairs and in the cells before I could gather my wits. I thought about demanding to see Father and David but it's a horrible experience and I froze. It was almost a relief when they started the birching. I should have stopped them touching me but I couldn't. I'm still feeling bad about it but the van driver brought the bids so I've identified another."

"I'm sorry about the birching." Lord Markham said, "We

didn't know about it otherwise we would have intervened."

"I would have let you at the time." Miles said, "I'm not as brave as David but now I'm glad you didn't. It doesn't seem so bad because it achieved something."

The following day PC Pritchard filed his reports. Nothing happened except an Inspector visited a day after.

"You're only a constable." he said, "I know these people are important but they've let you get carried away. There's enough to ask PC Blackman to resign and you should rewrite your reports according to this draft that I've brought along."

"I've orders not to do that, sir." PC Pritchard replied nervously.

"I'm your superior." the inspector exclaimed, "No-one else has the authority. Just do as you are told."

"I can't, sir." PC Pritchard almost squeaked in his nervousness, "I have orders from the king."

As he spoke, he took an ornate letter from under the desk and handed it to the Inspector who read it with increasing shock and disbelief.

"So do you intend to keep PC Blackman under arrest? Am I under suspicion?" the inspector asked.

"I don't know. I don't even know who's taken over the investigation. My orders are to carry on as usual."

"I see. I didn't like my orders and I'm glad that you've got such powerful backing. Just out of curiosity, what's happened to the real Robin Cashman?"

"He'll be held here for a week then transferred to Dartmoor according to the sentence. All of Sir Cloudsley's cases are being reviewed including his. However, Blackman has indicated that there's more between them than a simple bribe and he might deserve twenty years anyway. Even so, he'll probably be released when his case is reviewed but I'm quite happy for him to be out of circulation for a time. It'll give me time to put together an honest case and arrest him properly."

"I could almost feel sorry for him." the inspector said.

"Not when he frames kids, that lot liked the look of."

"Is that your assessment, *Constable?*" The inspector asked, "Or is it somebody else's."

"It's mine, sir. I say good riddance to Cashman." Constable

Pritchard replied, unperturbed by the inspector's reminder of his position, "Maybe I shouldn't speak badly of our superiors but a lot are going to get what they deserve as well."

"You are out of order, Constable, but let's hope you're right. Carry on and good luck. Just out of curiosity, are they just going after a couple of rotten apples in London, or is it nationwide?"

"Honestly sir, I don't know but I get the feeling that two impeccable witnesses is something of a breakthrough. They've not been so lucky elsewhere."

"A pity." the inspector replied, "Still, I suppose that they've got to start somewhere."

Both Miles and David felt humiliated by their experiences They tried to talk to each other but it was not easy. In desperation, David tried talking with the portal.

This experience was not part of your training. Interference possible. Have you learned by it though?

David thought for a moment, "You say that our world is declining. It's rotting away within and I didn't realise how far it had gone."

And about yourself?

"Despite my rank and position, I'm still a boy. I'm as vulnerable as Freddie was with Brian Allen."

You and your friend Miles had hope, and reason for experience. They gave strength. Freddie had neither. His experience was worse.

"I see that." David replied, "I should stop my friends travelling. I don't want them to have a similar experience."

Friends understand risks. You less cautious on own world. See how Miles reacts to journey.

"What? To another world. He's too much of a clown. I wouldn't take him."

Clowns play. Play would be good for you. His experiences also bad. Perhaps knowing would help.

"You're saying that it would be some sort of therapy. The king has summoned us so I'll think about it until we get back. What did you mean by possible interference?"

Creators have enemies. Enemies know portal technology. Manipulating people like Blackman, their style. Usually need time though. Caution necessary.

"So it was a trap. The whole idea of going to St. Justin's Circus was a scheme to get me."

No! Opportunity; exploiting weak point; luck, all possible descriptions. Strength of friends showed weak point not weak enough.

"I don't like it though."

No. You receive language and information when you travel: facts. Enemies play on emotion. Harder to use unless subject willing. Creators need to explain but unable to visit now. You have trip to palace. Be wary of enemies and trust your friends. Business as usual.

David was not happy about the revelations but there was little he could do as he and Miles prepared to see the King. There was a sense of expectancy when David and Miles arrived at the palace. Most courtiers hoped that David would finally be put in his place.

"Our court is not pleased with you." King Charles said sternly, "It feels that you pander to the masses and forget your peers. Please do not meddle in affairs that do not concern you. Legal matters arising from your last escapade require some discretion so we must continue this discussion in private."

As soon as they were alone in the ante-chamber, the king held out his hand to Miles.

"That was very brave of you and I wish I could recognise it publicly." he said to a startled Miles, "Unfortunately, one of the curses of helping David is that much must remain hidden. You know the areas where these animals preyed, perhaps you don't know that two pubs have already been renamed the Duke of Barabourne so at least some recognise your efforts. I meant what I said about meddling in affairs that don't concern you but this business did and you did well. David, two magistrates as well as Sir Cloudsley are about to be arrested, so are several senior police officers of various ranks. "

The king paused inviting them to sit.

"So far as our court is concerned, your sin was in making it so public." he continued, "They couldn't quietly go abroad on holiday until it all blew over. Your complaints of sexual assault and intimidation are not going to go away."

"I still don't understand, sir." David said, "There's nothing in the news and it doesn't seem as if anything is happening."

"We've been trying to stop this corruption for years and I'd say that it was part of the great decline you talk about. I'd already called in investigators from Scotland to find out why work on installing electricity was delayed but without success. Your approach was far more successful but your arrest opened the door to a far wider investigation. We've got two witnesses who cannot be bought off and the case is not going to collapse. The gentlemen in the other chamber know that there's an investigation in hand. They do not know who is doing it. Many of them are scared that they'll be next to feel the long arm of the law on their collars."

"So it's being kept secret to help the investigators and it's a lot bigger than we know but how did you get to hear about it so quickly, sir?" David asked, "No-one really knew who we were and everyone thought that it was this Robin Cashman being convicted at last."

"You underestimate your friends. Those at St. Justin's Circus started a near riot to keep P.C. Blackman busy while young Skeffington Tamzon's ride across London to find Lord Markham is already the stuff of legends. Lord Markham may be a conservative by your standards but he is no fool. He had my instructions to assist you and he sent word that you had been arrested in peculiar circumstances. I sent agents to observe and intervene if necessary but you all had your own plans. The only real mistake you made was relying on PC Pritchard's superiors to deal with it. An agent made contact and insisted on him making copies of everything."

David grimaced, "So you've seen reports on what happened to us."

"I've seen reports on two young boys who should have been protected by the adults responsible for them. It was not your failure but theirs. You were helpless then but it's your betrayers who are in your power now."

David nodded as the king continued, "I've sent your friends home. I think I'm fully briefed on helium. Killing you or Miles would be a bad mistake but frightened people are desperate and not necessarily rational. You should take Miles to Barabourne and stay there. Be careful who you trust. Admiral Smythe might seem like an ally but his interest in girls is being investigated because of the shadier individuals he seems to associate with. I don't know what Miles knows of your other adventures but you have a hideaway that might be worth using."

"I think we'll be safe enough at Barabourne, sir." David exclaimed.

"You signed witness statements and doubtlessly, copies have fallen into the wrong hands by now. I'll send agents to look out for you but I'm ordering you to stay within the legal boundary of Barabourne."

So far, Miles had been listening, enthralled but now he repeated David's lead in saying, "Yes Your Majesty."

"We wish that we could recognise your efforts because you may have saved our realm from rebellion. You may be aware that there is considerable unrest in the industrial cities and mining areas in the North. Agents have picked up on allegations of similar corruption as well as the notion that it is enough to be thought of as a union agitator to be sentenced to long terms of hard labour."

David felt as if he should respond but the king continued, "Factory owners and mine owners will resist any change and may well support their own rebellion so I have inherited a very volatile situation. Word of your activities is spreading through union pamphlets and owners who accept your ideas are doing very well."

The king paused again, "Though you may not realise it, you are calming the situation enough to give us a breathing space. Don't worry, this is a matter that doesn't concern you so you shouldn't get involved but you deserve to know how successful your efforts are."

David could almost feel the agents closing in on him as he boarded the train but he had to concede, he had not spotted one.

"David." Miles said when they were alone on the train, "What was that about staying within the legal boundary and what hideaway have you got?"

"Finally, you've dropped that stupid nickname." David said.

"It just seemed strange hearing His Majesty calling you, David. So, what about this hideaway?"

"You got involved in my stuff and ended up getting birched." David replied, "You don't want to know anything else."

"I've got a terrific story for the chaps at school. I've had tea with the king and now you've got this mysterious hideaway. You're fun to be with. I want to know all about it."

"It's too dangerous." David said, "Stick to what you know. It's safer. I'd stop Danny and the others visiting if I could."

"Now that just adds to the mystery." Miles laughed, "I know

Danny's an odd bod but where does he visit from?"

"LEAVE IT!" David yelled, "I'm sorry. I've got others to worry about and I've got things to sort out."

Miles stayed quiet worried about David's anger and wondering how much worse David's experience had been. David contented himself with walking from the station. Miles noticed the familiar way in which the locals greeted them but seeming surprised by David's surly response. However, the exercise cheered him up and he spoke in a much friendlier way as they neared the hall.

There was nothing dignified in the way they arrived at the hall. To Miles, it seemed as if they were mobbed by a gang of teenagers but at first, David cheerfully accepted it.

"I should have been there for you." Godfrey said, "I'm hardly behaving like your protector any more."

David shrugged, "You couldn't have done anything. Skeffington knew what to do. That was, stay quiet and get help; he also knew his way around London. If Blackman had worked out who I was before Lord Markham and Cooper Tamzon arrived, I'd have had my throat cut and it would have been made to look as if the locals had turned on me."

They made their way inside to be greeted by Wilson who said, "Welcome back Your Grace. Is your guest a West Wing or East?"

"Just show him to his room and see that his bags are unpacked. Don't you dare question ..." David tailed off, "I'm going to lie down. I do not wish to be disturbed."

The boys glanced between Wilson and Jethro who had just come out of the library.

"All of you. Come through to the library. You too, Wilson." Jethro said, "Make yourselves comfortable. Miles, we're very informal here so let me explain."

Jethro recounted the events of the previous year. He omitted mention of other worlds but there was still enough to make an impressive story.

"I've heard of his hideaway. That's where he gets all his information from. His Majesty seemed to suggest that we'd be safer hiding in it until the trial." Miles said.

"It might be an idea." Jethro said, "He takes too much on and it's wearing him out. This latest escapade certainly isn't going to help."

"And we're having this conversation with two farm hands and a boot boy. I'm surprised that the butler hasn't sat down."

"It's easier to clip your ear if you get too cheeky, Mr. Markham." Wilson replied to general laughter though Miles glared angrily at him.

"As you can see, the staff are terrified of us." Jethro chuckled, "However, I've yet to find a situation that they can't handle and that's down to Wilson. Now let's hear your story."

In his turn, Miles recounted events in London.

"I knew that Father and Cooper Tamzon were nearby but I was still scared that something might go wrong. David didn't know if help was on its way or not."

"Then please excuse his rudeness everyone." Jethro said, "He needs plenty of rest."

"Mr. Markham might have an interest in riding." Wilson said, "He might encourage David to show him around."

Miles glanced at Billy, "Will the boot boy see that my boots are ready each morning?"

"You look after David and I'll do it." Billy replied.

"Father and my older brother would have heart attacks if they saw this gathering." Miles explained, "Give me time to get used to it all, please."

"The West wing is David's mother's domain." Jethro said, "You may be more comfortable there."

"Yes but David's adventures start here, don't they. There's this big secret about his hideaway."

"You can come with me." Billy said, "You've got more of a toff about you. Bran might take to you more."

"It's a bit risky there." Jethro said, "The Spring Equinox isn't so far away. Isn't there going to be trouble?"

"Nah!" Billy exclaimed, "Cradawg's followers are the top ones since we fixed the screens in the ring. Iain and Megan are regarded as Elders because they appear every day to greet visitors but disappear every night to shag in their room upstairs. Bran wants to murder me because me and Cradawg is so close. If he's planning something, then he's going to try to wreck the Spring Equinox festival. If I've got a servant who knows what's what, then there's less point in killing me."

"What are you talking about, boy?" Miles snapped, "Sorry,

45

but I didn't understand a word of it."

"There's a situation where Billy's life might be at risk." Jethro explained, "He thinks that there'll be less risk if he has a successor that can just continue his work."

"It's not all work with Cradawg." Billy smirked, "He'll be happy to sit and discuss politics and philosophy with you though."

"Oh!" Miles exclaimed, "I think that I see what you're talking about. Cradawg isn't a young girl's name, is it?"

"No, and I'm not sure that I approve of their relationship." Jethro said, "Are you still keen?"

Miles smiled, "It sounds like the devil of an adventure. Seriously though, is this Cradawg really an invert?"

"In his culture, it's the duty of adults to teach children about life, including the pleasures and he sure has taught me a lot. He's happily married, and his wife and his children love him. I told him about Blackman and he offered to lend me his castration knife. You see, Blackman was about taking his own pleasures and denying them to the kids.

"No-one castrates people." Miles gasped, "Are they gypsies or something?"

"I don't think it's been used in centuries." Billy explained, "He was just so bloody angry at what happened to you and David. He reckons you're a hero though because you offered yourself to smoke them out. He says that he'd be honoured if you seeded one of his children."

"God in Heaven." Miles exclaimed, "Er are they boys or girls?"

"Both so you can choose." Billy chuckled, "I explained that you wouldn't understand his offer because on our world it's for you to ask permission and it's a solemn event."

"Asking for her hand in marriage, you mean." Miles said, "That was clever."

"You could ask for *his* hand, if you preferred." Billy chuckled.

"That'll do Billy." Jethro said sternly, "Miles is not interested in that sort of thing."

"Look! That world is like nothing what we could imagine." Billy said, "Yeah, it's dangerous, but in case you haven't noticed, so is London. If he wants to come, fine, but it won't be one of Her Graces' tea parties."

"I see that." Miles said, "I'd still like to go but I'm not that much of a hero. I didn't think that they'd even pull my trousers down until it happened for the birching."

"Yeah and you could have yelled for your dad or someone." Billy said, "You didn't and we got more of the buggers."

Miles smiled his thanks, "Very well, when do we go?"

"Tomorrow at dawn." Billy said, "You'll be wearing just shorts and t-shirt for most of the time but wear something warm that you can slip off. If someone takes a fancy to you and you like them, go for it."

"Really Billy." Jethro said, "You'll scare the boy off."

"It's what David doesn't understand." Billy said, "They don't just turn a blind eye to more, they think differently. It's all right to be shy or nervous but if you just reject them or seemed to be offended then it's an insult. A couple of times I've said that I belong to David and Cradawg and I can't handle any more. That's OK because I'm not saying that I don't like them."

"It's a bit primitive, isn't it?" Miles asked.

"They're more complicated than you realise. They can teach us a lot about electricity. They've even got holographic TV." Billy paused, "It's to do with electricity and I'll save it as a surprise."

Miles nodded thoughtfully. His school chums and their families thought that all sorts of groups were inferior. It was not prejudice so much as the superior feeling that their class helped to rule the largest empire that the world had ever seen. Billy and Godfrey were just servants, gypsies were horse traders who knew little else and so on. His perception of the world had been jolted by Cooper and Skeffington Tamzon. They came from an inferior class but had saved him from a member of his own. They were also both obviously intelligent and easy to talk to.

Billy might just be a servant but again he was obviously intelligent and being left to ... That was the trouble, Miles still was not sure what this hideaway was, who the people, Billy was talking about, were or how Billy had got to know them so well.

Miles liked David because he was popular yet he did not like the bullying and general oppressiveness of school. Despite David's own opinion that he took part in the bullying, Miles noticed that David chose his moment to divert the bullies before things got too rough. It seemed a more effective approach than direct confrontation.

47

Like any fourteen year old, Miles thought about sex. Amongst his school friends the general attitude seemed to be that girls would beg to service them. David however spoke politely to any girl he met, irrespective of position.

Miles himself, stayed out of trouble by being the buffoon that no-one took seriously. He stood back from the bullying by seeming unconcerned and cheerfully flirted with any girl not believing that she was interested.

The problem was that he had come to believe his own image of himself so it had come as a shock to realise that even men could be so interested in him. He was sensitive enough to see that he was being talked about in the same way that his friends talked about girls. It was unpleasant to be on the receiving end, yet an inferior like Billy seemed able to have an affectionate relationship with the most unlikely or unsuitable partner. He also realised that he had badly underestimated David who had been laughed at for *hiding* on his estates rather than mixing with his peers. David wasn't hiding, he was doing things that made adults listen to him.

He had a few days of the half-term break left and he could spend them aloof from the activities at Barabourne or he could become involved and his life would never be the same again. It also occurred to him that he had the king's blessing to stay for some considerable time. However, if he stayed he would probably become the boot boy's assistant.

The others were looking at him as if waiting for a response.

"Very well. I suppose after spending a day as a hardened criminal I can cope with anything. What about David though, won't he be annoyed that I've gone charging off with Billy."

"He'll be furious so we won't tell him until we're back." Billy said, "He expects us mere commoners to use our initiative though and I reckon that you'll be good for him when he calms down."

Just then the door opened and David came into the room.

"I suppose Miles knows about the portal and visiting other worlds by now. I should have taken him to mother."

"He knows about it because you've just told him." Billy chuckled, "I'm going to take him to see Cradawg tomorrow but he thinks we're going to some gypsy encampment."

"Miles, I said that you weren't to get involved. Billy, you're no longer welcome in the house. Move to the stables for now."

David yelled.

"That's enough, David." Jethro snapped, "You've made it clear that Billy is his own man so you do not complain if he offers his friendship to Miles. You didn't mean to but you've involved Miles in your adventures so again don't complain that he's volunteering for another."

"This is still my house ..." David began.

"David, you've discovered that you're as vulnerable as the rest of us." Jethro said, "Billy's brother was broken by those people; you're not broken but you've been hurt. I've said before, not even adults always know when they need help and you're not yourself even if you don't realise it."

David relaxed a little, "I know. I seem to panic if someone looks at me wrong and I keep getting angry for no reason. How about you Miles?"

"Imagine if you were at school; I can't believe that no-one's laughing at you because you say you're scared. Your Uncle's not saying, 'Be a man, boy. You need to move on'. Father and I knew that they were going to look but I was a prisoner and I couldn't believe what else they would do. I just wanted to bathe afterwards too. If you're going to admit to things, then I should. I volunteered for it as if I wanted it and I feel ashamed."

"If I may say so, young sir, it's pointless telling you that you shouldn't feel bad." Wilson said, "You won't believe it. Maybe you should accept that you saw an adventure but didn't believe it could go so badly wrong. It's a lesson all youngsters have to learn and you're no different."

Miles nodded, "Thank you. That does help. I've had an audience with the king which was not something I expected and I've got this trip with Billy to look forward to. I'm just going to watch though. I'm not going to volunteer for anything."

"And that is a lesson, ordinary soldiers quickly learn." Wilson said to a ripple of chuckles around the room, "Godfrey, Billy and you other boys, the rest of the estate does not need to know the details of what happened. It is sufficient to say His Grace is unwell and is not to be bothered. You may well be angry with me, Your Grace, but you have charged me with keeping order. The staff will be happier knowing that there's a reason for your behaviour and you need not bottle your feelings up."

David did feel another flash of rage but just as suddenly it vanished leaving him depressed so he contented himself with a curt nod.

"David," Danny said cautiously, "Are you dining with your mother tonight?"

"No. Why."

"Why don't we ask Mr. Barton if he'll take us for a coke and a pizza at the Blacksmith's Arms. You, Miles and me, I mean."

"I said that Miles shouldn't become involved. Doesn't anyone listen to me any more?" There was a hysterical edge to David's voice which worried everyone."

"Miles isn't going to sit back and ignore everything that's going on." Danny said, "My world's the safest one of all and Mr. Barton's not going to hurt anyone."

"NO!" David yelled still with a hysterical edge, "I'm burying the portal. It's got too many people hurt."

"Like who?" Billy asked, "Iain and Megan would be dead by now. That whole Roman World was going to be wiped out. Todd's talking about becoming a doctor. He had fat chance of that before. If it hadn't been for the portal, the smogs would have carried on killing folk, PC Blackman and Sir Cloudsley would have carried on. Hell, it was that Robin guy who set you up, wasn't it. If you hadn't been there, some other kid would be looking at 20 hard."

Billy paused, "Stuff happens. I bet a good few of the female staff know how you're feeling too because it happened to them before they came here. Barabourne is probably one of the safest places in the country for any servant and it's because of you and what you learnt through the portal. The real question isn't whether you should close the portal, it's whether you can cope with the fucked-up world we've got."

David stared at Billy, fury gradually being replaced by despair. He ran out of the room, sobbing.

"That was well said, Billy." Jethro said, "I'm afraid that you're visiting at a bad time, Miles."

"I was warned what could happen and father wasn't that far away. David was taken by surprise. I wasn't and it helps that I've got all this new stuff to take in."

"If I may suggest, My Lord." Wilson said, "You take Mr. Miles, Master Todd and Master Danny to dine at the Royal George.

Master Danny should fire up the brake."

"I'm afraid that my luggage hasn't caught up with me yet." Miles said, "I won't be able to dress."

"In case you haven't noticed, none of the lads are even wearing ties." Jethro said, "We'll treat it as your first night at sea. You need not dress and perhaps Todd could lend you some clothes. He's closest to your size."

"No problem." Todd said, "I don't like going back but I like to know I can so I order my stuff on-line and Danny's dad delivers it."

"Order it on-line?" Miles queried.

"It's our world and it's all ordinary for us." Todd grinned, "You won't be the same again but at least you'll understand why Darren gets so excited by airships."

"You two fit in being chauffeured in a steam car. Danny and I will change into our steam punk gear." Todd exclaimed, "You can drive over there, Uncle Jethro."

"David's not going to like it." Jethro said.

"I shall explain, My Lord." Wilson said, "I shall point out that you did not wish to dismiss His Majesty's suggestion out of hand."

"What about it, Miles?" Jethro asked, "Are you ready for a strange new world."

"Definitely." Miles replied, "It's all so damned intriguing."

On Danny's world there's nothing unusual about a meal in a pub. As with other first time travellers, Miles was just bewildered. From seeing his first car to the jukebox, all he could say with each new wonder was, 'Electricity?' All was going well when David arrived with Godfrey driving the other brake. The others tensed waiting for David's reaction but he had convinced himself that there would be another disaster if he allowed Miles to travel so he was genuinely relieved that they were enjoying themselves.

"It's silly." he said, "Nothing feels safe any more. Billy was right though. I've got all the advantages. I should be able to cope."

"I don't think that he meant that." Jethro said.

"No, but so far, the portal has just been a game. Could I cope with real danger or a real threat?"

"David," Danny said, "You've got to cope with what happened to suit yourself. Don't try to suit us or the portal."

"Is that one of your mother's pearls of wisdom … Sorry. I can't help it."

"Don't try. We'll cope." Danny replied cheerfully, "Our food's on its way so you'd better order if you want some."

"I'll wait for dessert. How about you, Miles. Enjoying yourself."

"You are so full of surprises, Pebbles." Miles laughed, "I thought the electric light at Barabourne was amazing enough."

"I'm sorry, Miles. You had a bad time as well. I was wrong about not letting you travel."

"Well you can't have every Tom, Dick and Harry travelling can you. Are you allowing Billy to take me along tomorrow?"

"It's up to Billy. He's in charge of that project and don't underestimate him. He's obviously not fooled by the front you put up."

Miles stared at David then nodded thoughtfully and the rest of the evening passed quietly off. The next morning found Miles nervously excited as he waited for Billy.

They set off in silence until Billy asked, "You saw my London, where I grew up. How did you like it?"

"I like Cooper and Skeffington Tamzon." Miles replied, "PC Pritchard seemed so pleased that we were tackling things. David would invite them here to stay but I wouldn't invite them to tea with my Father. Sir Cloudsley was more our sort of person but I hope he hangs. That's not answering your question, but I didn't see much, did I?"

"It's good enough. I was the boot boy. Now I'm a guest just like Lord Westerham. I mind my Ps & Qs on Sundays but today I'm in charge. You look after David, and I'll do your boots because I'm still better than the lazy sod who took over from me. You want to drive the brake and Godfrey will teach you but he'll be in charge. That's Barabourne. At your place, you'd sack a servant who knew more than you."

Miles smiled, "We wouldn't because we wouldn't know, would we? I've heard about the Great Decline. Is that part of it?"

"David can't do it all." Billy said, "He needs help. Your dad sees getting electricity as something posh. David and the King think that helping folk to use their talents is posher. What about you? What do you think is posh?"

"I think I understand. David and the King approve of you being so disrespectful because you're honest. You're asking whether

I can get used to it and help."

"Could you get used to it with your own servants?" Billy asked, "What about the guy sweeping the street outside your house?"

"Most of the people here remember their place though. Well, they seem a bit forward but that's all."

"And if your servants tried it, you wouldn't be all shocked and them let go?"

"Yes I see." Miles said, "Even that's pretty revolutionary, isn't it."

"OK, Miles. Decision time." Billy said, "We're at the portal. Cradawg insists that divine travellers like us are elders. However, even a high priest like Cradawg or Bran show their trust in the gods by being naked in the ring. It's a place of the gods but it's not a church or a temple as we know it. A couple of farmers might come here to negotiate the sale of some pigs. They're naked so they have nothing to hide and the gods see their souls just as easily. The idea is that there's no point in trying to cheat, because it'll be spotted."

"Does it work?" Miles asked.

"Bran's after all the power. He says he's a believer but I don't think he is, yet even he seems to be a bit more careful in the ring."

"And I should strip off as well."

"No. Looking uncomfortable or being embarrassed is just as insulting to the gods because you want to hide something. Wear as little as possible but feel comfortable. Once we leave the circle, we can dress again. Starting something in the ring is like having it blessed by the gods but you can go off and carry on with your business somewhere else."

"I don't want anyone looking at my privates again but sports wear feels all right. Will that do?"

"If I understand right, you've got a reason for staying fully dressed while you ask for the gods to help you relax."

"I'm Anglican." Miles said, "I couldn't pray to pagan gods even if I believed in them."

"Cradawg runs this ring. Bran is a sort of overseer responsible for a number of places. Where he's all powerful, they follow the rules and no-one questions the wind gods or his servant, Bran. Cradawg's a big wheel because his ring has a direct link with the gods' messengers, that's us."

Billy paused, marshalling his thoughts, "He believes that we were sent by them to repair the ring but he knows the *magic* is something mechanical. He's happy to believe that we're sent by the Christian god who must be pally with his gods. To him, Gods are gods and men cannot understand everything about them. If you knelt and said the *Lord's Prayer,* Cradawg would kneel beside you and wait for you to finish. Bran would accuse you of defying the wind gods and stop you because he wasn't in control. The odd thing is, the ring does feel good, I could believe it's something special and it even holds Bran back."

"Are you helping Cradawg to beat Bran?" Miles asked.

"Cradawg doesn't think like that." Billy replied, "I think that I'm helping him to find the god's wishes. Bran claims to already know."

"Very well. Do I have to behave all saintly or something?"

"No. Behave all human. Cradawg's no fool. He'll know if you're putting on airs and graces and he'll think that you're the fool. That's another thing. I really do think that he's all spiritual like - like the ring."

The previous evening, Miles had not really noticed when they had crossed the portal but today he felt the ground shake and saw the view shimmer. His first reaction to his new surroundings was to blush furiously at the sight of others *enjoying* the benefits of the ring. A youth, not much older than Miles hurried over to stand respectfully, head bowed.

"Hallo Kendal." Billy said, "This is Miles. It's his first visit to a new world, he's getting over a bad experience and he needs a friend more than a servant."

"The one who sacrificed himself for others." Kendal exclaimed, "I'd be honoured to serve him and be his friend if he'd allow it. As you are, with Elder David."

"At the moment he's overwhelmed by the beauty of your people." Billy grinned, "It takes us time to get used to it."

"Elder Miles, would you like me to show you around the town? We'll need clothes and no-one looks beautiful wrapped up like a sack."

Miles nodded gratefully as Billy said, "I'm off to find your Dad."

Where last night, electricity had left Miles stunned, so today it was the heliport with helicopters and autogyros coming and going

Miles and Kendal sat in a café watching aircraft taking off and landing.

"I'd love a ride in one of those." Miles said, "I don't suppose it's possible though."

By answer, Kendal called a waiter over.

"My Master is Elder Miles, a traveller on the Divine Path. He wishes to go for a flight. Find someone who can arrange it."

The waiter stared wide-eyed at Miles as Kendal spoke, bowed respectfully and hurried off.

"I'm not an elder, you know." Miles said, "And I'm not your master."

"Then we don't get a helicopter ride." Kendal retorted.

"Ah!" Miles exclaimed, "I'm not very religious though I suppose that I am a traveller."

"I can honestly say to my father that a helicopter ride would benefit us because it's educational, a new experience as well as fun. It's not worldly because it won't bring us wealth or power."

"I thought that we had to be very respectful of adults." Miles said, "You seem to be ordering them around."

Kendal stared thoughtfully at Miles, "I've never thought about it before. It's the waiter's job to serve customers and we're customers and being a traveller on the Divine Path makes you an elder. In the street, he would just be an adult and I'd step aside for him. You're an elder so you wouldn't have to but there might be problems if he didn't recognise you. I just take it all for granted."

"That's what we do." Miles said, "We take our worlds for granted and don't even question the bad bits."

"Revered Bran says that to question our world is to question the gods."

"Let's take that ride." Miles exclaimed, "It'll be fun. Tomorrow, we'll be serious and see how the poor live."

Kendal looked at him quizzically but did not say anything.

It was a few days later that Miles joined David and Todd as they headed for the village school joined by a group of older estate boys. He was far less of the buffoon and his innate intelligence and curiosity shone through. Although David was even more worried about being manipulated since his discussion with the portal, he was a good judge of character and had seen something in Miles when they had been in school together.

"I bet you never expected to be going to school with the likes of us." Todd said, "It's all a bit of a come down, isn't it?"

"I like those autogyro things they've got on Billy's world." Miles said, "After school, I'm going back there and learn to fly one. Godfrey's already looking at that oil stuff they use for fuel on Danny's world and reckons he's ready to start building lightweight engines. Just imagine, the next time I'm invited to some country house, I could fly there. Billy and Godfrey are making it possible. I'm going to be first to have all the latest gadgets, my best friend is going to be a boot boy and we'll take tea with the king. I'll still be the fop who leads fashion but I'm going lead them in a whole new direction."

"Do you think that you will?" Todd asked.

"David has to fight society to get electricity where it's needed. I can prance around in front of them and the idiots will just follow."

"You've changed." Todd said.

"That's the thing, I haven't. The idiots at school believed me if I said blue was the season's colour and stopped beating a 1st former while they listened to me. What happens if I go back to school in an autogyro and say that the boot boy got me the lessons?"

Billy had been half listening as he chatted to another boy and dropped back.

"The idiots start wondering if their boot boy is worth listening to. The trouble is, there's a lot who aren't so what do your mates do when they're disappointed?"

"True but I'll need a servant who knows how to look after it. If I let him fly it, just so that he shares the risks of course, but we also spend time discussing it all, isn't that leading by example?"

"You liked flying that much." Billy asked.

"Oh yes. I was hanging on so tightly while he spun up that big rotor and then we rolled forwards. I'd swear that I'd left my stomach behind as we shot up into the air. Then I was looking down at the town. I could just about see the people in the streets. Then he throttled back. It was so quiet, the sun was shining and even when we were really low no-one spotted us until he opened the throttle again and when we got a bit of height, he let me fly it. I did a few turns and went down a bit. It doesn't sound much but it was something that I could never have imagined."

Meanwhile, David was looking for the king's agents. He did

56

not spot any which left him with mixed feelings. On one hand, he was pleased that they were so discreet and were not interfering with his life but on the other, it irked him that had he not spotted them by the time they reached the school.

"Welcome Miles." Mr. Rogers smiled, "I have an idea what you would be studying if you were still at school so I'll try to keep you up to date with your subjects. When it comes to the sciences, you will have problems as most of the boys here advise universities while your school is training you for entry as a student. Do you have a particular interest in any field?"

"Yes sir." Miles replied, "Aeronautics and, I think that they're called social studies, it's looking at how our country works."

"Yes, Todd has mentioned social studies and I believe that this class is an experiment in the field. I wish you well."

David was still a little suspicious of Miles' new relaxed views. Before, he would never have become so friendly with Billy and the whole set up at Barabourne should have scandalised him. Although Miles had struggled at first, he had adapted surprisingly quickly.

It never occurred to David that part of the reason was that Miles admired him; also Miles had discovered something that he could become passionate about, flying. However, Miles had not changed that much; he was still a snob but as he said, after his experiences, it was his values that had changed.

Chapter 4

Although worried about Miles, it was Billy who was concerned and sought out David.

"Bran doesn't like me having an assistant especially one that can behave like a toff but he's hanging on 'til the Spring Equinox."

"Do you know what he's planning?" David asked.

"I think so. He's going to muck up the seeding."

"You'd better explain." David said.

"Right, they call spring the 'seeding time'. Some of it's what you expect. Some of it'll shock you and some is pretty disgusting.

Billy paused, "Bran is saying that I'm abusing Mother Earth by using the divine path for my own pleasure. The portal's buried in her, by the way. She's going to snub us by making our offerings sterile and worthless.

The seed is planted around the ring and this is the disgusting bit. It is fertilised by human waste to signify our part in the cycle of life. The shocking bit is that Megan will be expected to get pregnant."

"I get it. It's all to do with fertility and giving life." David said.

Billy nodded, "It's not so different to our farming but I never thought shitting would become a religious ceremony but that's not the problem. Bran's got a load of chances to kill the plants and we ought to get Iain and Megan checked out."

"Why?" David asked, "Bran can't do anything to them, can he?"

"Their doctors are better than the ones on Craig's world. If Bran's got one on side, then ..."

As Billy trailed off, David nodded.

"Are you going to take part in the ceremony?" David asked.

"Probably." Billy replied, "That don't bother me. It's keeping everything safe until the Autumn equinox that bothers me. If the plants die, Bran will say that my stuff poisoned it all. If I don't do it he'll say it's because I'm a demon and not of the earth and I'd give myself away by poisoning it. Either way, it makes me evil. I suppose that you'd better take over."

"No." David said firmly, "It's your project. On Danny's world, places were protected by cameras. See if he will take you there to find out what else we could do.

Billy suddenly hugged him.

"You're the greatest." he whispered, "I won't let you down."

David was startled and as the panic at being touched welled up, he pushed Billy away. Billy looked at him, worried but as David got his breathing under control so the panic subsided.

"I'm sorry." he said, "I couldn't help it."

"Don't worry about it." Billy replied, "You are the greatest, you know. I 'ope they 'ang Blackman."

David smiled, "I might go for a ride. I wouldn't mind a nice obedient servant who wouldn't speak without permission coming with me, but I don't think that I've got one."

"Try Jamie." Billy said, "He wouldn't sneeze without permission and he's been learning to ride or do you want more than a light canter?"

"No, that'll do." David said, "As long as I don't scare him to death."

Although David's ride proved to be uneventful, he was unaware of the real excitement of the day when a group arrived at the servant's entrance. As always, Wilson was ready to deal with any problem. Four of the men could have passed for civil servants in their dark three-piece suits even though they had a strangely military bearing. The remaining two obviously came from a lower class and they stood nervously although the older one carried a cane that would have made a vicious weapon.

One of the *military clerks* held out a warrant card though not for long enough to allow Wilson to read it.

"These two arrived by train. They didn't know their way around and were asking for directions here. Do you know them?"

Wilson shook his head, "No, I don't. May I ask your names?"

"Cooper Tamzon and this is my son, Skeffington." Cooper replied.

"Ah, Mr. Cooper. A pleasure to meet you and your son. Forgive me, but since these gentlemen are so suspicious, do you have any proof."

"No sir." Cooper replied, "I don't need it since I'm well-known in my usual haunts."

"Excuse me sir." the agent said, "He did ask us to vacuum

Lord Markham. It'll be some time before I get a reply though."

"Mr. Tamzon does have a distinctive scar so I think that's sufficient for now. I'll arrange for you and your colleagues to be shown to the staffroom for refreshments while I show our guests to the library."

He beckoned a footman before leading the Tamzons through the house.

"My apologies for your treatment gentlemen." Wilson said, "It's my first encounter with those people."

"That's all right." Cooper replied, "It's good to see that David, I mean the duke is looked after so well."

"In this part of the house, even I call him David, sir." Wilson said, "It's not a good idea in front of the dowager duchess, though."

Skeffington had been nervously looking around the room as if seeking danger until his eyes settled on a book lying on a table. Forgetting his fear he hurried over to pick it up, thumbing through it. Wilson noticed how his face screwed up with pain until he became absorbed in the book. Finally, he was distracted by his father murmuring his name. He looked up, to see his father frowning.

"You must forgive him, sir." Cooper said, "He forgets everything if he sees a book."

"Then I'm sure that he'll be doubly welcome in here, sir. Please address me as Wilson. Some of our more nervous guests try to call me Mr. Wilson, but that is for the staff. Please, enjoy the book. I'll enquire whether there's a spare copy for you to have."

"Sorry." Skeffington said, "I didn't mean to be rude but I'd read *A Lady Is Curious* and had heard that John Sanders had written another. I didn't know that it had been released though."

"Lady Isabella has a few advance copies, sir. It takes time to distribute them to the wholesalers."

"Lady Isabella? Yes I'd heard it had been written by an Isabella Darrow. Why does she release them under a man's name?"

"I believe that it is assumed that the ladies can only write light, vapid romances. Dark mysteries are supposed to be well beyond their capabilities and would not sell."

Skeffington nodded, "That's true, I suppose. Don't worry, I won't touch any more."

"Oh feel free, sir." Wilson said, "His Grace makes it clear that books are for anyone who can appreciate them."

Skeffington smiled his thanks and chose another which happened to be one of Todd's old schoolbooks. He frowned as he examined it.

"I've never seen one like this before." he said, "Look at all those coloured diagrams and illustrations and the cover's little more than thick paper."

"It's known as a paperback, sir." Wilson said, "You will find a lot of items here that are either prototypes or known as proof of concept. Some may be years from being commonplace."

"And this is all about electricity. A new kind of manual for a new science."

Jethro arrived and Wilson made the introductions.

"I'm delighted to meet you." Jethro said, "Please relax. People still talk about your ride across London."

"I feel bad about leaving him, sir." Skeffington said, "It felt like I was running away."

"You must be careful with David." Jethro said, "He is affected by his experiences but from the moment he was arrested, they were bound to happen. If you had stayed, you would have been arrested as well and would have watched, unable to help while far worse happened. You did not hide but acted decisively to save the situation. I take it that this isn't a social visit."

"No sir." Cooper replied, "Skevi was attacked and he's got a couple of cracked ribs. He'll be all right and it's not his first fight but it's the first one where a comely lass attracts his attention and a couple of bruisers are waiting in her room."

"Yes, I see." Jethro said, "He's a potential witness, isn't he?"

"Yes sir." Cooper replied.

"Then he's lucky to get away with cracked ribs."

"Yes sir. They moved a bit too soon and Skevi was able to defend himself. Like I say, it's not his first fight and he takes after his old man. The thing is, he's got his mother's brains and knew when to run. His brother Chris would have kept smashing into them."

"Yeah, I ran again." Skeffington muttered morosely.

"You were already injured." Jethro said, "While you were knocking one down, the other would have time to recover. Your father is saying that your brother would have allowed himself to be worn down and beaten to a pulp. Alternatively, he would have killed them and would be facing the noose. I'm sure the girl would have made an excellent witness for the prosecution."

"That's right, sir." Cooper said, "I chose him to look after David, because he's got the brains. Chris would have flattened PC Pritchard that night and made David run, handcuffs and all but I doubt that they would have got far."

Just then David entered the library but as he saw Cooper and Skeffington, the blood drained from his face.

"Why are you here?" he asked, for David, very rudely.

"I'm sorry to disturb you, sir." Cooper replied, "We should go."

David took a deep breath, "I'm sorry. You were the first people I saw when I got up from that table. I didn't expect you then and seeing you unexpectedly again brought it back. Please! You are welcome even if I am being rude. Oh, and call me David."

Jethro recounted events finishing, "It seems that we're being guarded, very effectively. He should stay until the trial."

"You did well uncovering four agents." David chuckled, "I've never even seen one."

Cooper smiled, "I've always been able to spot the rozzers."

"We'll find you a cottage and you should bring your whole family here." David said, "I know, you'll lose business on your stall. I'm sorry but if you become associated with Barabourne then you can't go on trading in suspect jewellery. How about spending your time here learning about electricity and becoming some sort of agent, selling equipment?"

"Chris is a bit wild to bring here, sir." Cooper replied, "Like I said, he's a bit too free with his fists, especially when he's had a drink."

"Billy said that about his brother." David retorted, "He's as scared as a mouse but the constable does have trouble on pay day with others so it'll be nothing new."

"It's kind of you, sir." Cooper said, "I'll think about it."

"Wilson, will you work with Billy to find accommodation, please." David said turning back to Cooper, "You're welcome in the house for a few days but with so many new people we'd be overflowing if everyone had to stay. We've not had any complaints about our new cottages though. Skevi, have you seen a doctor?"

Whether it was tiredness from the journey, or relief at being safe Skeffington was struggling to hide the pain he was in.

"No sir." he replied, "There's a decent one in the next parish but I wouldn't trust the drunk that we've got."

"Send for Doctor Hastings." David commanded, "We've got doctors closer by but they are specialists in diseases. Dr. Hastings is used to injuries and physical damage."

Skeffington nodded, "Thank you, sir but you needn't trouble the doctor. I'll be all right."

"Dr. Hastings is on a retainer. He'll send me a bill for further treatment so at least let him earn some fees."

Skeffington smiled as he nodded again, "Thank you, sir."

It was later in the day that David spoke with Skeffington again.

"Dr. Hastings said that I was to speak to you, sir." Skeffington said, "He gave me these pills and said that you would get more."

"Just out of interest, what did he say about you?"

"That these pills were safer than laudanum and I should take them regularly. They're called painkillers and they let me breathe and cough more easily."

David nodded, "I'll get you a supply. Do they help?"

"Yeah, I can move a lot easier. How come only you can get them?" Skeffington faltered, "Sorry, it's none of my business, is it?"

David thought for a moment.

"Would you find your father, please. When I can get everyone together in the library, I'd like to talk to you." He called a footman over, "Would you tell Wilson that I need Godfrey, Jimmy, Miles, Todd, Danny as soon as possible. Would he inform Skeffington when they arrive?"

The nights were already drawing out and although still cold Danny would visit as many evenings as possible. Danny's parents had relented about him cycling to the portal but Darren was still not allowed. For some reason, even doing his homework in Barabourne's library made it an adventure for Danny.

Miles was found after his latest flying lesson and finally they were all assembled. David was not surprised to see Billy and his uncle also there.

"Very well." David began, "Barabourne has some secrets. Nothing bad but you may find them interesting. It has, what the king calls a hideaway and I can guarantee that none of Sir Cloudsley's people or Pritchard's will find us there. Now, at the moment, it's a badly kept secret, and I don't want anyone else discovering it. However, I didn't take the idea that we were in danger seriously until today. Now I think that it might be a good idea if Miles, Skeffington and myself are ready to use it."

Jethro nodded as David continued, "I don't think that we can be kidnapped unless we go out on a public road at night. However, we might be at risk from snipers and there could be some sort of highly organised raid but the king's agents would probably get wind of it and warn us."

David paused again before looking towards Cooper, "You're not a witness and providing your family's at Barabourne, they can't be used as hostages because the takers would be trapped here. Cooper, you can stay while we discuss some of our plans but please don't be offended if I ask you to leave before we're done. I'd also ask you not to interrogate Skevi about what we discuss."

"I understand, but are you sure that you want Skevi to stay?"

"He can't use the hideaway if he doesn't know where it is, can he?" David asked.

"No sir, and thank you."

"First, I want Miles and Skeffington to have bedrooms as close to mine as possible. Jimmy, I want guard posts with radios and an operator indoors. The further out the posts are the better. Godfrey, I want a steam tractor at instant readiness at all times. If necessary, it must be able to smash through the gates to get to the portal. Next question, with all the generators and lights you're building can we give the guard posts lights, er, searchlights are they called?"

"Are all these preparations necessary?" Jethro asked.

"I hope not." David replied, "It might be a demonstration of our new equipment though."

"It's a thought." Jethro said, "It's not like you though. You don't normally like turning Barabourne into an armed camp. Neither do you like hiding."

"I suppose I'm shocked that Skevi was attacked and it was because of me." David replied, "Now I want him and Miles to be safe. The question is, am I staying here simply because I don't want to run away or do I want to close the portal down but suppose something goes wrong and I'm needed here?"

"Right!" Jethro exclaimed, "That was terribly muddled and

that's not like you either. If Cooper brings his family here, then he's going hear about your trips. So I may as well mention them now. You need to rest. As I keep reminding you, adults would struggle to cope with what you've dealt with and you're only fourteen. Be proud of the way that you do cope but you need to rest. It's still too cold to spend time at the waterhole but maybe you could find somewhere warmer, set up a tent and not have any responsibilities.

"For tonight, Godfrey, take Skeffington to the Royal George. Try not to get arrested for being drunk and disorderly over there but otherwise just relax and enjoy yourselves. That's to introduce Skeffington to the hideaway. Danny, speak to your Mr. Barton, see if David, and Miles can have an equally relaxing evening. Jimmy, we'll discuss this sentry post idea when it's quiet. Cooper, send for the rest of your family or do you really have no-one who can run your stall? David, I understand what needs to be done. You've done your part, now let the rest of us do ours. Go and have fun."

David felt relieved that his uncle had taken over so decisively. Seeing Cooper and Skeffington had been a shock and his uncle was right, everything he did, seemed to create problems. He should let someone else run things.

That evening neither Skeffington nor Godfrey got drunk, Miles, Danny and David enjoyed burgers in an arcade before the three boys got lost in a car racing game at which, surprisingly, Miles excelled.

"It's my flying lessons on an autogyro." Miles explained, "I've got used to not calling out 'Whoa' and pulling on the reins to stop."

The following day, David was strangely detached, not interested in any of the work in progress, preferring to spend as much time as possible in his room. When Jethro could not find anything that could have upset David, he became concerned and remained concerned when David was equally quiet the next day and the day after.

The following day, Jethro called David's friends together, describing his concerns.

"He's all over the place." Godfrey said, "First he didn't want anyone using the portal, now he doesn't care who uses it. Skeffi's been in the Royal George every night, playing pool."

"How does he get there?" Jethro asked, "I thought that it

needed three of you to open the portal."

"A couple of us go as far as the portal then leave him to it." Godfrey explained, "He prefers going alone because he drinks wine. It's too pricey over here and he could get himself beaten up if he tried drinking anything so pansy in his usual haunts."

"Can we get back to David, please?" Jethro asked, "Any thoughts?"

"How do you feel, Miles?" Godfrey asked, "Do you feel anything like David, do you think?"

"I don't like anyone getting too close to me and I don't think that I can get undressed in front of anyone. It'll be hell back at school when we have sport or anything." Miles paused, "Kendal doesn't care whether he's dressed or not. Neither does his girl friend and when they hug …

"I'm getting used to it and I feel a bit silly wearing shirt and shorts now but Cradawg insists that I do. He says that I'll know when I'm ready to properly respect the gods."

"But you don't get panicky or anything? You don't want to hide in your room?" Godfrey persisted.

"Possibly I do but then I want to finish my flying course. Ever heard, 'spare the rod, spoil the child'? Well the masters at our old school didn't believe in spoiling us. They also believed that a bit of bullying toughened us up and prepared us for the real world. Think of ways to humiliate some sprog and you'll see what I'm driving at. Do you know what I think made it worse for David? Blackman didn't even need someone looking out for a prefect or a master. He was the top man."

"You make our schools seem pretty grim." Jethro said, "You're saying that Blackman had such complete control that he swamped David."

"Pebbles is the bod in charge." Miles replied, "Suddenly he isn't. Think about it."

"It makes sense." Jethro said, "Apart from letting him rest, do you think that there's anything we could do?"

"I don't know." Miles replied, "I told you, our teachers would just tell him to pull himself together and get on with it."

"Right!" Billy snapped, "We've discussed this before but nothing happened. Miles, young gentlemen like you should go for a morning ride. Get David to show you around. Godfrey. Get some lads down to the swimming hole. Get them to make some noise under David's window but don't force it."

"It's still a bit cold for that." Godfrey said.

"Tough." Billy retorted, "I'll join in if you like but I already do CPO Hammond's physical training course as well. He's going to get pretty lonely if we're all out playing around and too busy to visit him."

"That might isolate him further." Miles said, "Let me talk to him."

"It can't hurt." Jethro said, "See what you can do."

"No time like the present." Miles said as he headed for the door. Miles tapped on David's door but opened it to peer in before David could reply.

David was lying on his bed but smiled when he saw Miles who sat on the edge of the bed.

"I still can't believe all of it here." Miles said, "It's fantastic. Thanks for including me."

"I didn't want to but I'm glad that you're happy."

"The thing is Pebbles ... No it's not school, The thing is, David, I'd like to stay on permanently. I'd like to go exploring with you."

"I'm not exploring any more. Uncle Jethro has taken charge and he's right. I've messed everything up and I should just keep out of the way. Billy's doing a better job on the stone ring world than I did. I'm useless and see that now."

"You mean the street urchin and thief who became your boot boy and is now as important as the Archbishop of Canterbury on another world. Tell me, how did you mess up with him?"

David stared at Miles but did not say anything.

"I got you birched and those inverts pawing over you. God, I hated it when Blackman touched me."

"Your cousin is becoming established as an authoress and Godfrey is marrying her while becoming the richest stable boy in the country. That's a right mess, isn't it."

David smiled, "All right but it all started because I fell over. It's all luck, I didn't plan any of it."

"Really?" Miles queried, "I'd say that everyone knows what you want and it works. The likes of us don't belong in that part of London and you thought it would be like a stroll through your village. You know what though, I now like that warehouse accommodation you're building. That was your idea, wasn't it. Skeffington says that people trust you and want to help now.

Miles could see that David was listening so he continued, "Boy's have been birched at school and you probably would have been by now if you had moved up. We both got the cane in prep school, didn't we?"

David nodded.

"Well then, for once it achieved something or am I messed up? After all, I don't see Skeffington as a shifty waster any more. I see the value in helping people like them."

"All right." David snapped, "I've been lucky but let's face it, my luck's running out. It's time to stop."

"Survivors leave." Miles said, "Did you ever take it?"

"Huh? What are you talking about?"

"Sailors get leave if their ship sinks. Danny talks about something he calls Post Traumatic Stress. Let's agree that you need to rest but you're not really happy just lying here are you?"

"I do sleep a lot and I feel better for it but no. I'm not happy but it's just not fun any more. Next time, someone may be killed."

"A cousin of mine was killed when his horse bolted." Miles said, "Are you sure that the rafters aren't riddled with woodworm. Could the roof come crashing down on us? Those flying lessons, they're not about flying, they're about safety, learning the correct procedures, checking everything, they even got this flight simulator thing. It's a sort of room that makes you think you're flying for real. I pushed it too far, chopped the rotor off and nosedived into the ground, it was so real I nearly wet myself. That's the thing though. I made a mistake and learned something. You got careless and made mistakes and you're learning. That's my instructor's line by the way. He says something else. The gods may be perfect but we're not gods so we keep making mistakes. Personally I'm not sure that their gods are so perfect but I don't say it over there."

"How about taking me for a ride." David asked, "It sounds like fun."

"Sorry, I can't. I fly solo now but it's still under supervision and I can't take passengers." Miles paused and grinned, "You've messed me up after all. I'm not an idiot any more, I'm a responsible young man."

68

David smiled in his turn, "Fair enough, maybe things aren't so bad, after all."

"Look, I don't want to be touched either. Every so often I feel dirty and need to bathe. Sometimes I get up in the middle of the night for a bath. I'm glad I'm not at school, they'd say I was weak and that's when they're being kind."

David laughed but became serious, "Aren't you angry with me for putting you through it?"

Miles was silent for a time then replied, "I need your permission for something. May I bring through one of their autogyros and support equipment?"

"What about fuel? We're nowhere near ready to build suitable engines and we don't produce the right fuel."

"They've got battery powered versions. They're good for about an hours flying but then need about five hours charging. Do you know what solar panels are? They'll charge it with fifteen hours of daylight. Godfrey reckons that we can run the charger all right and I've had to learn a bit about the battery theory so I don't blow myself up with them." Miles paused and smiled, "They're not worried about me, they don't want it to happen at a thousand feet so that it wrecks the village or something."

"You say that you've learnt some theory. Does that mean that we could develop these batteries?" David asked.

"I think so. Your people are looking into it and I've been talking to Godfrey. It seems that once they know what to look for, making discoveries is easier."

David nodded, "You've started it without my say so?"

"I was surprised but Godfrey said that the first step was to do a feasibility assessment. The more parts that need their own development projects, then the less feasible batteries become but he's hopeful. You or your Uncle Jethro become involved when it needs funding. It's amazing how your people just get on with things."

"You have changed, Miles." David said, "You missed Lady Stanton's ball and you're missing the social season. Don't you mind?"

"When the highlight of my new season is defecating in a ditch?" Miles laughed, "Father is impressed that I seem so favoured by His Majesty and when I do go back to school, I admit it, I want the autogyro to show off with. There's something else. There's a couple of girls on the stone circle world, er, you can't just take a girl there like they say at school, er, they have to like you, er, and ..."

He trailed off.

"Don't be shy, it doesn't suit you." David laughed, "Uncle Jethro seems to guard the corridor to my bedroom when Olivia visits while the father's over there would leave you alone. Still, I don't see Olivia wanting to visit again."

"Why not?" Miles asked.

"After what happened, she won't think that I'm a man. I've put her off so it'll be easy for her to break up with me."

"Idiot." Miles scoffed, "We're heroes. There's still not much in the papers but according to father's letter, we're the talk of the town. All the girls want to meet us."

"Maybe I should invite her again. It's just that ..." he trailed off uncertainly.

"It's just that you see yourself as allowing a lower class oik to beat you and play with your privates while everyone else sees you as getting rid of the scum."

"And you. I can't believe that you volunteered. You're so different to when you're at school."

"It wasn't a game, was it? Danny was complaining because it would have never been allowed on his world but it taught us something about our world, didn't it? I couldn't get out of it by making them laugh, could I?" Miles shuddered, "When you visited, Father suggested I find somewhere to play while he talked to you and found out what the King wanted. I didn't like that he saw me as a child and you as an adult. I had to show him that I was as grown up as you. I felt so good when Cooper said that Father should be proud of me."

"Come on, Miles, let's go for a ride." David said, "Let's get out of here but do you mind if we swing past the portal? I'm going to ask it how to turn it off."

"Make sure you don't trap anyone." Miles said, "I've got fond of that damned boot boy and I'd miss his cheek."

David laughed as he dismounted. Miles also dismounted curious about the display that had appeared. Everything seemed to tremble and both David and Miles found themselves in a woodland glade. There was no sign of the portal.

They looked around, startled. Miles recognised a jump through the portal and assumed that David knew all about it. David had no idea what was happening and felt a knot in his stomach as panic set in. He glanced at Miles but before either could speak, they were distracted by the sound of a hunting horn echoing through the forest. A man in his thirties and a boy of about twelve charged into the glade. Both were dressed in rags, were barefoot, breathless and desperate but as the man saw David so a look of hopeless despair enveloped him and he fell to his knees. The boy looked at his father and with the same defeated look, also fell to his knees but David noticed that the boy kept glancing at him.

More men dragged by hounds appeared. They also stopped and knelt, but they were respectful rather than terrified and then riders dressed in chain mail arrived.

The leader dismounted approached David and, also knelt.

"Sir David, how did you get here. We thought that His Majesty had summoned you."

David thought fast, "I was summoned by the king and now I'm waiting in the woods. What do you think I'm doing?"

The soldier was thoughtful as he considered the question, "You're here in secret? Are you expecting someone? We're about halfway between London and the coast so a spy from France? And you so young that nobody will think that it could be you?"

"Now go and pray that your blundering has not ruined everything." David commanded, "Never speak of it again. I will test you and if you even admit to seeing me you'll all be hung, drawn and quartered. Do you understand?"

"Yes Sir David. We'll take those two somewhere else." the soldier grinned, "They won't talk once we've gutted them."

"No. Leave them here. I heard you charging around but I didn't hear them. They may be useful."

"Sir David?"

"You're still here." David said menacingly, "Go or it won't be just those two who are gutted. Go!"

The soldier remounted and the men hurried off.

David turned to the father, "Do as I say and you'll live. Run or cause trouble and I can't help you."

"You help us? You like us dancing from a rope's end too much."

"Dad, that's not the earl's son." the boy said suddenly, "He's a wood elf. Maybe he can help."

"Interesting." David said, "What makes you say that?"

"Where's your sword? Your clothes are strange. You look like the Earl's son but you're bigger and, er, look stronger."

"Very good so let's play a game and pretend that you're right except that we're in human form." David said, "That means we could be killed if those men get suspicious and catch us."

"Follow!" the father commanded and he set off at a fast trot.

Miles looked at David who nodded. They looked around hoping to see the portal but there was nothing there so they obeyed the stranger and followed. The man kept to a steady trot and the boys learned to follow his footsteps exactly to avoid the thorns and branches ready to rip their clothes. Even so they were breathless when they reached a river where the bank was over one and a half metres high on the far side. They helped the son over then scrambled up themselves. As they pushed through the undergrowth, so the man slowed and stopped.

"We're safe enough here." the man said tersely, "Rest."

Miles looked worried so the boy explained, "Dogs can't climb banks and handlers are too old to be soldiers. They're slow and tire more easily. "

David nodded, "Very well. Let's play the game guessing who I am some more. I'm a stranger here so who do I look like?"

"The Earl of Brabon's son." the boy replied.

"You're not in trouble with me so why did those men want to hang you?"

"I told you, the Earl likes to see us dance but he says we were taking wood from his hunting grounds."

"Oh!"

"OK, I'm David and my friend is Miles. What are your names?"

"I'm Will and dad is William."

"You know that we're not wood elves, don't you?" David said.

"Yes, you are. You're not men. You're stronger, bigger, your skin is softer and your clothes haven't been torn. Much the miller talks of you. His son was declared an outlaw for killing a deer. He's the same age as me and we used to play together."

"Where do you live?"

This time it was William who answered, "We had a farm but the land was poor, always sodden and we were close to starvation. We couldn't pay the taxes and we were driven off by the Earl's men. Now we live in the forest with others."

"I don't suppose that you rob from the rich to give to the poor, do you?" Miles murmured.

William grinned, "We steal more food than gold but Robert of Romney has strange ideas. He saves gold so that one day we can buy land but he gives some to the farms around the forest, not much but it makes them friendly."

Miles and David stared at each other.

"The names have got the same rhythm." Miles whispered.

"What has?" Will asked.

"Robert of Romney and Robin of Loxley." David explained.

Will shrugged, "Never heard of this Robin. Have you, Dad?"

William shook his head and they fell silent for a time.

"Right!" David exclaimed, "We need to get home. I can take Will with us and he'll have a good life. I'm sorry. I can't take everyone."

"You want to take him from me?" William asked angrily, "We helped you."

"I'm sorry, it came out wrong. I can offer Will a life where he won't be an outlaw, where he can work the land or explore the world, whatever he wants. Yes, I'll be taking him from you and you'll never see him again but he'll have a good life. It's an offer and, you and Will can accept it or reject it. It's your choice."

"Who would his lord be?"

"Me!"

"Forgive me sir, but may I know your title?" William asked.

"I am David Pevensey, Duke of Barrabourne." David replied.

"And you are hiding from David, Earl of Brabon? His family has lands granted by William of Normandy near Pevensey. You look like him but I agree, you are not him. Is it witchcraft?"

"No. I don't know what's happening but it's not witchcraft. How soon can we get back to the clearing where we met?"

"Before sunset. The men will already be heading for the manor. They don't like the forest at night. Will and I will lead. You follow. I'll talk to him about your offer."

73

"Is there anything that you can explain to me?" Miles asked?

"No." David replied, "We're in the greenwood with one of Robin's Hood men. What's wrong with that?"

"Nothing except that it sounds as if you're the evil Sheriff of Nottingham."

"Thanks!"

They trudged on in silence until they reached the glade. David looked around and saw the portal almost hidden by tall grass. He strolled over murmuring, 'I need a bag of gold'.

He found one on the ground beside the portal.

Returning to William and his son, he said, "This is for you. Whatever you decide, don't stay here if the Earl's after you."

"Thank you, Your Grace. Will's place is with me." William replied, "My grandfather came from Nottingham but he took the lands that were offered when he returned from the Crusade. My son earns coppers by the stories he tells and I could make my way as a tinker. We'll go North."

Will looked back as he and his father walked off and waved but then Miles and David were alone.

"Can we go home now?" David asked.

The world shimmered and they were back in the field with their horses still waiting for them. It was as if they had only been gone a few minutes. They looked at each other, puzzled.

Chapter 5

"What was that all about?" Miles asked.

The screen appeared with the message, P*lay.*

"So it was all imagination." David asked, "It wasn't real."

It was real. You met origin of legend.

"You're still playing with us." David snapped irritably, "Explain properly."

Yes. See benefit in filling circuits with inconsequential data. Forces real data to be filed and clears orphan routines. Now for the sensible answer.

Time is like a river, it flows, has currents and eddies. Your timeline is caught in an eddy and is looped. You crossed the loop. Will, or William of Braborn as he became known, was famous as a story teller around Nottingham. He was forgotten but his stories were remembered long after his death and then were written down.

You saved his life, then stimulated his mind to play games which then meant stories or plays. As you suggested, Robert of Romney became Robin of Loxley, Will remembered your clothes so he became Will Scarlet, they both liked fine clothes. He remembered you by forgetting evil ancestor and the Sheriff of Nottingham became the villain though he appeared later.

"Are you saying that we helped start the legend of Robin Hood?" Miles asked, "Without us, there'd be no legend."

Yes you helped. Without him legend would still exist because of other worlds. You made the inevitable easier and saved Will.

"Very well." David said, "I didn't like the sound of my ancestor much."

No. You would be him but you stronger, responded to Mother more.

"Huh?"

When villager was sick, who sent for doctor, who took food? Mother can't always hide gentleness.

"So you arranged for me to spend time on Danny's world so that I could learn about the lower classes and to treat them properly."

Instinct in you. Needed bringing out. Hitting head accident though. Appropriate word – apologies.

"Fair enough but why arrange today's trip?"

Attempt at humour. Only danger was when you were talking to soldiers. I would have brought you back if needed. Didn't need so you had your own version of Robin Hood to play with. Therapy.

"Okay, I thought you needed electrical equipment to know a world. How come you got the timing on this one so right?"

Temporal parameters flexible. Adjustment possible.

"You can travel through time?" Miles asked.

You travelled back to the late twelfth century because of the loop in the time-line. Natural Phenomena. I could adjust within eighty-nine year span so found suitable moment. Choice depended on inter-universal information and cannot explain further. My question, you took journey very calmly.

"I could speak the language easily." David replied, "That had to be your doing."

Very good. Physiological responses improved. Therapy worked.

"OK yes, I suppose it did." David conceded, "It felt weird wondering how I'd got caught up with Robin Hood, and now it seems funny."

Practising humour. Glad it's working, but high demand, need to recharge now.

"OK but one quick question. Was Skeffington's beating anything to do with the creator's enemies?"

Events being agitated. Must stop now.

The screen disappeared and assuming that they had been dismissed Miles and David rode home.

"It's been one hell of a ride." Miles said, "How do you feel?"

"Tired but that's understandable, this is turning into a long day."

Once home they were greeted by Jethro who asked them if they had enjoyed the ride.

"Yes thank you, Uncle." David replied, "We spent some time in the greenwood with Robin Hood's men."

"Do you know, I would never have thought that you and Miles could let go to play like that."

"Have you ever heard of either Robert of Romney or William of Braborn.

"No, I can't say that I have. Who are they?"

"Just people we met, Uncle." David replied.

"Very well." Jethro said, "You're so much more cheerful – you must have had fun. How about you, Miles?"

"Well yes, I did. David always surprises me with his ideas on the right people to know or the right place to be."

Jethro looked at them as if he wanted to ask a question but finally said, "I'm not sure what mischief you're up to but go and have fun."

When Jethro had gone, David said, "May we keep today our secret? I'm just not sure how to explain it and we've got nothing to show for it. Oh, and thanks. I'm glad you were there."

"I didn't do much except watch." Miles said, "You just seemed so accepting and you knew what to do."

"I didn't but you were calm and it steadied me." David said, "I was wrong about not involving you. It still bothers me that I've got to stop this world from declining and I worry about how much the portal manipulates me or if someone else does. I wouldn't have chosen you because you seemed so stupid and empty at school but you're not. I only asked for your father because I thought he was a pompous idiot and he isn't. I'm sorry, I know that's all so rude and I do know differently now. You see, you understand society, I don't and I can see why you'd be useful and it all comes back to manipulation again."

"Yes, I do understand. It was a shock that father thought me so immature compared to you. It's another reason that I don't want to go back to school. I won't be the buffoon so the bullies will take me seriously. To be honest, I don't care whether the portal is manipulating me because I like what I am now but school won't like me being so different."

"That's the problem, I do care." David exclaimed, "Imagine if someone had planned that business with Blackman. The portal said that it was possible."

"I don't know about this enemy but could they involve so many people? Supposing situations are set up and you're left to respond. Billy and Godfrey are good choices. Supposing that there's a village boy who would be an even better choice but you haven't spotted him yet. Nothing is certain."

"I could live with that." David said, "It doesn't feel so inevitable if the planners can stuff up but they were beaten by this enemy. Does that mean that the enemy is cleverer? There's something else. I was close to Todd, Billy and Godfrey but they took advantage of my friendship to do their own thing."

David paused as Miles frowned then continued, "That came out wrong, didn't it. You're a new friend but you're already working on batteries and autogyros so you'll move on. I can't keep bringing new friends here."

"They're still your friends but it's not like school where we're in the same class, playing the same sports, doing the same things. That's the problem with school, we'd have to conform again. We all study together but I can't make a light bulb and Godfrey hasn't met Robin Hood or was it, Will Scarlet? They're still your friends, they just seem more distant compared to school."

"Maybe you're right. You know, despite what the King said, I'm not going to stop the decline if I hide down here. I've got to be in London."

"Any thoughts?" Miles asked.

"Yes but it comes back to being manipulated." David replied, "We start a fashion for being inventors and having educated servants."

"And I'm the bod who could do it so I mysteriously turn up, Pebbles." Miles laughed, "I'm going to find Skevi. He's already famous, he's learning about wine, even Wilson's helping him and if he can help with my battery project then we've got a reason for associating. I'll write to my father about introducing him to our set."

Miles thought for a moment, "You could also consider open days here. There's so much coal, oil and soot that visitors would wear coveralls which would make them classless."

"We tried something like it Christmas Eve." David said, "As a result, Godfrey's getting a lot of enquiries for lightweight tractors. We've set up a sales office so that Lord Muck-a-Muck can discuss the tractors and his man sorts the sordid details like money with the office. I give Wilson shares in each of our projects and he serves Godfrey's and Todd's guests as if they were Mother's."

David frowned and thought for a moment, "That came out wrong again. He takes our projects as seriously as Uncle Jethro and me. It's right that he profits out of them."

Jethro was a little concerned that both boys went to bed early that night but the following day, David was bright and cheerful as he sought out Godfrey.

"Have you chosen a best-man?" David asked.

Godfrey shook his head, "Your mother cannot decide what station he should be; stable hand or noble."

"Then I'd be honoured if you'd consider me." David said, "I'll warn you, I have an ulterior motive."

"I'd be honoured if you would agree, but can we take the honoured bits for granted?"

"Good idea." David agreed, "Now, we've got to fill your side of the church. Who do you want to invite?"

"Ah! Your mother is allowing Billy but she wants to shorten my list."

"There's a surprise." David retorted, "Let's start with a couple of suggestions, the king and Lord Markham."

David laughed as Godfrey stared but continued, "And the Tamzons. Then there're the guys we went swimming with last year, now who else?"

"I'd like to ask Wilson; he has been good to me but he'd be too worried about the house collapsing about us. Why do you want me to include the king?"

"Normally he would be invited because of my position and technically, Isabella's parents send the invitation. However, again there is something scandalous in her marrying a stable boy so maybe it would be better not to invite him. Look, you know it's not how I see you but it's how a good few of the guests will think. However, if we do invite the king then we could also invite him to the stag night. First, the question is, do you want the usual village event where you get as drunk as a skunk and then find out which village girls are available."

"No! I don't, not any more. I was going to ask about taking my closest friends to the Royal George for a meal though."

"How about the Savoy in London?" David asked, "The grown-ups could go on to a club of some sort."

"That's your ulterior motive. The king would be seen mixing with commoners but it wouldn't work. Billy knows how to behave but the others would feel too uncomfortable. I'm still not sure which fork to use."

"Wilson will provide lessons." David said, "It may sound a bit snobbish but your friends won't be embarrassed if they know what to do. Don't forget, it's the first year that Uncle Jethro or Mother hasn't stood nearby to tell me what to do."

"Yes, I see but the other thing is, I want to do something that we can all do. I don't want to just dump the youngsters, especially Billy. I know it's tradition to let rip before I settle down, but I already have. The Savoy is part of Isabella's world and I'd like to show that I can fit in there as much as Isabella and your Olivia fits in here."

David was startled for a moment then nodded, "Yes she does fit in and I wish that she could visit more often."

He was still thoughtful as he sought out Miles and repeated the conversation.

"Pebbles, that would be utterly bad form." Miles replied, "You do not involve the king in things like that. What you do is, have your meal and mention to the king when it will be. If he is willing to help then he may well dine there at the same time, maybe on his way to or from a tennis match. Now when he's eating in public like that it's not done to acknowledge him. However, if he notices you and deigns to speak to you, that is another matter. I'm sure your meal won't go wrong but if it does, then he's not involved and will not speak to you."

"I thought that arranging this would be easy but I'm getting it all wrong – *again.*" David exclaimed.

Miles heard the despair in his voice, "No, you're not getting it all wrong. It's a jolly good idea; now delegate. Let me deal with the protocol and let Godfrey deal with his friends."

David nodded, "You're right, of course. It's just that I'm still all over the place."

"Rest. Have fun." Miles said, "We're not at school so you don't have to pull yourself together and act like a man. The portal expects you to be a boy and play but how would the others have coped with meeting Will Scarlet?"

"That's the long way of saying that I'm still ill but thank you. I'm going to talk to the portal. Come along if you wish."

Once the screen was visible, David asked, "Am I ill?"

A better word, convalescing.

"So my judgement will improve."

Thinking clouded by emotions. They swing between optimism and pessimism, hope and dread, over-confidence and self-doubt. Convalesce and they will calm. Learn to think without emotions but accept that for now, they intrude.

"Have you got any more games for me to play?"

Warning. What seems like a game, can have dire consequences, even death. If you had met the Earl of Brabon, you would be dead.

"So you can't help. Oh well!"

Did not say that. Travel dangerous. Always risk. You ask for adventure without risk but perceived risk makes adventure.

"Perceived risk? I get it. Last time, I didn't know what was happening so I felt at risk. Next time I won't. Or rather I will know that there's no risk so there's no adventure."

"Even I understand, Pebbles." Miles laughed, "Let's move on."

See world and I know much of it. Know locals better because of sensing them. May find something local but real, not game.

The world shimmered but at first it seemed that nothing had happened but then a girl screamed. They hurried to the lane to see a girl of about seventeen being chased by a group of youths. David recognised Godfrey amongst them.

The girl saw David and faltered, her terror obvious. Maybe she saw something in David's face for she ran on past the two boys and on up the lane. David stood in the middle of the lane with Miles by his side. The gang of youths cased to a halt.

"Is she one of your father's, sir?" Godfrey asked, looking nervous, "We didn't know."

"She's one of mine." David said, "At least, she will be. I suggest you all get back to work."

"Sir?" Godfrey replied, "Mr. Allen's overseeing the slaves while they clean the stables. This afternoon, we'll exercise the horses."

"In any case, you can go back the way you came." David said, "I have other business here."

"Yes sir." Godfrey replied, "Good hunting, sir."

Once they were alone, the world shimmered again. They looked around then returned to the field finding their two horses. A message appeared on the screen.

Situation unexpected but manageable. What did you learn?

"Ah! I didn't sound very nice over there. Neither did Godfrey. We have slaves?"

No! They have slaves. The idea disgusts you. You sent Allen away, they do not care about his interests in slaves.

"Is that world in decline?"

No. It is developing slowly.

"So I can't help."

You can't interfere. Help is only when it is wanted.

"OK so I've learnt something but it wasn't much of an adventure."

Apologies. It was the only event within acceptable dimensional parameters.

"Whatever that means." Miles muttered.

Temporal displacement possible. Event maybe time ahead or behind. Displacement varies world to world and takes more energy.

"Are there places that you could send me but you'd have to recharge so I'd have to stay there for a day no matter what?"

Yes.

OK. We visit Danny's world and the stone circle world regularly. Do we move through time?

Answer not straightforward. Best reply; take shortest route.

"That'll do. How many worlds developed the portal?"

One. Others try but inter-dimensional consciousness blocks them. I hope that does as well.

David smiled, "In theory, would I have to fight an evil world that was building a portal?"

You may have to fight you. You understand that now but you are not ready. Remember, search for right successor to creators took many years. On many worlds, your father died in war. Lord Carlton became protector and he is a bad guide to life. Others, dukedom never happened. Other influences affected family. No two worlds identical.

"Is this how the creators were destroyed?"

Yes!

"Oh!"

"And all the baddies are waiting until Pebbles is ready to slay them." Miles interjected.

Foe is gaining influence, trying to stop you but is still weak. Creators not ready. You not ready but time is coming. Not stopped, enemy will control many worlds. If it controls you through Lord Carlton, it controls me – disaster. Wait. Situation developing.

Returning you.

The world shimmered and although he was used to jumps, it took a few moments to take in the scene for he was watching himself beating Godfrey with a riding crop. As David recovered, so he leapt forward, grabbing the other's arm.

"How dare you touch me. Let me go ..." the other David yelled but trailed off, confused as he recognised his assailant. The other was slightly chubbier than David but there was a hard, cruel look to his face though David thought that he detected something else. The other David looked around for help but paused startled as he saw Miles.

"Markham!" he exclaimed, "What are you doing here? Is this your man?"

"Hardly, do you intend scrapping or can I have a go at introducing you two gentlemen?"

"A gentleman would not interfere between master and servant." the other David exclaimed angrily, "I say that he's no gentleman but a family bastard. I'm the Right Honourable David Pevensey. My father's the Earl of Brabborn. You are?"

"David Pevensey, Duke of Barabourne. Sadly my father died."

"Don't be facetious." the other David snapped, "Now tell me who you really are."

"I'm afraid that he's quite correct." Miles said, "You should visit the dukedom, it's something else. Tell me are your carriages steam driven? Do you know about electricity?"

"Are you suggesting that I live in some backwater and rely on horses but what is electricity?

"I'm just trying to get my bearings. This is dreadfully confusing you know, Pebbles."

"You were always an idiot, Markham, but wait until the chaps at school hear how you've been taken in by this liar."

"David, I mean the duke, why don't you see if your Godfrey could fetch one of his vehicles down to the field. Let's compare worlds."

"Why not?" David chuckled. The other David looked on bewildered as David took out his phone and spoke into it. The other David could see it light up and could hear a voice emanating from it but could not pick out the words.

"He says that he'll send Todd. He has to change to escort

Isabella."

"You claim to be noble, yet you let a servant talk to you like that. What is it with village wenches? My servant thinks that I care about one and you allow yours to escort one as if she's a lady. I'm not putting up with any more nonsense, Godfrey, take him. The constable can deal with him."

"That's not a good idea." Miles said quietly, "Todd won't be long and you won't be disappointed. On second thoughts, you might be, I'm not sure that you could understand the significance of Godfrey's devices."

"I am not an idiot." the other David yelled raising his riding crop, "Godfrey, do as I say, take him."

"Portal, get us home." Miles snapped and the portal complied.

"Portal send us back but in a different location." Miles commanded again.

Again the portal complied, and both Miles and David had to stifle their giggles at the others' confusion. Godfrey just stood turning to his master while the other David seemed to want to speak but could only gulp in air.

"How did you do that?" he finally managed to splutter.

"I'm a duke so I outrank you and I prefer not to be questioned." David said, "Suffice it to say, that some information is not meant for bullies who abuse their people."

David took out his phone and took a picture of the scene before showing it to the still perplexed Earl's son.

"My people help me develop all sorts of strange devices and they're going to make us all rich. Your people fear the whip. They're too cowed to help you, is that what you really want?"

"They're servants and they do as they're told." the other David said though he spoke with less conviction.

"Then I'm not wasting any more time on you." David snapped, "Portal, take us home."

David, the earl's son, stared in amazement as the visitors vanished again.

"What do you know about all this, Godfrey?" he asked.

"Nothing, sir." Godfrey replied, terrified.

David, the earl's son, smiled, "I wasn't accusing you. I was curious. Do you have ideas that could make us rich? Do you know who those people were? Do you know anything useful?"

"Er ..." Godfrey began but trailed off, glancing at the riding crop. David's eyes followed his look and nodded before dropping it.

~~~

On the other side of the portal, David and Miles stared at each other before bursting into laughter.

"And there was no danger." Miles said, "I like adventures like that."

David was still laughing as a thought crossed his mind, "Portal if we had been grabbed, could you have got us home?"

Once grabbed, could only transport all.

"So it was Miles' quick thinking that saved us."

Miles' skill is anticipating trouble. One effect, he deflects trouble by being buffoon, fop, allowing himself to be laughed at. Another effect, he protects you while you deal with problem. You made Earl's son see servants as people.

"Another lucky find, a coincidence."

Superficial thoughts accepted general opinion of Markhams. Deeper thoughts knew them better. Why else did you ask for their help?"

"I'm sorry Miles. The portal's right. I didn't see much beyond your reputation."

"If I understand the portal correctly, you did see more in us but it didn't surface until it was needed."

You understand correctly. Consider this. Others were helped by you but none spoke except the Tamzon's. You accepted their protection. Skeffington has demonstrated his abilities on two occasions. Cooper is devious. He wants his son to have prospects and found an excuse to bring him here yet he has lost face by going into hiding. Manipulation, Skeffington was brought here by his father. I'm informing you that he would be good replacement for Godfrey. Decision yours.

"You're saying that Skeffington displayed his qualities but didn't know where they were leading. His father saw something in David and hoped that he would help Skeffington." Miles said, then added as it occurred to him, "Others lacked the courage to even speak to David."

Correct.

"My father said that as head of the family and the estates, everything revolves around us. You keep making it clear that it doesn't. No-one is going to knuckle his forehead and say, 'Yes Your Grace. Anything you say Your Grace'. I don't suppose I want that, but I do get the feeling that things keep running away and I'm losing control."

Logic says that looser control is more effective. Don't understand feelings but understand conflict in thoughts. You were still in control in London. You had defined events and they followed their course even if you were prisoner and did not feel in control.

"Fair enough. The creators have this quest for me. They've suggested Danny's friend, Craig because he's so interested in science but he hates me. Supposing I look for someone else."

References.

"Huh?"

Portal can supply reference or not. So can your deep thoughts. Both need time.

"Fair enough. I thought that Skeffington would know what to do when Blackman arrested me. Even Wilson speaks highly of him though I think Wilson just likes being treated like a wine connoisseur."

"What's this about a quest?" Miles asked, "You've mentioned the portal's creators and their enemies but what about the rest?

"I have to save the people who built the portal."

"And you want our help. Aren't we a bit young for that sort of thing?" Miles asked.

Able to absorb new ideas and new thinking. Experience would be good but no-one has any for your quest. Are you ready to begin, David?

"I'll sound out Craig. Miles and I have to be ready to give evidence here. There's Godfrey's wedding but that's all."

You forget Lord Carlton. He may be idiot but he's also intriguer. Encouraged to hate you. You have given King incentive to introduce changes. Allow him time. Creators also need time.

David nodded, mentally reviewing the situation at Barabourne. One day, he would have to ask why his Uncle Jethro preferred to live quietly at Barabourne rather than in town or obtaining his own estates. However, the general care of Barabourne was in his capable hands so there was no problem there. Todd was a typical teenager, one day wanting to be a doctor, the next a pilot. Whatever he ended up doing, at present he was proving an excellent link between the scientific knowledge on his birth world and the research being undertaken in his adopted world.

Billy was David's biggest concern, unhappy about the relationship between him and Cradawg who was worldly enough to understand electronics and engineering. However, he believed that he was guided by the gods and spent much of the time trying to understand their wishes. On David's or Danny's world Billy would be considered in moral danger. On Cradawg's world he was learning how to understand his deepest thoughts and feelings by a wise and gentle mentor. In return, he shared Cradawg's efforts to moderate Bran's attempts to control everything.

Finally, there was Godfrey and Isabella. Godfrey was now manager of the stables and garages. He was busy developing light tractors and vehicles and offering Isabella a more equal marriage than was usual on that world. He fully supported her efforts to become an established authoress and was delighted when she pulled on a pair of overalls to work with him.

"Right!" David exclaimed, "I don't want to start anything except see about Craig. Once the court cases and the other stuff are over, I'll think about the quest. Portal, is that acceptable to the creators?"

There was an unusually long pause before the portal answered.
Creators also have problems to deal with which is why they need time. You will be informed when quest can begin.

One problem changed. Sir Cloudsley Pomfret-Smythe committed suicide. Using the courts to obtain 8-10 year old girls created a scandal that no-one could openly support, not even to close ranks against the lower classes. By taking his life he had avoided fines and penalties that would have left his wife and children destitute.

As it became obvious that anyone who might have helped him was either under arrest or covering their tracks, PC Blackman agreed to plead guilty and turn King's evidence against his former allies. The only concession was that he would be held in a Scottish prison away from anyone who knew him.

With the threat against them disintegrating, David and Miles could visit London again. Skeffington and Danny accompanied them.

"How are your ribs?" David asked, "You understand where the

portal takes us and I need a team to help me with a quest. Are you interested in joining?"

"Why me? I left you and ran. I know everyone says I did right, but you need someone who doesn't run."

"You're as bad David." Miles exclaimed, "You both think that you're gods who can do everything. David wants another go at visiting those warehouses. It's too dangerous for David on his own so he needs a protector. At least he understands that now. You need to understand that you can't take on crooked magistrates and police. You leave that to us."

"All right, my ribs still hurt a bit but I can handle it." Skeffington said, "And thank you. What's your job, Danny?"

Danny looked uncomfortable as he sought an answer.

"He's always there when we need him." David interjected, "If we found ourselves on Mars, he'd be gathering rocks while the rest of us get over the shock. He'd also be the first to spot that the Martians are taking aim and get us under cover. Miles is a bit like that as well."

As Danny grinned happily at David's opinion of him, Skeffington nodded. There was no question of David going under cover this time so they piled into a hackney cab, a four wheeled growler. It was Skeffington who was the least used to travelling by a horse drawn coach. Danny was used to the broughams on David's estate but at first he was confused by their nickname, growler. He was still the seasoned traveller though, while Skeffington revelled in the unusual luxury.

As they turned into the yard, the visitors could see it was full of activity. Workmen were collecting materials from stored piles while stalls were full of goods and knick-knacks for sale. David was sure that an outbuilding had been turned into a pottery.

Rather than go straight in, David led the way in browsing the stalls. Someone hurried into the main building and a chubby businessman came out to stroll over.

"Welcome, gentlemen." he said, "Are you looking for anything in particular?"

"No, thank you." David replied, "I didn't expect to find a market here, so I'm just looking around."

"This is a new venture, we encourage residents to find hidden talents. If they do, then there's a potential source of income."

"Mr. Jones, is it?" David asked and as the man nodded, continued, "I'm David Pevensey, Duke of Barabourne. I approve but I'm wondering about the financing."

"Ah!" Mr. Jones said, "The budgets provide for quality supplies but some suggested suppliers are somewhat expensive. I shop around, and find cheaper sources but I don't skimp on quality. Local businesses are also willing to help and donate materials. That's how we got the kiln."

"Most firms would see you as a rival undermining them and giving their workers ideas."

"Some do." Mr. Jones responded, "Some think that helping us will give them an edge in getting electricity and we've convinced others that we won't compete directly. If a furniture maker produces chairs in the finest mahogany, we'll make stools that are cheerfully painted."

"Skeffington, take a look around inside will you, please? You should know residents so they'll talk to you." David said, "Mr. Jones, you appear to be running this place exactly as I envisaged but I do need to be sure and I'm not trying to find fault. I do believe that you have problems recording your activities so I'd like Sir Douglas to visit and help you organise the books. That way you'll be better covered and maybe be able to expand."

"You're not coming in." Mr. Jones asked, "I'm sure the residents would like to thank you for your kindness."

"No. It'll be too phoney. They'll be duty-bound to say 'thank you very much for your kindness'. I'll be duty-bound to say that it's my pleasure and you're all doing very well."

Mr. Jones laughed cheerfully, "You're right of course, Your Grace. It's all forced and not sincere, but I can assure you, they do appreciate what you're doing."

"That's enough. I had a bad experience the last time I visited this area and I think that I need to lay a few ghosts."

"I know what you achieved and what it cost you. The locals love you and would not understand your wish to be in the background."

Luckily, Skeffington arrived and ended an awkward conversation for David.

"I gather Sir Douglas Mayhew has visited." Skeffington said, "Mrs Hawkes isn't how she was described to me."

Mr. Jones smiled, "This is her first job in a long time and she was scared of losing it. When Sir Douglas visited for the first time he explained that audits would take in more than the books and said that I should detail what I did even if I couldn't produce a chit for everything. It put Mrs Hawkes' mind at rest and she really looks after residents now."

Skeffington nodded.

"One thing, Your Grace. There's a family in there and all three children have the measles. Apparently there's no budget for doctors or medicines."

David took out his wallet and handed Mr. Jones the cash.

"Will that do for a start? I'll ask Sir Douglas to work something out for medical bills."

"Yes Your Grace. Thank you."

"How about other children. Are they at risk?"

"I don't think so, Your Grace." The family has three cubicles side by side. There's double beds in each of them and room for a table, chairs and a dresser. It's not overcrowded by any means."

"I'll make an official visit sometime." David said, "Today though, I just want to be sure that all's well."

As they left, David asked Skeffington, "How was it, really?"

"Bloody good." Skeffington replied, "It was almost like your village, everyone helping out."

"OK! Dorrit Street next. Miles, Danny, this isn't really your problem. Do you mind coming along?"

"You're doing all this and you want me along." Miles exclaimed, "I don't feel like the village idiot any more. Lead on."

"Same here. I want to help." Danny replied.

There was a guard at Dorrit Street.

"Yes?" he said tersely.

"We're just visiting friends who are staying here." David said.

"Visiting hour is between five and six. Come back then."

"It's not a prison." David snapped, "Residents can receive guests when they like."

"Clear off now, or I send for a policeman."

"I suggest you send for the manager instead. I am the Duke of Barabourne. Please give him my card."

The guard studied the card, then looked at David, before muttering, "Wait here please," and hurrying off.

When he arrived, Mr. Serling looked like a bank manager, stern and unsmiling until he saw David but even then his greeting was hardly warm.

"Thank you, Eastman. You should have recognised him. We have his picture in the main hall. My apologies, Your Grace, please come through to my office."

"No thank you. After Mr. Dobson, I assume that you were appointed for your business skills. That's fine, I'd like Skeffington to talk to one or two of the residents but it's not an official visit. He's just visiting friends."

"Yes of course. Everything is in order and accounted for. We can make an exception for your friend."

"Mr. Serling, you are not running a prison. You are running accommodation for people who have fallen on hard times. I know that some may be drunks or drug users, others have mental problems but many just need a helping hand. They don't need being regimented."

This time Mr. Serling's smile was warmer.

"I'm sorry Your Grace, it's mine and Mr. Jones' fault. You see we work together and send the fit and able to Stable Row. Here we have children as young as ten, youngsters who are, shall we say, a bit simple and older folk whose brains have been addled by drink or drugs.

"We have strict rules that require them to er, lose any habits that they have acquired on the streets. Those that can't we try to hand over to organisations better able to cope and some may need support here for life."

"I see. I must have missed the report."

"There isn't one yet, Your Grace. It's something that's developed and we're preparing one to send to Sir Douglas. I'm afraid that Sir Douglas did say that we should use our initiative and I'm sorry if we've gone too far."

"No. You see your role as protecting the vulnerable and I can go along with that. Skeffington, take a look around please."

They waited in silence until Skeffington returned.

"There are small dormitories instead of individual rooms." he said, "They were being cleaned and the bedding changed. The youngsters were in classrooms doing their letters and the older ones were doing basket weaving. It felt like a school but it was all right."

"That's all I want for now." David said, "My only suggestion is that you make the reception a little friendlier. How about getting plans for a proper reception room?"

"Yes thank you, Your Grace. Perhaps we should be more welcoming."

"Getting the balance right will take experience. Just do what you can."

"Right" David said when they were back in the carriage, "Next stop, the police station."

The young police constable behind the desk looked up nervously when they entered. David was pale, clenching his fists as memories flooded back and it was Miles who spoke.

"P.C. Pritchard please."

"Sergeant Pritchard, you mean, sir. Your names, please."

"Tell him, assorted Robin Cashmans. Don't worry, he'll get the joke when he sees us." Miles interjected.

"Stop being an ass." David snapped.

"Do you want him to turn out the guard?" Miles asked quietly, "I thought a light-hearted announcement might be in order."

Sergeant Pritchard seemed just as angry when he came through the door but when he saw his visitors his face split into a wide grin.

"So I've got all three in my station again. I hope it's a quieter visit though."

"Robin Cashman is here?" Miles asked in surprise, "I'd have thought that he'd be in Dartmoor or released by now."

"He's on remand, pending an appeal, but also being questioned on other matters."

"Do you have much on him?"

"PC Ian Jarvis owned an expensive pocket watch. We found it among other trinkets in Cashman' room. If we find more evidence, then he's heading for the noose."

Miles glanced at David whose breathing was rapid and shallow. He was still ashen and his knuckles were white from his clenched his fists.

"Thank you, Sergeant. It's time we went."

Sgt. Pritchard glanced at David and nodded.

"No." David gasped, "I want to see that room where ..."

"Do you think that's wise?" Miles interrupted as David

faltered.

"I need to see it."

"Maybe you do." Sergeant Pritchard said softly, "It's an interview room again."

"Very well. We'll interview Cashman. I am a magistrate, so I'm entitled if we ignore questions of jurisdiction." David said, his breathing more relaxed.

"I think we'll have to ignore more than jurisdiction but I don't see why not."

Chapter 6

David faltered again when he saw the table but relaxed as he was invited to sit behind it. It was Miles' memories that were rattled when he saw Robin Cashman dressed in the hooped cotton shirt and trousers and in chains.

"Hello Robin." David began in a conversational, almost friendly voice, "I'm David Pevensey, Duke of Barabourne and you planted a diamond necklace on me to frame me. I'd like to know why?"

"That was stupid, wasn't it?" Cashman replied in a surprisingly cultured voice, "Father always said that the devil is in the detail. Unfortunately it was not the time to be properly introduced, so I missed that particular detail."

David chuckled, "Do I hear a Yorkshire accent, but you've been to public school?"

"Very good, Your Grace."

"And your family?"

"According to Father, I have no family. You know, I still like the old boy so I'd rather not embarrass him further."

"Further?"

"I like girls, you understand, but father insisted on closeting me in all-boys schools. After three schools, and three expulsions, he would not accept that others willingly offered to give me relief which comes back to you."

"I'm sorry, I don't understand." David said.

"It's part of my dues to Blackman. I either find alternative entertainment or satisfy his needs personally."

"Why did he need your help? Surely he could have just arrested me."

"Witnesses. I bet he made a great show of searching you and finding the necklace. The grateful owner would identify it and maybe even give him a reward."

"Did you think about all the lives you ruined?"

No, I did what I had to do. Do you think about the lives you ruin when you close a factory and leave everyone destitute?"

"David doesn't do that. He's converting warehouses so people have a chance." Danny interrupted.

"How about PC Ian Jarvis?" David asked.

"Stupid boy." Cashman exclaimed, "Just because he was planning to get married, he didn't want any part of it. If he was that stuck on girls, he'd have got on with Sir Cloudsley and his police friends; he'd have been an Inspector by now. How is Sir Cloudsley? I used to provide a warm-up entertainment with his girls. You know, to get him going."

"Sir Cloudsley's dead." David said, "The evidence against him was overwhelming so he took his own life. What's wrong?"

Robin had turned deathly white and would have fallen if Sgt. Pritchard hadn't held him. There was a tremor in his voice as he spoke.

"He promised to help me. He knew that you weren't Robin Cashman when you stood before him. The police would have had a body at Dartmoor and I'd have had your name. It doesn't matter now, does it, but he did look after his friends."

"So he sentenced me to a birching, knowing that I was telling the truth?" Miles exclaimed angrily.

"Who are you?" Robin asked, "I don't understand."

"It doesn't matter. You thought that Sir Cloudsley was going to rescue you to perform for him again?"

Cashman nodded unhappily but then looked pleadingly at David, "What's happened to Blackman?"

"Earning a lighter sentence by telling us everything he knows."

"About what happened to Ian Jarvis?"

"Probably. I'm only talking to you because you framed me. I don't know anything about the police investigation."

Robin Cashman glanced at David's three friends, defeated.

"I've got nothing to offer, have I? You've already got a selection."

"It's something that you wouldn't understand, they're friends. I don't want what you're offering from anyone."

"No-one's that perfect. Are you sure that you don't have a price?"

David was now calm enough to realise that Robin was desperate.

"Let's just say that no-one has ever offered enough." He replied.

"All right. Have you got enemies? I can deal with them you know? Sir Cloudsley didn't like Jarvis snooping around."

"You know, that could interest me. Lord Carlton for a start." David said, "You are being interviewed by a fourteen-year-old boy. It's hardly going to sound convincing in court, is it? Why don't you tell us what you're capable of?"

Cashman seemed to have forgotten that Sgt. Pritchard was still in the room or maybe, he thought that he was now in David's pocket. Either way he had seen a way out and had nothing to lose.

"Jarvis was easy. He thought that he could search me but once he was close enough I knifed him. There was a reporter snooping around and he thought that I was an informer. Do you know, the idiot thought that we were shaking hands. I almost pulled him onto the knife."

"You sound as if you could be useful but I need a bit more. What was the reporter's name?"

"Jack Cunn …" Robin suddenly remembered where he was and glanced towards Sgt. Pritchard who leaning unconcernedly against the wall.

"Jack Cunningham?" Sgt. Pritchard asked unconcernedly, "What did you do with the body?"

"In the river." Robin answered and Sgt. Pritchard nodded in confirmation, "So am I what you want?"

"No. I've got my own ways of tricking people. Listen!"

David pulled out the phone he carried and played back a recording. If Sgt. Pritchard was startled, Robin Cashman was devastated to hear his own words condemning him.

"Don't worry. This can't be played at your trial but I'm going to see if it interests the king's special investigators. If it does, then … they don't use torture but it can be pretty close."

Cashman collapsed to his knees in tears.

"No please, I'll tell you everything but please help me." He sobbed, "I don't want to hang."

"I don't suppose Ian Jarvis or Jack Cunningham wanted to die, either." David said, "Oh and I do know that Sir Cloudsley's girls could be as young as eight and you admit to being part of that as well. It's sad, because in a way I do like you.

"Here's the best that I can do. Make statements to Sgt. Pritchard and you can stand trial as Robin Cashman instead of your real name to protect your family name. Help the investigators and I'll send my family solicitor to represent you. I'll even send a tailor to dress you in smart clothes. Don't cooperate and you'll be in those prison clothes, chains and smelling of lye. It's not much but it's all you're going to get."

As they left the police station, David took a deep breath.

"That room looks so ordinary now." He said, "How about you, Miles? Are you all right?"

"It gave me the creeps but what about Cashman?" Miles asked, "I agree that there was something likeable about him."

"I know but he was playing with us." David retorted, "I see now how he could charm anyone and why do you suppose Ian Jarvis and Jack Cunningham dropped their guard so easily? I was sent a report about him. Apparently, Sir Cloudsley found pairs of girls. He watched while one was tortured and raped and the other could either be very willing or be … er, encouraged. Cashman was often the torturer. Despite what he said, he would rape the footman just as easily as a maid at Barabourne and not care. He'd slit my throat if Lord Carlton offered more than me."

David paused thoughtfully before continuing, "His father is a factory owner, a pillar of the church and makes large donations to the local alms houses. He is known as a kind gentle man and his other children love him. What upset the father, was that even then, Cashman's victims were younger and one almost lost an eye after a bad beating for 'snitching'. I'm happy to keep the family out of it all."

"So why did you want to see him?" Danny asked.

"I didn't know that he was there but when Sgt. Pritchard told me that he was, I was curious. I'm glad that I did see him because I understand more."

Their final visit was to St Justin's Circus where he greeted Jeremiah and Lindsay as they worked on their stalls.

"It's good to see you, sir" Jeremiah said, "I 'ope you're well."

"Very well, thank you." David replied, "I believe that it's my round, would you care to join me?"

"It's not snowing, today, sir. I should stay open. Lindsay, you remember David, 'Is Grace that is."

"Course I fucking … Hof course, Hi do." Lindsay replied, "Hit's hay pleasure to see you haygain."

Danny started giggling, "I'm sorry. It's just that Lindsay needs to give Jeremiah some of her aitches."

"Allow me to introduce Danny Lambert. His family looked after me when I was lost and they're down-to-Earth people. They wouldn't change how they spoke for the king."

Lindsay smiled, "You were fucking all right the last time you were fucking here and I fucking was putting it on a bit."

"Don't bother on my account." David replied, "I felt at ease here otherwise I wouldn't have said who I was."

"That's kindly said, Your Grace." Jeremiah said, "And it's good of you to visit again."

"How are things around here, nowadays?" David asked.

"Better, sir." Jeremiah replied, "I like electric light in my 'ouse even if the landlord wants to put up the rent."

"Tell him that you'll form a tenants association and you'll have Sir Douglas Mayhew representing you."

The girl who had acted as messenger on his last visit was standing close to Lucy. Suddenly she piped up "They want to name the pub after you. Someone said call it *David's Haven*. I like it but everyone says it's not respectful."

"I like it too." David laughed, "The sign should have a picture of us all enjoying a drink together."

"What do you say, Ebie?" Jeremiah asked

While they had been talking, a small crowd had gathered around. Reassured by the friendly atmosphere they had stood content to listen but Jeremiah had turned to a lad of about fifteen.

"'e's a clever one, 'e is and an artist." Jeremiah explained, "'e's labouring now and it's ruining 'is 'ands."

"I gotta look after me mum and sis." Ebie said, shrugging.

"Ebie?" David queried, "What do you say about the pub name."

"Ebenezer Frazer, Your Grace." he replied, "I like *The Incognito* with a picture of you in all your robes and another sitting with us like you said."

"I take it that you're an artist." David said, "Let me see your hands."

At a nod from Jeremiah, Ebie complied though he obviously resented the public examination.

"OK." David said, "They are getting torn up, aren't they?"

"Whoa there, Pebbles." Miles exclaimed, "I know what you're thinking and you need to stop."

David turned angrily to Miles but before he could speak, Skeffington interrupted, "Miles is right. You've mentioned education before and now you've got a reason for doing something. What are you thinking, schools for the country or just the whole of London?"

"Excuse me, sir." Jeremiah contributed, "You're doing enough, I didn't ask Ebie's opinion to push 'im onto you."

David smiled, "And none of you think that I'm big-headed enough to want another pub named after me. I like *The Incognito* because it tells the story but it's up to the pub's owner. If he's willing, I'll pay Ebie to come up with some designs. If they're good enough, then I'll sponsor him to be apprenticed to a sign-writer and I want something in return.

"We're training electrical artisans and we're going to need other sorts of artisans. The problem is they need to read more than just the bible. That's my fellow peers idea of education. I need ways of improving education and I'm wondering whether communities like this could invest in their children's future."

There was a thoughtful silence.

"If your Mr. Serling and Mr. Jones can 'elp, we'll try." Jeremiah said, "You understand, there's plenty 'oo just want to earn enough for the pub."

"I know." David answered, "I'm using this area to test ideas. If other areas like what we're doing then help them start their own schemes but I don't have to be involved. Does that suit you, Miles? Skeffington?"

"Be 'onest with us. Do you profit out of all this?"

"I will do." David replied, "I could be become the richest man in the world."

"But not at the moment."

"No. Everything goes into development and investment."

"Do you consider us an investment?"

David thought for a moment, "Yes I do. My fellow peers are content to sit on their backsides and do nothing while everything stagnates. You can't do that or you'd starve but you have little incentive to improve things or to change them."

"I understand. You're saying that you gain if we gain. It makes you 'uman if you want something. You're staying at 'is place

Skevi, is 'is Grace and this other toff genuine?"

"Yes they are." Skeffington replied, "I've seen a posh doctor talking to a tramp who knew a bit about healing herbs. Miles here doesn't look like a toff when he puts on overalls and helps the stable hand build a new engine. David lets me use his library and his butler teaches me about wine."

Jeremiah nodded, "We'll 'elp and you can leave Ebie to us. We'll see that 'e gets that apprenticeship. You just leave us to our own affairs."

David nodded. It was time to leave but as they walked up to the main road, Miles said, "That's gratitude for you. They more or less told you to go."

"It was the best thing that they could say." David said, "They know that I'll not cause hardship if they start getting above themselves so they want the chance to try. Let's see what happens."

In fact, David was far less certain than he pretended to be. The portal expected him to save his world from the stagnation that he mentioned but it was an impossible job. True, he had convinced the king that he could be more tolerant, now he had persuaded a small community that they could do something about their lives but it had barely scratched the surface of the problem. The king might still be worried about rebellion in the north but for now though, he had done what he could. It was time to turn his attention to the next problem he could do something about.

"OK." David said, "Danny, I'd like you to return to your home-world and invite Craig to spend a few days with us here in London. I'd like you to give him a journey he'll never forget. Steamer from the Royal George to the airship mast, airship to St. James' park then growler to Eton Square. Oh and if Darren can make it, then I'd like him to skipper the airship."

Danny stared for a moment then grinned, "You want to blow his mind, don't you? You want it to come as a complete shock, don't you?"

"Will it work?" David asked.

Danny nodded, "If his Dad allows it. He's a control freak and he checks on everything that Craig does and it's never good enough. He reckons that I'm rubbish bringing Craig down."

He paused thoughtfully, "I have to meet my uncle, and I'm having dinner at the Savoy. I call Jethro uncle so if we stop long enough to introduce him I won't be lying will I? Mum doesn't want me travelling alone but reckons we're old enough to go in pairs. Mum might help out with a story like that."

"Do you want to dine at the Savoy?" David asked.

"No, I can say that we changed our minds and stayed at his place in Eton Square. Craig's dad will be impressed by that. Do you really want him though?"

"No, I don't but the creators know people and they think that he's a possibility. Let's find out."

~~~

"I shouldn't encourage you to lie," Danny's mother said the following morning, "But that man's a nasty piece of work. I reckon Craig knows and is unhappy about it. I'm proud of you, and David for that matter for giving him a chance. I'll phone him for you."

Danny caught snatches of the conversation.

"Yes, he doesn't get to London very often, that's why it's such short notice … Danny's very responsible but it's his first time going up there alone, I'm thinking that there's safety in numbers … Yes I did say that they'd be staying in Eton Square."

"You're lucky that he's such a snob." She chuckled as she hung up. "Once I'd mentioned the address then Craig was going whether he wanted to or not."

Not long after Craig was on the phone complaining about being pressured.

"I just wanted to get your old man on side." Danny said, "Look, before it's all decided, I need your word. You won't tell anyone where we're really going. My mum knows and she's been there but there's no way that your dad can ever know."

"Why?" Craig asked and Danny could hear more curiosity than anger in his voice.

"Promise first and you'll find out."

"So we're not going to meet a rich uncle."

"I said, promise first and then you'll find out. I've got a sort of adopted uncle who is very rich and you'll probably meet him but that's all I'm telling you."

Curiosity now dominated and Craig was waiting, backpack already over his shoulders when Danny arrived in a taxi.

"Royal George, Barnbury Lane, please." Danny told the driver as Craig clambered into the taxi.

"Why not the station?" Craig asked, "There's a direct service to Victoria."

Danny glanced pointedly at the driver and whispered, "Not yet. This is phase 1 of the journey, just go along with it until phase 3, OK?"

Craig realised the driver was trying to listen and his love of spy stories took over. He nodded. As they drew up at the Royal George, Craig saw the brake driven by Godfrey and looked quizzically at Danny.

"That's phase 2." Danny said, "Ready?"

Craig was beginning to believe that he would end up on a remote farm surrounded by steam-punk nutters but he had to admit, the steam brake was fun, and he would like to drive it. For now, he relaxed, enjoying the view from a novel position.

His fears about a remote farm seemed to be confirmed when they turned into a field though he gasped as the hall came into sight until his attention was drawn to the airship that they were approaching.

"Ready for phase 3?" Danny asked.

"We're travelling in that?" Craig gasped, "Is it your uncle's? Is he flying us to London?"

No, it's a naval ship. Darren will be skippering it but don't worry. The Chief Petty Officer is training him."

"Who's Darren?" Craig asked, "I know it's stupid but for a moment I thought you meant your brother."

"I did." Danny answered, "It's like a different world, isn't it?"

Danny was extremely pleased with himself for planting the idea of a different world in Craig's mind. He was pleasantly surprised when Craig grinned and nodded.

Craig already had a sense that things were not right. The chief petty officer's uniform seemed better suited to a 1940s war film and Darren even had an air of being in charge as he bent over the chart table. He smiled a greeting to his brother and Craig, then gave his orders.

He was still confident as the airship rose and turned onto course, steadily gathering height and speed while CPO Hammond dutifully handled the controls. Neither did tapping a message on odd looking radio equipment and noting the reply seem to worry him. Craig read enough to know that they were expected, somewhere, but he was not sure where. When he turned to look out of the window, his sense of unreality increased.

A train was pulling into Chasebourne Station. The problem was that it was a steam train and Chasebourne was little more than a village. There were no dual carriageways linking the town to the motorway, Craig could not even see the motorway though they had to cross at least one to reach London.

"Chief, I think we're over the wrong town. It looks more like Bromley than Croydon." Darren called out, "Is it OK if we turn 20^0 to port."

"Mr. Lambert, I know that you're just a passenger on this trip but will you take over the helm please?"

"Yes Chief." Danny replied, "Come on, Craig. You take the wheel while I handle the flight controls."

Craig stared wide-eyed but followed Danny, gingerly taking the wheel from CPO Hammond.

Danny glanced at his position then spoke to Craig, "The arrow thing shows that the rudder has 5^0 of port. That's because of the wind. You'll feel the rudder trying to turn and you hold it. The compass shows the course so if we start turning, I'll tell you how to compensate."

Craig nodded, unable to speak. Of all the possibilities he had considered for the trip, steering an airship never entered his thoughts.

"Increase rudder to 15^0." Darren called out and Craig suddenly found everyone looking at him. He spun the wheel and the indicator duly moved then he looked up, watching the sun move around.

"The correct answer is to say, '15^0 of port helm, Skipper'." Darren said, "You then repeat it when you're done."

"15^0 of port helm, er, Skipper." Craig duly repeated.

"Darren's a Captain Bligh when he's in charge." Danny laughed, "Go with it though, because he's good."

Craig nodded. It was all too strange but he was enjoying the novel experience. CPO Hammond was also enjoying himself. He took a lot of ribbing about becoming a schoolteacher but he was impressed with his young squad, especially Darren.

As they approached St. James' park, he should have taken over but Darren was fractionally ahead of him and giving the right orders. Instead, he positioned himself beside Craig to keep an eye on the newest crew member but again, Danny was explaining things and Craig was coping.

"Drop anchor." Darren called out then, "Stop engines. The crew is relieved."

Darren turned nervously to CPO Hammond who contented himself with a nod. Craig was shaking.

"Wow!" he managed to exclaim.

"Phase 4." Danny said, "We hail a cab."

Craig looked at the horse drawn brougham then at the rest of the traffic.

"It really is a different world, isn't it?" he whispered, "What's going on?"

"Not yet." Danny said but before they could climb in Lt. Worthington hurried up to them.

"His Majesty wishes to see you." He gasped.

"Us?" Danny exclaimed, "David's not with us."

"He knows. The exact invitation is that I should ask Mr. Lambert and Mr. Williams to visit him. It's more of an invitation than you think because normally it's 'attend him'."

"Come on." Danny chuckled, "Attend or visit, it's not the sort of invitation that we can refuse."

Craig did not appreciate the joke but he had picked up on something.

"His Majesty?" He queried, "It's still 2018 isn't it?"

"Do you remember when you laughed at David for being so confused by history?" Danny asked, "He wanted to explain but we've been summoned by King Charles VII and I hope I remember when to bow."

"David? You mean his stories were true? He hates me, why am I here? Is he a duke? How did we get here?"

"David doesn't hate you and you're here because he needs your help. We tricked you a bit because we had to convince you that David really is the Duke of Barabourne, at least on this world. There is an uncle, Lord Westerham and David's real uncle but all of David's friends call him uncle because it's respectful."

"OK!" Craig muttered, "I get it but what's going on now?"

"I don't know." Danny admitted, "He's OK though."

As always, Danny felt the angry eyes of the high and mighty in the land burnt into his skull. For all practical purposes they were just a couple of badly dressed guttersnipes with privileges that they could only dream of. Danny tried kneeling as he saw the king and Craig even more uncertainly followed suit.

"Thank you for the courtesy." Charles said, "I understand that it's not your way. Is something wrong?"

"You usually say *we* not *I*, sir." Danny replied.

"Well spotted. My father said that King and state were indivisible. I no longer believe that to be true, and I think that it's a personal matter if I choose to have sausages for breakfast instead of kedgeree."

Danny grinned, "It makes sense, sir."

"We, that is the state and I do have agents keeping an eye on Barabourne, the boy and the estate which is how we learned of your visit. You, Mr. Williams, are not of this world yet we assume that you are here to assist His Grace so you're welcome."

"I don't know, sir. I don't really know what's going on."

"Danny?"

"Craig thought he was visiting his own London. We thought that he should figure out for himself that there really are parallel worlds."

"Ah, so you are still in a state of shock."

Craig nodded, feeling he should say something but Charles VII seemed satisfied as he called a young man in his mid-twenties over.

"I obtained your names from the airship's complement list so I have the advantage. Allow me to introduce my middle son, Malcolm Stuart and no, don't bow please. He wishes to be incognito."

Danny held out his hand to Malcolm with a cheerful, 'Hi'. Malcolm looked startled, grinned then took the proffered hand.

"Most people that we try this with, say 'Yes Your Majesty then hope that they can ignore me." Malcolm said, "Let Father explain further, though."

"Of all my children, Malcolm supports our reforms more than any. My oldest son may slip back into the old ways when he becomes king which is why we need to see our schemes firmly entrenched."

"Since I met your dad, er, sorry, His Majesty, I've become interested in what our royal family does." Danny said, "They become patrons of good causes and they're seen where it counts."

"And where does it count?" Malcolm asked.

"I don't know." Danny replied, "Sometimes it seems forced and a stunt and other times it seems as if they really care. David wants to open new warehouse accommodation but can't afford it. If you became involved and helped with running it, it might help. At home there might be pictures of you rolling up your sleeves and helping with the conversions."

"Would that be one of the stunts you mentioned?" the King asked.

"David says that when he stayed with me he started to see people. How do you see people? Do you think that they'll sit on their backsides until it's all done then just move in? Or do you think they'll be working beside you?"

"Blunt and to the point as usual." the King said, "Our agents say that His Grace has enough to contend with without further damaging his health. William might be more amenable to the changes if the mob cheers him more loudly and he took the credit for Malcolm's efforts. I suppose that's a bit false for you."

"It's politics though. I know you have to do it. David mentioned something about civil unrest so are you trying to get people on side?"

"We are. His Grace does inform us of all his activities and we do have agents looking out for him because there are hotheads on both sides of the argument. However, electricity is turning our industry into a world leader, and no-one else can keep up with the developments that your world supplies. Even the most extreme capitalist sees the potential profit but it makes Barabourne a prize to be won, not an ally. This quest that he has described is also dangerous but we cannot stop him for fear of jeopardising the portal.

"Giving Godfrey a knighthood gave him status before the commissioners and indirectly showed our support. It does not apply to you and technically you may be foreigners. Your brief is to look out for His Grace and should you need anything you may call on us through Lt. Worthington. We will recognise your efforts at some stage, even if only on this world and please note. I am using *we*."

"I wish I could tell my dad all about this." Craig muttered then looked up, "Sorry."

"Your father should have the chance to be proud of you. Speak to His Grace about it and I will assist if I can. Malcolm?"

"Father and I have discussed this and we agree that the warehouse scheme is giving His Grace a lot of support and a dangerous power-base. We don't doubt his loyalty but there's that fear that someone may seek to control him. We can either stop him or beat him at his own game and we have the resources to beat him because the less of a monopoly he has, the less useful he would be. I think that you see where this is leading, a trust named after me, but I take an active part. It's all a bit egalitarian for us so your views and assistance would be welcome."

"And is trying to be incognito a first step in your plans?"

"Very good." Malcolm smiled, "

"I don't know much about this sort of thing." Danny replied, "Visit St Justin's circus and ask for Jeremiah and Lucy. David, er, His Grace trusts them and they might help. I suppose that you take it for granted that people will help but they'll be wary of you until they see that you mean it. I think that they'll trust you more if you tell them about the publicity you want."

"And, very well, David, he won't be upset that we're stealing his project?"

"No way! He worries that he can't do enough to stop the great decline. He'll be delighted if you do more."

"Thank you, Danny." King Charles said, "Transport is waiting for you. His Grace will be wondering where you are and Malcolm must consider his plans. This discussion need not be kept from His Grace but if we need further discussion, we will send for you."

"I think that Skeffington Tamzon might be better. He knows the area and he visits our world. Malcolm, should meet him, I mean …"

"We, Malcolm and I, know what you mean and it is an idea. I don't expect you to understand court etiquette and I did say that my son is incognito."

"Thank you, sir." Danny replied, "I know I do everything wrong and I'm sorry."

"Don't be. This meeting has been more productive than any other I've had this week. I suspect that this is Malcolm's first conversation that treats him like a human being and he hasn't fainted in shock."

The courtiers in the room beyond wondered what Danny was laughing at as they left. Craig was just too confused as images of his day flashed around his mind and he stared at the steamer waiting for them.

"How come the king wanted to talk to you?" he asked, "How come you know all this stuff? I don't know anything about any of this so why am I really here?"

"You're here to help us steal a nuclear bomb." Danny said, "David has been chosen to help worlds. Don't ask me why because we're all kids."

"What do you mean, steal a nuclear bomb?" Craig yelled, "What the fuck are you talking about."

"When the brake picked us up from the pub, we travelled through a portal. Now that portal does other pretty cool stuff like teach us all sorts of stuff like languages when we go to a different world. It gets to know you and the kind of person you really are. It wanted us to give you a chance so here you are."

"OK but like you say, we're kids, still at school."

"Mr. Barton at the library says it helps because we can learn new ways of thinking. He could be right because you remember how Clarisa Young sounded off about how Brad Pitt had spoken to her when she got his autograph? David is the celebrity here and gets pubs named after him because he's helping people. He nearly got raped by a bent copper but he turned it all round so the copper and his mates are in jail and here they could be hanged but David's a hero. Jake's cousin's got a Porsche, so what? Darren's got an airship and is an expert on helium, Miles has got an autogyro, he helps in designing batteries and lightweight engines. How do I show off and say that my Dad is in inter-planetary trade or that I have tea at Buckingham Palace?"

"Don't you want to, though?"

"Sometimes, I suppose. You're OK, you like spy stuff so you like secret codes. I get laughed at because I take it seriously and everyone reckons that my phone is out-of-date. So what? I'm an honoured traveller on two worlds and on one of them people try to kneel for me. Billy's a bit younger than me, but he's being taught gay sex by Cradawg. He's a high priest on another world and really is holy. Billy and Cradawg's son are friends even if he knows what Billy and his Dad get up to. Look what happened to Will Thompson when that nude picture got out. His girl-friend just thought it funny to embarrass him but I don't see what the fuss is about. On

Cradawg's world I see everyone naked and I get naked too."

"So that's why you got all friendly with Will." Craig said, "I wondered and I get it. You've seen and done more so you don't even understand why his Dad grounded him. How about it? Have you been with anyone?"

Danny grinned, "The girls know what they're doing on Cradawg's world. It's difficult to refuse or deny anything if you're both naked."

"God! Your folks would have a fit if they knew." Craig exclaimed.

"Let's say they know that travel has broadened my mind. Dad tells me to be careful because the father's there might not like it." Danny laughed, "One father did walk in on us. He said something about my cock doing his daughter proud and left."

Craig stared open-mouthed then nodded, "You're adapting. They can't."

"Mum won't let Darren cycle out to the portal because the lanes are too dangerous and said how proud of him she was when I took a video of him giving orders on the airship. That bit is still not real to her. Dad has trouble coping with alternate worlds though he probably wouldn't if there were customs, immigration control and the like."

Craig was silent for the rest of the journey. Although he tried to be a strong part of the gang in school he knew deep down that he was just average and no-one took any real notice of him. He was suffering from a dual shock, firstly that his friend Danny was having adventures that he scarcely believed possible and secondly, he was considered worthy of joining in.

His father disapproved of his friendship with Danny because his family was working class and fostered kids who would be *tomorrow's druggies and criminals*. Craig was rebellious enough to reject the children of slightly richer, slightly higher status families that his father wanted him to be friends with just as he rebelled against the school and its discipline.

Suddenly, it was his friends who were the *right people*. Instead of being steered into a nice respectable job, helped by his father's *very important* friend who ran an accountancy office, he was mixing with kings and dukes. He also faced a challenge that would tax even his adventurous spirit but maybe his father would be less impressed by that. Being on a different world was a minor detail, he was fourteen years-old and beginning to see how far that he would be going in defying the narrow-minded, bigoted man that his father truly was. It was that more than anything that scared him.

He was quiet when he greeted David and was introduced to the others, scarcely listening as Danny described their meeting with the king.

"It looks like Skeffington might have a new job." David said cheerfully, "That's good news, Danny. I thought that the king might start backtracking on the reforms as he got used to the portal so I'm glad that he's pushing them forwards but I'm sorry Craig. You got a bit deeper into our affairs than I intended today."

"It's all too weird." Craig replied, "I want to go home."

"Are you sure?" David asked, "Sorry, yes of course. Skevi, would you take Craig back to Barabourne, please? I've got an appointment with Sir Douglas this afternoon. We'll follow on the evening train."

Craig was thinking in terms of booking a flight, customs and the other rigmarole they went through when his family went to Spain. He also understood just what was involved in preparing a space launch to another world but it was easy coming through, wasn't it? According to Danny, that was why his dad had trouble coping so why shouldn't it be just as easy going back?

"Can I wait for you at your place, please?" Craig asked, "I need to get my head around all this."

"Skeffington, could you be the strong, silent servant? You know your way around so if Craig wants to, he can wander around as much as he likes and get used to it all."

As Skeffington nodded, Craig said, "Thanks. I'd like that."

"How come he's struggling so much?" Miles asked when they had left, "He doesn't seem to be coping."

"You and Danny had some warning before you travelled." David said, "I didn't and I was so confused, everyone thought I had concussion or something. Craig had no warning either, he's done a lot more on his first trip and is just confused."

"It's more than that." Danny said, "His Dad puts him down a lot, I've seen him do it, and Craig was a bit of a bully, trying to be in control of things to make up for it. He can't control this lot and he can't put up a front."

Chapter 7

Once they were outside, Craig snapped, "We'll walk to the station. I want to look around."

Skeffington nodded and they walked on. Craig felt a little more in control when Skeffington did not argue and it occurred to him that he needed friends.

"Sorry," he said. "You needn't be that silent. I'm a bit rattled, that's all."

"I remember visiting the Royal George for the first time. Electricity and cars were enough for the first trip. I've got to like pool though."

"Thanks. So this is your world and you travelled to mine. How are you and David friends?"

"It's a long story but we met when he visited my part of London."

"OK but I'm in London. It's covered in soot, stinks of horse-shit and sounds like a preservation railway gone mad. How about telling me the story while I get used to it all."

As Skeffington related the story, Craig listened enthralled.

"Wow!" he exclaimed, "It's amazing. Is that the station up the road? What's it called?"

"Victoria." Skeffington replied, "You look surprised."

"I just didn't expect you to have a Queen Victoria, that's all."

"I don't think that we did, it was named after the Roman god of victory."

"How about Charing Cross?" Craig asked and Skeffington nodded.

"Waterloo?"

"Never heard of it." Skeffington replied.

"Kings Cross?"

It was a conversation that Craig could relax with. Both had heard of Paddington, Euston and Fenchurch Street while Craig had never heard of Marlborough, Caledonia Road and Aldgate except as an underground station. Skeffington had never heard of Kings Cross, Liverpool Street or Waterloo.

"I tell you one we've forgotten, London Bridge." Craig exclaimed.

"Oh yes." Skeffington agreed, "We've got one too."

Craig was aware of porters bustling around delivering parcels and luggage. On one platform was a train of windowless carriages marked Royal Mail. On other trains, carriages were marked 1, 2 or 3 and painted in a dark green livery. He could have been on the set of a film based in the forties but no film could afford so many trains arriving and leaving.

A train pulled into the station beside the platform that they were waiting on. Craig watched as the engine was uncoupled then he hurried to the end of the platform to watch another engine arrive and be coupled up. He was enjoying himself cheerfully accepting the novel experience of being on another world. Equally novel, was being greeted by a butler when they finally arrived at Barabourne and being shown into the library.

Craig was tired after his day and was content to sit though he was cordially greeted by others coming and going.

"Hi," one said. "I'm Jimmy. Lt. James Clark if you want to be formal but since Darren's pinched my airship again, there's not much point."

"Lieutenant?" Craig exclaimed, "Sorry, but you're not much older than me."

"True. I should still be a midshipman at Dartmouth." Jimmy explained, "Here I'm just Jimmy designing a new kind of airship: helium filled, electric actuators for the control surfaces and radio."

"And the oldies don't like change." Craig said, still trying to understand.

"CPO Hammond is good but he always says something about returning to report when we're on an exercise. He never remembers radio."

"Back home, all my mates are at school and get into trouble if they bunk off. Here it seems as if you're running the place."

"We're not though." Jimmy replied, "We just show what's possible. There're all sorts of engineers and scientists that take over the work."

Craig stayed quiet even when David, Miles and Danny returned, content to relax and listen to the chatter.

"Skeffington, you're wanted at the palace. His Majesty is moving far faster than I expected otherwise I would have had you stay in London."

"I'll see if I can catch the last train. Er, what do I do when I get there."

"Danny seems to be the expert." David laughed, "Let him brief you tonight and catch an early train tomorrow."

"I'll radio Lt. Worthington." Danny said, "He can look after you, Skevi. Now let's see ..."

Craig was still content to listen to Danny while the others settled down to chat or read. Back home, it would have been computer games or TV but he was startled when the others all stood as a striking young lady entered the room.

"You don't have to do that." Isabella laughed, "I always feel as if I'm interrupting."

"It's just habit." David responded, "Where's Godfrey?"

"Hosing himself down after a day in his workshop. If someone can see us through the portal, we've arranged supper at the Royal George."

"I'll go with you." Skeffington said, "I'll not disturb your meal but I've got to tell them that I may not be here for the pool match on Wednesday."

Skeffington's remark strained Craig's credibility to the limit. Exploration; yes, trade; possibly, study; yes, they were all reasons for travelling to another world but to play pool? Then it occurred to him; it was useful. One of David's projects was social reform and Skeffington was learning how a more relaxed world could work.

The following day was Sunday and Craig watched as the Duke of Barabourne was greeted by his *people,* the tenants, staff and others who made up the estates as they attended church. He felt as though he was being sized up by David's mother as they took lunch afterwards. However, it gave him an idea for confusing his Father.

As Craig expected, his father had been to the golf club. As usual, he was just sober enough not to attract attention as he drove home but was drunk enough to be belligerent and aggressive.

Needing to take control of his son, he snarled, "So what is Danny's uncle, a servant or a hanger-on?"

"Neither Dad. I need your help though."

"Go on." his father replied, "What sort of trouble did you get into?"

"None. It's my morning suit. The trousers will crease if I fold them over a hanger. Have you got anything so that I can hang them properly?"

"Show me!" and to his amazement, Craig complied.

"Danny and Darren leave theirs at the hall." Craig explained, "I brought mine home in case you wanted me to go with you and your important friends."

Craig's father's abuse was verbal rather than physical and he was sober enough to see that his son was making fun of him. However, for once he could not think of a put down. Defeated, he stomped to his bedroom to sleep the drink off.

"Nice one." Craig's mother chuckled, "I'll get some clips so that they can hang from an ordinary hangar. Is that a hat box? You haven't got a top hat have you?"

Craig nodded, "Look Mum. I don't have to keep it all secret from you but I don't want Dad to know."

"I don't blame you." His mother replied, "If you got into trouble at school or you were rude to him, you know, the usual stuff, I'd support him. He does his share around the house and he provides us with a good home."

Craig nodded.

"He just doesn't like the idea that you are your own man and not an extension of him. Now I've heard rumours about that David and his friends. Are you in danger if you visit? All I want to know is, should the child welfare people be interested?"

Craig thought for a moment then replied, "Not that sort of danger, Mum. If I said that David lives on another world, I flew to London in an airship and David wants me to help him steal a nuclear bomb, you don't have to believe me. What I'm trying to say is that there are different risks."

Craig's mother glanced at the morning suit, "That's more than just a figment of your imagination, isn't it, but you're right, I don't fully believe it. I was worried that you'd escape your Dad by running away or when you're old enough, joining the army. If you've found another escape then go for it but tell me what you're doing even if you do have to wrap it up."

"What do you suppose Dad would make of this, Mum?" Craig asked, "I've been in Buckingham Palace and talked to their king."

"Now imagination or not, that's something I'd like to hear all about." Craig's mother smiled, "Not now though. Put your stuff away while I start the tea. He'll get grumpy if he thinks that we're having a conversation without him."

Craig went to sleep that night happier than he had been in a long time. Where his mother was strong, his father was weak. They loved each other and for much of the time his father could spend his time playing golf, attending his allotment while his mother organised their lives. Where Craig's mother could not help his father, was at work. He had been promoted above his abilities, sought further promotion and blamed his juniors for the poor performance of his department making him more and more unpopular and further affecting morale and performance. It was the resulting stress that affected his attitude to Craig, making his son equally stressed.

Suddenly Craig was living in a different world, not the physical one that he had visited but the one where he felt good about himself and had a way of dealing with his father. Even his teachers and fellow students saw the effects the following day. From maths to history, suddenly a range of subjects had become interesting and useful. His new friends accepted the discipline imposed by their tutors, especially CPO Hammond so school discipline seemed easier to accept. In fact, he was simply more relaxed knowing he could deal with his father.

~~~

Other matters changed. Towards the end of the week, Cooper Tamzon announced that he wanted to take his family back to London.

"We don't really belong, sir." he said to David, "We'll sell electrical goods on our stall and even Chris has learnt about it. We'll do all right. Skeffington is no adventurer even if he's got guts and is good in a crisis. As you know Prince Malcolm sent for him and he's becoming some sort of advisor."

"Good for him." David said, "I wish you all well and you'll be welcome here anytime."

David felt as if he was working through a checklist when Billy spoke to him. He had seen Billy on occasion but it had not registered just how little time Billy spent at Barabourne. Miles still went for flying lessons whenever he could and there was nothing to suggest that Billy was in danger so David had concentrated on other things.

"Bran's dead." Billy announced, "We caught him sabotaging the crops then something really weird happened."

"Tell me about it." David said, "Are you all right though."

"I'm fine." Billy replied. "Do you remember suggesting cameras?"

David nodded

"I've seen them cameras and they stand out a bit. Anyways, I asked the portal about drilling holes in the stones for them and it asked me why I didn't use the holographic generators."

"The what?" David exclaimed.

"2D TVs are a bit old-fashioned for that world. The stones have their own stuff. Not only that it gets piped through to the portal."

"Ye Gods." David exclaimed.

"Don't blaspheme." Billy snapped then in a softer tone, "Sorry but I'm kinda fallin' in with Cradawg's ways. He wouldn't like it if you said that but he wouldn't say anything. You'd feel it though."

"OK and I'm sorry as well. I didn't realise."

"It's what people don't understand. Yeah he teaches the stuff they all snigger at but he teaches me a lot more. There is something. He'd adopt me and the sex stuff would have to stop and I don't want it to."

"You understand that I'm not happy about it. I'm still the duke, you're one of my people, I'm responsible for you but I'm putting you in moral danger."

"Yeah, I know that you don't approve but I am all right."

"Yes, you are. I can see that. Now what about Bran?"

"However you look at it, watching crops grow ain't the most exciting job in the world. You're waiting for trouble, hoping it won't happen and glad when something does to give you something to do."

David grinned as Billy continued, "The portal don't get bored it just watches and when something does happen, it records it and no-one on that world knew that it could. Anyway nothing happened until the shoots started appearing. Blokes arrived each night and sprinkled patches with something. The shoots didn't die but they looked all deformed and underdeveloped. The portal said wait before I did anything and Bran started saying that it was my stuff doing it because everywhere else was healthy."

Billy paused for breath before continuing, "Cradawg told me not to worry about it because the gods would show the truth. Both Cradawg and the portal were telling me to wait but people were getting pretty narked with me. Then, Bran called for a Council of the Stones."

"What's that?" David asked.

"It's a sort of court of enquiry. Bran wanted to prove me a demon but he said that it was to find out what was wrong with the crops. Cradawg said that my time was coming, be ready. That's what's weird about him. He knew I could do something but he didn't know what. They've got holographic TV so technically he knows what it's about. He just believes that a divine traveller is guided to use it wisely."

"I see. Go on." David encouraged.

"There was a big crowd standing beyond the circle and crops. It was not very mystical as Bran set up a speaker system so that everyone could hear. He described what was happening then finished up with, 'It hasn't happened in other years and we must deal with it before the evil spreads'. He pointed to me and said, 'He came at the start of the year and disturbed the divine path with his evil. That evil is now spreading into Mother Earth'."

"That must have been scary." David exclaimed.

"Kind of but I was waiting for it. Remember that I'm getting into Cradawg's ways."

David nodded so Billy continued, "I think everyone else thought that I'd be scared because I'd been found out. I asked Bran if I could answer and he said, 'Of course, make your denials'. When I got to the microphone I tried to be calm but I think I squeaked a bit as I called out, 'I call on the stones themselves to show the truth'. Whoever built them stones, weren't half-hearted. The hologram appeared over the full cultivated area and everything was full-sized and bright enough for it all to be seen in bright sunlight. It was that black and white image, you know, what you get at night, something-red. There was a guy sprinkling and it was directly over the affected area and when he looked up, you could see the face. He was not only in the image, he was standing near Bran for real and suddenly everyone was looking at him."

Billy paused again, marshalling his thoughts, "I feel a bit sorry for him because he just didn't know what was going on."

"Well done, Billy." David said, "I felt a bit sorry for Robin Cashman but he was willing to hurt people. This guy might have been Bran's servant but he must have known that it was wrong."

"That's what he said as he collapsed. He knew it was wrong but Bran kept saying that the wind god needed his help. It didn't make sense because the god was all powerful but how could he argue with Bran?

"Now this is where it got real scary. Bran yelled out to the gods to defend their priest and this wind blew in and knocked us flyin'. I was knocked back and Bran fell where I had been standing. There was a bang and when I stood up, there was all this blood around Bran."

"Bloody Hell." David gasped.

"I was a bit shaken but Cradawg and his family looked after me. It happened yesterday. A doctor gave me a sleeping pill and I went straight to bed when I got home. I've been back today, to find out what was happening and there're all sorts of investigations going on. We had these painted circles to stand in, they were to do with making the arrangements more orderly or something but mine is now a hole and Cradawg said that Bran was holding a remote detonator."

"So he was going to kill you and that wind saved your life. How did that happen?"

"We don't know. The stones use air-curtains but they couldn't be deflected like that. The portal said it didn't do nuffin' and it would take a bloody great fan to do it anyway."

"Cradawg's got no idea?" David asked.

"All Cradawg says is that Bran asked the gods to defend their priest and they did."

"They defended you." David said.

"Yep. Everyone's looking at me a bit funny now."

"I'm not surprised. So what do you do now?"

"Dunno." Billy replied, "Anything that happens at the stones is world news. There's nothing to stop spectators from filming. I didn't find out until now but our first arrival was worldwide news for a week, then we fixed the screens and that got them even more excited. Now all this."

"So do I start calling you, Your Holiness?"

"Stuff that, Your Grace. It's all happened so fast, I've got to think."

"Are you all right though? Is there anything you need?"

"Nah. Thanks though." Billy replied, "I haven't seen much of you lately but you're there, not far away and it feels good. That's Barabourne and what I need more than anythin'."

"At least I'm preparing for my quest. You sure have been thrown in at the deep end."

"Tell me about it." Billy exclaimed, "I want to talk to Uncle Jethro though. I think this is where I need a grown-up to tell me what to do."

More than anywhere before in his life, Billy felt safe at Barabourne. Wilson expected him to work hard but somehow it had never been more than he could handle and Wilson's quiet, patient demeanour encouraged Billy. Until a year ago, David and Jethro had been remote figures but ones to be respected, not feared and then he had become involved in David's adventures culminating in nearly being killed. He was still shocked and upset but there was still Barabourne to protect him.

Billy had not been fully ready to talk about events but although David was busy with his own affairs he still had time to listen. It made Billy feel good about himself, talking to David had cleared his mind and it was enough so he was quietly confident when he returned to the stone circle world.

As he arrived, everyone turned to him and knelt.

"Greetings, Divine Guide." Kendal said, "I'm waiting for Revered Miles though I don't suppose that he needs any more flying lessons. You will wish it known that he is competent."

"That's for his instructors to say. You forget, we arrived as children so we will study as children with no special favours." Billy raised his voice so that everyone could hear, "Bran was killed to protect the true priest. If he had won, he would have used his position to destroy others. In my heart I don't believe that I'm the Wind God's priest but it's someone else who was saved."

"And that guidance is as divine as it is wise." Cradawg said, "Is your heart on the Divine Path and not this world?"

"Somewhere along it, where I truly belong."

"And you will suggest Cradawg." someone called out, "You're too close."

"Where I come from, people in high places have chaplains to guide them. The Wind God's priest has a lot of worldly power because he's in charge of many places. I think that Cradawg would make an excellent chaplain and prevent the Wind God priest from

119

forgetting his spiritual duties."

"Cradawg is right. You do have divine wisdom." This time it was a woman who spoke. Billy recognised her as the Earth Priestess as she continued, "You were knocked clear when you could have been killed with Bran. Like it or not, you are in our god's favour and that qualifies you as a priest. Besides, we have no candidate to replace you yet

As Billy smiled, the priestess continued, "This part is interesting. As a priest, we must respect your views that you should not be a priest. Putting it more sensibly, if you say that it is not your destiny then so be it. However, will you stay long enough to help the High Council find your successor?"

"Bran's successor."

"No. We do not want another like him. Like Bran, you have a strong mind and a will to achieve much but he lacked a light heart, a sense of fun or great wisdom." the priestess explained, "You have balance."

It was the priest of the Fire God who spoke next.

"You worship a different God, will you bring him here?"

"I see him as the one who created all." Billy said, "He's already here but content to let your gods look after your world. After what happened, I can believe in both."

The Fire God priest frowned, "You see our gods as inferior."

"You are part of the scheme of things, so are your gods and so is my god. Am I calling you inferior?"

"You are too good to be true." the priest said, "No boy your age can have so much wisdom."

"I don't. I'm a boy so I have lessons as well."

The priest nodded, "So you have, you also have a quick wit and considerable cheek which we do not normally tolerate but I won't oppose you. Those that your god has appointed to look after your world favour you and maybe it's as well that your god is a god of all. I don't think that one world will hold you. What are your plans?"

"You know about Bran's schemes so my original task is done." Billy said, "Miles will still be visiting to complete his flying lessons so he can tell me when I'm needed again. Until then, I have other duties."

"May your gods and ours protect you." Cradawg intoned.

It was later when Billy was describing his experiences that a reaction set in though at first, he chatted quite happily.

"It's a good place." he said, "I could move there but I'm no priest even if their gods do favour me."

"You don't believe all that guff, do you?" Danny asked.

Billy thought for a moment before answering, "I think that I do now. Bran should have easily finished me and Cradawg, but all it took was that gust of wind and it all changed. I asked the portal what it detected and it said *nothing*. I would like to keep on visiting but I suppose you need me here."

"Maybe Godfrey does." David replied, "I don't seem to need a travelling servant for now. What's wrong?"

Billy was trembling, nearly sliding off the chair. Miles rang for assistance but he was already recovering as Wilson arrived.

"Sorry." he whispered, "I keep seeing Bran lying there. I don't want to see anyone's innards ever again. I cut myself a few days ago. It's all right, I've healed but I thought about the blood then sort of jumped to Bran."

"Your other-world friends may understand better than this world but I suggest that rest, light duties and knowing that you can talk to anyone may be enough." Wilson said.

"That's right." Danny exclaimed, "Mum's dealt with all sorts of screwed up kids. She'll talk to you as well."

Danny paused looking sheepish.

"Sorry." he said, "I didn't mean that you were a screw-up. I meant that it's a screw-up experience, I mean ..."

"I know what you mean." Billy laughed, "And thanks. I suppose soldiers get used to seeing that sort of thing. I should cope."

"Soldiers can have problems for years after, some for the rest of their lives." Wilson said, "Your experience was worse because it was personal; you knew Bran. A part of you may be glad that he's dead while another part regrets it. You may never have another reaction or you may need this counselling that Master Danny mentions. Either way, your friends will support you."

To everyone's relief, Billy seemed fine the next day, at least until the dowager duchess sent for him. A footman carrying a tea-tray followed him in. The duchess dismissed the footman.

"I'm not happy with servants waiting on other servants so I shall pour." she began, "Dear me, that sounds wrong, but I wouldn't even trust David to make my tea. How do you like yours?"

"If it's your usual Lapsang Souchon then as it comes, Your Grace." Billy replied, "I like the aromas."

The dowager duchess looked surprised, "I add milk so this may be a little weak for you."

"No, it'll be fine. Sometimes, it's too strong and I have a bad aftertaste for hours."

"I'm so glad that I listen to David and not my friends. They offer tea ranging from the most expensive to the cheapest and serve according to the visitor but this is where I need help. I find Godfrey a delightful young man with charmingly simple yet good manners. You also are a young man of taste and I know that it's me being crass in referring to your class but it's why I asked to speak to you. I have decided that I should invite as many of Godfrey's friends as possible but there may be difficulties."

"You don't want half your guests looking down on the other half and sneering." Billy interjected.

"Exactly." the dowager duchess beamed, "Isabella's brother Jeremy will be one of the sneering classes, become falling down drunk and be quite unpleasant but he will be tolerated. If one of Godfrey's friends so much as stumbles he will be regarded as a drunken boor. I do so want this wedding to be a happy event for everyone concerned and I want it to be a vindication of David's ideas but I'm the last person to solve this problem."

"I'm not sure if I'm being rude but how many of your friends belong to the sneering classes and how many are your real friends?"

"Yes it is rude but you are right. Many just visit to say that they take tea at Barabourne. The more egalitarian that we become, the more their status is eroded."

"David's talked of being best man and inviting the king but Miles said that it would be bad form to invite His Majesty."

"I have many friends who I rarely see." the dowager duchess said. "One of them happens to be the queen; we were at school together and we still correspond. Normally, royal marriages are more political than romantic but they met at a tennis match and fell in love. Now, the present king's father would never have agreed to the heir marrying a non-royal but he was trying to forge alliances against France among the German principalities and Ann happened to be the god-daughter of a Bavarian prince."

The dowager duchess paused, "I hope you see what I'm talking about. We have a queen who flouted the same rigid conventions that David is challenging and one who enjoys my stories about you, Godfrey and his engagement with Isabella. The king does not discuss other worlds with her but I'm afraid that I do so she also knows about Danny and Darren."

She paused again, making sure that Billy was following, "I could invite Her Majesty and she would definitely be on the bride's side. I could also invite Skeffington and Prince Malcolm. I hear that Malcolm is far wilder than a prince of England should be, Skeffington is more refined than a barrow boy should be and they meet in the middle. I'm not sure what that means but according to the Queen, they make lively company when they're together."

"It seems that you have solved the problem, Your Grace. Godfrey got on with Skevi and so he won't mind inviting him. We'll still have to treat the prince properly, won't we?

"Your speech has changed." the dowager duchess said, "I still don't wish to be rude but you've lost your East London accent."

"I ain't lost nuffing but I 'ad an idea." Billy chuckled, "If the portal can teach languages, could it treat accents like languages? Speaking posher is just another language that I've learned."

"Very good. Going back to your question, Prince William already has a son. That now puts Malcolm as third in line. If Prince William has another, then Malcolm will be fourth. Second sons can resent slipping down the line to the throne but Prince Malcolm seems to enjoy the increased independence. We must still follow protocol but Prince Malcolm may prove far more relaxed than the King was on his visit. Now, would Godfrey's side of the guests have a problem with a prince of the realm mixing in?"

Billy shook his head, "They're used to David and Uncle Jethro being ready for a chat. The stable lads have got their own project with central heating and the new boot boy gets time for school and goes with David. What I'm saying is, we're all a lot more equal at Barabourne so the odd prince or two won't make much difference."

It would normally be too unladylike for the dowager duchess to chuckle but she came close, "Thank you, Billy. Queen Anne understands that there are problems in protocol and has unofficially accepted an invitation. However, we agreed that I withhold the formal one until I was sure that the event would go smoothly. His Royal Highness will escort his mother on the day. Now who's going to tell David that his mother is interfering?"

Billy grinned, "I'll talk to Miles. He was worried about David's schemes so he'll be happy to suggest an alternative."

"Yes, Miles. I'm surprised that he fits in so well. He always seemed so immature."

"He has though. I like him."

"I would have said that the Markhams were definitely of the sneering classes but it seems that I'm wrong."

"His brother belongs but Lord Markham shakes my hand and asks if I've come for the boots or for tea. If he has other guests I'm introduced as one of Miles' more interesting friends. Someone always tries to put me down but Lord Markham says something like, 'Billy knows that I'm joking, neither of us know whether you are."

"And is he joking?" the duchess asked.

"Oh yes. He doesn't go on about me being a boot-boy, but a lot of his friends would ask about my family, where I'm from and who I know. He picks his time then asks me whether I've spoken to the king lately. He could do a comic turn in music-hall; his timing's always perfect and instead of getting ready to embarrass me they have to figure out who I really am."

"Don't tell him about doing music-hall." the duchess exclaimed, "He'd be so insulted."

"Last time I visited with Miles, he tried out some gags he'd memorised. He was good."

"Good heavens above! I assume that David's attitudes are spreading and stopping this Great Decline of his."

"It all helps but not that much has changed yet."

"Thank you, Billy and I do apologise. You are not the boot-boy any more. You are one of David's closest confidantes and I should refer to you as such."

"Nah, Lady. It don't bother me none," Billy grinned but then became serious. "If I hadn't been a boot-boy, I wouldn't be talking to you, I wouldn't get on with Lord Markham, I wouldn't have seen other worlds and I wouldn't be a priest. Coming here as a boot-boy was the best thing that could have happened to me. It's something that Cradawg has taught me; don't be ungrateful of the path that leads to good fortune."

"You are an impressive young man. Now, I'm expecting Lady Greenham, you are welcome to stay but I doubt that I possess Lord Markham's comic skills."

Billy grinned again, "I shall leave so that you can maintain standards at Barabourne."

It was a little later that Billy managed to talk to David, Miles and Godfrey, recounting his conversation with David's mother.

"I thought that the invitations had to be out ages ago." Godfrey exclaimed.

"From Mother's point of view, Barabourne would be snubbed if an invitation was declined. She's put out feelers and watched to make sure that we could handle the visit. Now that both sides are happy, the official invitation can go."

"So that's how you do it." Miles exclaimed, "I knew it had to be informal but I wasn't sure how. The king won't be involved."

"No." David said, "He has engagements booked over two years in advance. It would be favouring us too much if he cancelled another visit to come here. Sorry about all the politics though, Godfrey."

"It's fine, I just wish that my parents could be here for the day. They wanted me to do well and I was at school when the gas leaked."

"I know your parents were killed but I don't know the details." David said.

"They had a shop. The fire brigade reckoned that Dad smelt gas and went down to the cellar to check. Something caused a spark and there was an explosion and it killed Dad instantly. The shop floor above collapsed and Mum and a couple of customers got caught in the wreckage. One of the customers was killed, Mum died a few days later and the other walked away from it all. There could have been a fire but Dad had turned the gas off. I was about six when it happened and Ma had taken me to school but I don't really remember them now. I grew up in an orphanage until I came here."

"Sorry." David said, "I didn't mean to pry."

"It's all right." Godfrey replied, "Look! I'm happy. I love Isabella and I want to marry her. Your mother has been fantastic, and I can talk to Uncle - it feels funny calling him that but I can talk to Uncle Jethro. A year ago I was just a farmhand, now we're discussing which royals are coming to my wedding. Oh and my first road car is nearly ready. We might leave the church in that. With all that, do you suppose that a little bit of politics will make much difference?"

"Put like that then no. Do you still just want a dinner party for a stag do?"

"No, but I don't want to be hung over, either. How about something in the barn but on the Thursday?"

"Why not, I'll ask the pub to supply some barrels and Wilson can supply the rest."

"Thank you." Godfrey said, "He's been good to me and I tried to invite him to the wedding but he says that he couldn't trust anyone else to do it right."

"He's probably right. I'll instruct him to organise refreshments in the barn and I'll also instruct him that he should assist in keeping the evening relaxed and friendly."

"Why not just call it a servants ball?" Miles asked.

"Because I want Godfrey's friends to be truly welcome. Some will have to work on the day, I'll have to be the duke, the horses still need looking after and so on.

"You're saying that if a groom has to stand beside the horses during the service, he could be sitting next to a duke discussing Ascot in the afternoon."

"It's more or less what I've said." Godfrey said, "My real mates agree. It's what David said that first time he came down to the waterhole, if Barabourne succeeds we all prosper. Isabella gets that as well and we want our wedding to show off what we can do."

David nodded, aware that on Danny and Todd's world he would be regarded as a dreadful snob while on his world, he was regarded as an anarchist. There's an expression about people wearing different hats to denote different jobs. In David's case, it was ties. Nowadays, he always had one in his pocket, and if he wore it then even Godfrey would knuckle his forehead and call him 'Your Grace'. If he took it off and undid his top shirt button, then it could be, 'Hey David, how about a hand with the milking'. Jethro also followed the custom, as of course, did Miles but as with any group, attitudes varied. Older staff did not have the confidence to respond, some resented the fact that they could not just skive off or were jealous of David's seniority. However, most understood what David was trying to do and that they had probably the best working conditions in the country.

Godfrey's guests included two or three stable-hands, a couple of children of tenant farmers together with two village girls and their current boyfriends. They would be sharing his side of the church with the Markhams, and guests from other worlds. Godfrey happily included Cradawg and his family for Billy's sake but they would be dreadfully embarrassed at wearing clothes for a religious ceremony. Although still virtually a stranger, Craig was invited together with his mother. They accepted provided they could manage without his father finding out. If Godfrey's part of the guest list presented some unique problems, the royals provided the most interest and even that was being dealt with.

Everyone involved agreed with Godfrey that it was a chance to show what Barabourne could do. Those closest to David understood that it was part of addressing the Great Decline so everyone was determined to make the day impressive.

Apart from the preparations, it remained quiet until the Tuesday before. Everyone was involved in their various activities. Even the dowager duchess was visiting sick villagers. Wilson was irritated to see a footman running in the hall but stayed silent until he explained himself.

"Mr. Skeffington is at the servant's entrance, Mr. Wilson. He has a guest and I think that it's His Royal Highness Prince Malcolm."

"And you left them standing there."

"Oh no, Mr. Wilson. Reginald is showing them to the library."

"Very well. Inform the staff that His Royal Highness is not here. You are either mistaken or he is incognito."

As Wilson entered the library, Skeffington hurried over to greet him, grinning, "I know, you're staff and I'm a guest but I am pleased to see you again."

He turned to his guest, "Malcolm, I shouldn't introduce the butler like this but he was so good to me on my last visit."

Malcolm stepped forward and offered his hand, also grinning, "I'm pleased to meet you, Wilson. I'm Malcolm Stuart."

Wilson would not grin on duty but there was a twinkle in his eye as he took off his glove to shake hands and said, "You should feel completely at home in Barabourne, sir. Mr. Skeffington, kindly remember that you are a guest. In the future, you use the front door."

"Yes, sorry. We turned up without warning so I wasn't sure."

"Expected or not, you are always a guest even if there is no-one to greet you. If you'd care to wait here, I'll arrange rooms for you. Reginald will look after you."

"Thank you and I hope that I say this right. His Royal Highness is not arriving until Friday evening and he will be with his mother. We won't be wearing ties so until then, Malcolm and I could use a cottage or even the stables to avoid confusing other guests."

"I'm not sure that the stables would be suitable."

"Wilson, I believe that you are one of His Graces confidants." Malcolm said, "Since becoming involved in the warehouse homeless scheme I have an office at Stable Row and I sometimes stay there. People have come to trust me and show me somewhat different sides to the city. To put it bluntly, I'm ashamed of my father's capital. Increasingly I agree with His Grace's ideas but I'm curious. Does he practice what he preaches at home and where do his ideas originate?"

"Yes I see. His Majesty was more concerned that order was maintained, you're more concerned with the substance of his ideas. I suggest Mr. Skeffington that you find Godfrey and then you take Mr. Malcolm to the Royal George. Perhaps you would take the brake because they should have cases of wine for me so you can bring them back."

"Australian again? Are you planning one of your events?"

"Just so, sir." Wilson replied as Malcolm looked puzzled.

"Wilson has his own scheme for encouraging equality." Skeffington explained, "It started among the staff of visiting guests but now guests themselves ask for invitations. At least if they look beyond the label, they do. I'm not an expert but I'm invited because I do try to learn more."

"I see. So the gentry mix with their servants and other riff-raff in order to enjoy rare and exotic wines." Malcolm said, "But Australian? I didn't know that they made wine."

"The answer isn't straightforward and again, the Royal George holds the key. Real wine buffs prefer the company of other wine lovers so they surrender their position for the chance. They also like the mystery of, shall we say, irregular imports."

"And the less discerning have no idea." Malcolm exclaimed, "Now tell me about the Royal George and how it got its name."

"Let's visit. We'll have our own wine-tasting while we're there." Skeffington paused, "That's providing that I can exchange currency. Wilson?"

"That will not be a problem providing you want to change less than ten pounds. I have a hundred of their pounds in my pantry."

"Currency exchange?" Malcolm queried.

"Yes indeed, sir." Wilson replied, "Regular contact with the Royal George requires some procedures to be followed. It will become clearer after your visit. I'll send for Godfrey."

"No, we'll wander down to the stables." Skeffington said.

In any house, news of a royal visit would spread, even if it was unexpected. Staff would be warned to curtsey or bow and there would be general hubbub in the background as staff did what they could to prepare so it came as a shock for Malcolm to be completely ignored. News had spread because one or two bobbed their heads but there was no other reaction.

"Hello Skevi," a lad of about seventeen greeted them, "Are you and Malcolm looking for Godfrey?"

"Yes." Skeffington replied, "Let me guess, he's in his workshop. Will you get steam up on a brake, please?"

"I'll light the fire but it'll be ready when you are. Do you need me to untap it or can you do it?"

"Wait for us will you? I'd do it, but I'm a bit nervous of all that steam."

"It's safe enough. The connection locks if the pipe is under pressure. You turn off the valve at the boiler-house end and raise the safety valve. Then you can disconnect at the brake. I'll wait for you though. I could do with skiving for a few minutes."

Skevi laughed as they headed for an open door but Malcolm said, "I didn't like that remark about him skiving. We shouldn't encourage that sort of thing, should we?"

"That's Mark and I've heard him say the same thing to David. He'll sit in the brake to watch the fire and quietly doze but I bet if we're back too quick, we'll catch him giving it a wipe down."

"I'm surprised he called me Malcolm."

"It's your name and we're not wearing ties. Do you want to drop your incognito?"

"No, but I feel as if I'm on a different planet."

"Not yet, you're not." Skeffington replied.

Chapter 8

Godfrey looked up and smiled as they approached.

"It's good to see you again, Skevi." he said as they shook hands.

"We'd like to visit the Royal George. Can you come with us?"

"I can go as far as the lane but I need to get this done. Is Mark around, he'll drive you."

"Mark knows about the portal?" Skeffington asked in surprise.

"The whole estate knows about it with all the comings and goings." Godfrey chuckled, "Even the portal reckons he's sound, he's old enough to drive over there and loves that cola drink. David agreed that we could do with more drivers and Mark's badgering him to get one of their cars. He reckons it would save on taxi fares."

Skeffington turned to Malcolm, "Are you satisfied that David practices what he preaches, yet?"

"Yet father found it orderly here. Strange. Father talks about parallel worlds and I assumed it was a reference to the strange ideas evolving at Barabourne but you're talking about currency exchanges and portals so what is going on? "

"We're trying to show you. Just be a little patient." Skeffington replied before turning to Godfrey, "Give my best to Isabella."

Malcolm just stared as Godfrey's assistant straightened up to reveal a strikingly beautiful young lady.

"You're too kind." she said then turned to Malcolm, adding, "I'd curtsey but it's difficult to do it elegantly in overalls."

"Ah yes. We're not wearing ties so it's not expected." Malcolm smiled, "Forgive me. Lady Isabella, I presume."

"Just Isabella. Dresses do for me, what ties do for the boys. I'd drive you to the Royal George but Mark does so enjoy his visits. His eyes still grow big and round when he sees a new make of motor car."

Skeffington and Malcolm strolled over to the brake seeing Mark grin as he received his new orders.

"How much do you know of David's adventures?" Skeffington asked.

"Not much, it still doesn't feel right calling him, David. They needed a driver to carry goods to and from that portal thing and after I watched stuff appear and disappear a few times I asked Godfrey what it was all about. Then His Grace and Godfrey took me to the Royal George and explained that they needed an extra driver who could cope and keep his mouth shut."

"So you don't go on any of their stranger journeys?"

"No, sir, that's for His Grace and his closest friends."

"Sir? We're getting a bit formal aren't we?" Skeffington asked.

"You're His Grace's guests and I know, it's not what you want. It's Dad, he goes on about how all that friendly guff is going to end in grief when those in the big house have had their games. His mates say the same so I suppose it rubs off. Me, I just enjoy it while I can but sometimes I get worried."

They had been driving while talking and Malcolm was distracted when the wheels started making a growling noise. He was surprised to see that they were now on a hard metalled surface which was rare away from urban side roads. He was drawn back to the conversation when Skeffington said, "David likes a more experienced guy as one of his travelling companions. He asked me but I thought that I could do more in London but now, I'm not so sure. Has he found anyone yet?"

"I don't know."

"So you're not joining in?"

"Of course not. His Grace wouldn't want me."

Skeffington thought he glimpsed a flash of excitement at the prospect and did not notice another flash on Malcolm's face. He felt his own though, he was beginning to regret his caution in refusing.

He was distracted from his thoughts when Mark suddenly asked, "What's an off-road vehicle?"

"One of Godfrey's designs?" Skeffington asked.

"Possibly. Does he call them Land Rovers?"

"Not that I know of. Why?"

"It was as we came through the portal. I got a strong feeling that David needs one. Long wheel base, towing hook, and a trailer."

"I can guess what it means. A large vehicle able to carry a lot of supplies over rough ground." Skeffington said.

"Yes I understood that." Malcolm exclaimed, "But what does it mean? I mean, why would His Grace need one?"

"I don't know, but I think that the portal is planning something."

"Mark, when we get there, take a look around the car park. See if you can find anything. Damp the fire then come and join us. We'll work out if there's anything we can do."

Both Skeffington and Mark remembered their first trips and allowed Malcolm time to adapt.

"Are you leaving young Mark outside all the time?" The landlady asked, "At least take him out a drink."

"No Mary. He'll be in shortly. How's the pool team doing?"

"It's short of a player for tomorrow, can I put your name down?"

"It shouldn't be a problem but I'll have to check."

"None of you lads carry phones, do you?" Mary said, "Jerry wants a chat with you. He's got it in his head that you want to buy his Dad's old Defender."

Both Malcolm and Skeffington looked puzzled.

"What is it with you steam nuts?" Mary exclaimed, "Don't you know about cars unless they've got steam coming out of chimneys?"

"It's not a type of land-rover or off-road vehicle, is it?" Skeffington asked.

"Oh, very good." Mary laughed, "I'm surprised you knew that."

"It's just an odd coincidence, that's all." Skeffington said.

"I doubt it. Go and get Mark then sit in that alcove. I'll join you and the first round is on me if you give me some straight answers."

Once they were all settled, Mary said, "You say that you live off Barns Lane yet no-one knows of any house down that way. The old boys talk about it being haunted and how odd things have always happened along that lane. Now you have to admit, you lot are different, you appear and disappear and the gossip is getting wilder. I'm doing business with you and I don't like mysteries with business partners."

There was an awkward silence before Malcolm asked, "I can understand your problem but we are just guests. David is the one who has to decide."

"Yes I know about David but why is a fourteen-year-old boy

in charge? You're adults and I'd appreciate some straight answers from you."

"There's a wedding on Saturday." Malcolm said, "Why don't you come as Skeffington's guest. It's quite all right, I outrank David. I just apologise that it's too late to send a proper invitation."

"That's very kind of you but I shouldn't intrude." Mary replied, "I do know about the wedding though, some guests are being dropped off here by taxi and collected. I'd just appreciate some answers."

"Believe me, when I make an invitation, no-one would consider it an intrusion." Malcolm said, "Let's agree that there is a mystery concerning Barabourne, you are a neighbour, in a way you're on their frontier. Now it would be far better having you as an ally than an enemy so treat the invitation as a peace offering."

He glanced at Skeffington and Mark, "What with currency exchanges, border problems are something I do understand."

"You make it sound like different countries. Barabourne! Your folk think that David is the Duke of Barabourne, don't they? Thank you, if you're sure that I won't be intruding then I will accept."

"Will Jerry be in tonight? If there's a match tomorrow, he'll want a practice session. I could do with getting my hand in as well." Skeffington asked.

"I'll ring him and let him know that you'll be here and I'll leave you to it."

"We should head back." Skeffington announced, "We're in over our heads."

On the way, Skeffington stopped at the portal.

"I've seen you talk to the others." he said, "Will you talk to me?"

The screen obligingly appeared.

Yes!

"What's all this talk of Defenders?"

Grabbing opportunity. Vehicle may be needed for quest. Aware of Jerry's sale. Purchased before father's first stroke. Little used. Remember licensing requirements, you are first visitors qualified to drive it. Hurry needed.

"I understand. Cars are expensive and David has limited funds over there."

Agreed. Other vehicles considered but negotiations with Jerry could centre around food, driving lessons and job.

"Trade." Skeffington exclaimed, "That would work."

Father managed shop until illness. Jerry trained in building firm which went broke. Now jobless. Focus of trade, care for parents. Jerry may want adventure.

"You mean he's a candidate for the quest."

Unpredictable dynamics. Four candidates together.

"Did you arrange this?"

Cannot arrange. Skeffington and Malcolm unexpected. Repeat, using unexpected situation. Mild disorder is also humour, is it not?

When they returned, David and Jethro were still out, visiting other estates and again, only Wilson was there to greet them as they headed for the library, Mark feeling very nervous at taking such a liberty. He relaxed slightly as Skeffington described events to Wilson, finishing up with, "We should wait for David or Uncle Jethro but they might not be back in time."

"Mary Styles is a fine woman. A widow, I believe." Wilson said, "It is the duchess who is sending the invitations, but speak with Godfrey. His side of the church is still sparse so I see no problem. His Grace is happy for staff to initiate their own projects and present a report for his consideration. Make it clear to this Jerry that you cannot decide there and then but see what you can do. Mark, go fetch a change of clothes and you may have a room to rest and prepare for tonight. You other two can be shown straight to your rooms. I'll arrange for a meal in good time for your visit."

"It's not your place to tell us what to do, Wilson." Malcolm exclaimed, "You forget yourself."

"His Grace has charged me with maintaining standards at Barabourne." Wilson replied, "You are to be involved in negotiations on its behalf so you should be properly prepared. Instructions and advice are the same in that they are either sensible or they are not."

"My apologies." Malcolm replied, "Please continue to do your duty and you're right, I am tired."

Although he had just travelled to another world for real, like Craig he felt that he had lived in a different world since meeting Skeffington. When Malcolm first mentioned visiting the warehouses, Skeffington had told him that David saw more by being incognito. Malcolm announced that he wished to do the same and from then on, he had adopted the tie convention. To the shock and horror of the court servants, Skeffington ignored his rank unless he was wearing one. It worked, Malcolm had not been recognised at the warehouse, with everyone assuming that he was some young aristocrat, cut off from the family wealth for some reason, now having to make his own way.

He was naturally warm and outgoing, tried to help with the renovations, becoming a reasonable carpenter's apprentice. By the time he began his real task of organising more accommodation, and it was revealed who he really was, his popularity carried over and he was still accepted. Malcolm took a genuine pleasure in the idea that he could cope away from court as a man, not hiding behind his titles. It felt good being accepted for himself and he remained firm friends with Skeffington. That friendship had brought him to Barabourne and the confirmation of what really happened there but dealing with an outspoken servant had caught him off guard. As he quietly dozed the real problem that nagged was, what did 'playing pool' mean?"

Malcolm was still content to follow Skeffington's lead when they met Jerry that evening.

"OK, I need your help." Jerry said, "I know that you'll think I'm weird but we live outside the village and it's easier to get here cutting across the field then up Barns Lane. Every time I walk along Barns Lane, I get this feeling that you need Dad's Defender at least someone to do with that David kid does."

"I get strange notions in Barns Lane as well." Skeffington said, "One is that you don't want to sell your father's carriage but you need money. Supposing we could offer a job, supplies and training in exchange for the use of it?"

"Since his stroke, Dad's changed and he gets violent. I've lost jobs because I've had to get home and help Mum. Because I was fired, I don't get benefits and our only money is Dad's sickness benefits."

"Fine. So food would be useful. We might arrange some money and we might be able to arrange regular staff to help your mother. I say might because David will have to agree."

Skeffington might have said more but Mark looked towards the door and turned deathly white. Skeffington also turned to look but only saw David chatting to Mary at the bar as he bought an orange juice before joining the others.

"Hello Mark." he said, "Please don't call me Your Grace like you did last time because people here think it most odd."

"Yes, er, sir. Er, sorry." Mark stammered.

"Wilson's briefed me." David said "The portal agreed that I need this thing of Jerry's so fill me in on what you've decided."

Skeffington duly brought David up to date.

"Usually vacancies are filled by people known to me or my uncle." David explained, "Once or twice, I've been given references by a source which I trust. That source is recommending you. If your previous training includes electrical skills, then we need you. Although it may be difficult paying you in cash, we can offer food, other goods and help to look after your father as Skeffington said." David said.

"Now it's difficult to explain more and if you've got any questions, I'm not sure if I can give sensible answers. However, if you're by that large metal gate in Barns Lane at about nine o'clock tomorrow morning, someone will meet you and bring you up to the house."

"That's what Skeffington said. What I don't like is that 'Your Grace' business and Mark being so scared of you. Mark's not the only one to call you that."

"Tomorrow." David replied, "If you like the deal we can offer then you need to understand the problems. For now, I'd like a quiet chat with Mark and it's pointless asking whether he minds being dragged away. He'll agree whatever he thinks."

Once they were on the brake, David said, "Over here, I'd be on the extreme right of the political spectrum. Your Dad's a radical which puts him well to the left. He goes on about the power I have and warns you about losing your job and how I could take it out on your family. You do relax at times but if your Dad hears about it then he has a go at you. It's not me that you're scared of but your dad. How close am I?"

"Pretty much, sir." Mark replied, "He reckons it's all a fad and you'll grow out of it."

They stopped at the portal.

"Portal, display the planet list." David commanded and three columns of numbers appeared on the screen.

"The green ones are safe for us to visit." David explained. "The red planets are lethal for some reason. Now, the scenery is going to change, we're not going anywhere it'll just be an image because it's from the red list."

Mark gasped at the sudden change in view. Instead of evening twilight, the bright sunlight put the time at midday but it was not the warm sunlight of a summer's day, it was harsh, bluish, bleak. There were the remains of a gate and what was left of the hedgerow, was misshapen and stunted as it struggled amongst the dead wood. Grass struggled to grow in what little shade there was but otherwise, the field was barren.

"I don't know much about radio-active fallout." David said, "About forty years ago, there was a war and their weapons produced it. It's still around, not in the air but in the soil and in the water. It's like a poison only more deadly. There's something in the atmosphere called an ozone layer which was also badly damaged. If we were standing here for real, our skin would have been burnt off and if we were still alive, we'd be blind. Turn it off, please, portal."

To Mark's relief, the image vanished and they were back in the real world.

"The Creators, the people who built the portal, made the portal highly visible to that world then when the government became interested, sent emissaries through but they were killed. The first emissary managed to warn their government but he was accused of trying to undermine their defences. They not only ignored his warnings; they shot him for sabotage. We did warn another world which took our advice but we didn't like them very much so we don't go back. Billy visits a world that's very strange but I think we've helped it. What I'm trying to say is that there's far more going on than you or your dad realise. I don't want people who remember their place, I need people who'll just shove me out of the way if there's danger. Can you understand that?"

Mark stayed uncertain, "Surely you want it like the army. You know what to do and there's no time to argue so the rest just obey orders."

"That's the thing. I don't know what to do. The portal will teach you to drive this Defender thing and then you'll be in charge when you're driving it because you'll know it's limitations better."

Mark nodded, "All your friends are experts in something and you have to listen to them but I'll just be a chauffeur."

"Just? You mean like Godfrey is just the stable manager."

"All right but why me?"

"Why me?" David retorted, "I always thought that Miles was an idiot but he's not. I nearly sacked Billy for stealing cider but cook insisted that it had always been done that way. I make too many mistakes to be in charge but when I say so, everyone argues with me."

David paused, "I am a duke so I have a bit of power, I got lost on the Royal George world and I learnt to deal with all classes but those are my only qualifications."

"Now I would argue with that, Your Grace." Mark laughed, "I've seen you and you are the boss when you need to be. Tim didn't like that rollicking you gave him. He moaned about some brat being able to talk to him like that but he sure bucked his ideas up."

"And are you going to buck your ideas up as well?" David asked, "OK you're not lazy but I need you to be decisive around me."

"In that case, come with me." Mark said, "We're going to deal with Dad."

Wondering whether he had released a monster, David complied and they drove to the village of Braborn, stopping at the pub.

As they entered, Mark looked around and strode over to a table where four men were sitting.

"Dad, David here might be the duke and our landlord but you know that the drainage in Longacre field is wrong and he won't know until you tell him."

"I think that you ..." David began

"Be quiet, David. This is between me and my Dad."

"You're not too old for me to take a belt to you." His dad snapped before turning to David, "I'm sorry Your Grace, I don't know what's got into him."

Suddenly, Mark was less certain, also turning to David.

"Mark has been caught between what I need from him and what you think I'm doing. We can't go into details but it seems that he's made his decision and now needs your support."

"So you can play your games then laugh at us all." Mark's dad said.

"They're not games, Dad." Mark said, "You know about all the strange stuff in Barns Lane. Nobody could call that a game.

David's shown me what's going on and I've decided to help."

There was silence for the whole pub was listening and Mark's father thinking furiously.

"Look lad, toffs don't care about the likes of us. I admit that His Grace is better than most but they've got all the power and they'll toss you on the midden without thinking twice. I'm sorry for speaking badly of you, Your Grace, but that's the way of the world. The best thing that Mark can do now, is join the army to get him away from here."

"If I'm as bad as you think then you've made a bad mistake talking to me like that." David said, "Do you really believe it, though?"

"No, not while everything's going so well but my Dad always warned me to beware the bosses especially when times are bad. Mark, go home and wait for me."

"Sorry Dad, I'm driving David back to the big house. We're then going to sit in the library while we discuss the new duties he has for me. Things are changing but it's something Godfrey said; like David, I'm young enough to accept change. You're too set in your ways. Come on, David."

David managed a quick shrug before hurrying after Mark who was standing by the brake, trembling.

"I went too far, didn't I?" he asked.

"I couldn't speak to my mother like that even if I am the duke." David said, "You're older though and you both give out mixed signals. He trusted me enough to speak his mind but was worried about you. You can speak freely to me then your nerve fails and you act like a frightened rabbit. Skevi and Malcolm can walk home while we have that chat."

"Oh God, I'd forgotten about His Royal Highness."

David struggled to get an answer from Mark on the way home and almost had to drag him into the hall. Once in the library and invited to sit down, he sat on the edge of a chair ready to leap up at the slightest sound.

"Two or three lads take goods down to the portal. I suppose that we were sizing up likely assistants but you're the first that the portal has suggested.

"Now I have some sort of quest to help the portal's creators. When Godfrey travelled with me, he felt like a bodyguard and he could spot trouble. He was older and I think that it made him sharper than me. Sharper may be the wrong word, maybe cautious or just experienced, but you get the idea. The thing is, quests can be dangerous and not everyone likes travelling. Uncle Jethro's assistant tried it and hated it. Carrying goods or chauffeuring my guests as far as the portal is estate work but becoming fully involved in my travels is far beyond that and you will be more than a servant. If you want to join in, then you need to sort yourself out. This room is where all my friends relax so you can start by sitting back in your chair."

Mark grinned as he complied then looked worried.

"Don't you think that I'm a cissy for being so scared?"

"You're confused, not scared." David replied, "If Jerry fits in then you should spend time with him. He's not a Barabourne man by any means, he may help you."

"There isn't a Barabourne over there, is there?"

"When their Earl of Braborn was executed, the estates declined and were broken up. The village shrunk and what was left was destroyed by the railway. There's a different village over there and although the Royal George is a little way out, it's the village pub. I think that there's a couple of hamlets around where Braborn used to be, so it caters for them as well. So far as I can make out, it's tourists and ramblers during the day and locals at night."

By now, Mark was far more at ease, enjoying his conversation with David. He was fascinated by the idea of visiting another world and wanted to do more. Others would accompany David out of duty, some preferred the security of Barabourne while Godfrey had enjoyed his adventures. Now he wanted to settle into married life and it was more difficult than David expected finding a replacement for him. Mark left to make peace with his parents, leaving David to ponder on how a simple problem could take so long to sort itself out.

If Mark was obviously excited then David was disappointed that Jerry failed to arrive the next morning, or so he thought. It was late afternoon that Billy and Miles burst into the staffroom, one of the rooms where he worked, with Jerry in tow.

"Sorry that we waylaid your guest Pebbles." Miles exclaimed, "Skeffington had the chance of a flight in the airship and we were due on the stone circle world. Todd came with us as far as the gate and would have brought Jerry back. He came across all right but had trouble with alternate worlds so we took him with us. I had a flying assessment, Billy had some sort of meeting so we left him in the circle with a couple of girls explaining the dress code. I think he ended up on a different world in more ways than one."

Jerry blushed as the others laughed.

"It felt weird stripping off in front of everyone, especially with Moira and Doreen offering to help. Then it turned out that Kayne was Doreen's boyfriend and suggested we all go back to his place. I was glad that we all got dressed to go there but we all stripped off when we got to his bedroom. Then it all got weird again when his mum walked in with a jug of lemonade and some fruit. She must have known what we were doing, I mean, my mum doesn't like it if I kiss a girl in front of her."

"You were on a different world." David said, "This is my world and the Royal George is on yours. Have you had enough or do you want to know more?"

"It takes a bit of getting used to. You want my help so supposing I said that I'll visit. I'll try to get to used to it all but I want all my meals here to save Mum money and I can drop everything if mum wants something. And that's something that bothers me, how come I've got a signal on my phone?"

"The portal can route calls. We've got a wedding, this weekend." David said, "Everyone's busy with that but you know Skeffington and Mark, they can look after you and show you what we're doing here. You could also show Mark how to drive the Defender. I'm still not sure what it is though."

"It's the sort of truck that you'd drive across the Sahara in. I assume you call it the Sahara Desert."

"That big beach in North Africa?" Miles asked, "We've got one. By the way, I'm due for my final assessment. I still won't be able to take passengers because I've got to log in more hours but they're giving me a couple of autogyros. Apparently, they've been told that I need one for a task on the Divine Path. The other one is so that I can build up my flying hours."

"Congratulations." David said, "I do mean it but I should be worrying about the wedding this week. I'm sorry if I don't sound that interested."

"Understood. Danny would say that it's cool."

"Okay, I can see that you're busy." Jerry said, "What with

airships and autogyros in the back garden and everything steam driven, I'd like to get my bearings."

"Good idea and get a shopping list for fresh food off your mother and give it to cook. If your Mother agrees, cook can prepare stews and stuff that can be reheated. We'll call it your wages for now, and figure out what else we can supply."

Preparing for his quest had been an unexpected interruption to the wedding preparations. He had not seriously considered it, but had assumed that Skeffington had been chosen as Godfrey's replacement. The portal always said that it could not manipulate people but David had not fully believed it until he realised that their were four options. The portal was right; it could not force people but it could give opportunities and wait to see who took their chance. David felt better for understanding more of how the portal worked but he knew that his enemies worked differently and he was not sure how and it was worrying. However, there was little he could do so he turned his attention back to the wedding.

Both David and Godfrey were relieved that the stag night could be a simpler affair. Godfrey was content with the barn; there was food, drink and the more musical hands played. No-one seemed to mind that village girls had also been invited and there was more than one romance in the air. Malcolm surprised everyone with his arm-wrestling skills, and came a creditable second in horseshoe-tossing.

The evening was not subdued but for most, there was a sense that it was the quiet before the storm. Barabourne had held other events but this one was special because one of their own was involved and it was not just for the *big house*. Maybe the *big house* was well represented by David, Miles and Malcolm, there was also Todd, Jimmy and Skeffington, not quite toffs but still more than just hands. There were even some engineers and scientists but it was all for Godfrey and he was one of them. The big day had to go well for his sake. David had organised the evening as best man and many were appraising his efforts. That such a diverse group could relax added to his stature as an effective lord and master.

At one point, Malcolm approached David chuckling.

"Young Nobby was telling me how we've all got to behave on Saturday. I'm sure that he was warning me not to forget my place."

David laughed with him, "He frowns at me if I speak to a

groom on the way to Church. I'm thinking of asking Wilson whether he could become a footman. With Wilson's training he'd be terrifying as a butler."

"That's your secret, isn't it? Making such a clear distinction between being on duty and off. Nobby would never have spoken to me like that, anywhere else but as a butler, he'd maintain strict order in the house."

"I also respect talent. Anyone may use my library and it doesn't matter what he does on duty. If he can appreciate my books off duty, then why not let him?"

"And no-one takes advantage of you?"

"I also respect Wilson's talents. Let's just say that they only try once."

"There's more to your methods than meets the eye." Malcolm said, "I'd like to study them. My brother takes after Grandfather more and hates anything that offends *God's order*. Heaven forbid that anything happens to Father anytime soon but when William succeeds he'll be far less tolerant. As you know, there's considerable industrial unrest. Father can see how just talking to people can make a considerable difference but it's not enough; we've got to give substance to our new friendliness and we have to spread it up North."

Malcolm paused, "But that's our problem. Yours is to keep Barabourne secure especially from Lord Carlton who's getting so much support from coal mine owners. He'll happily report to William about any troubles this weekend."

"Uncle Jethro wanted him taken off the invitation list because he's not welcome at Barabourne but Mother insisted that the bride's uncle be made welcome."

"You wanted father to publicly back you but you're stuck with me."

"You'll do." David laughed, "Godfrey wanted a meal where he could show off his social skills but Isabella talked him out of it. I wanted something in town where His Majesty could join in but Mother convinced me that it would be too contrived then we decided on this and you showed up. I'm enjoying myself if we don't stay serious for too long."

"Chalky's hoping for a rematch. Why not? The next time Prussia starts a diplomatic spat, I'll challenge the crown prince to an arm wrestling competition."

Godfrey was content to circulate, receiving the congratulations and the ribald comments that the occasion demanded. A few chose to get drunk; David heard rumours of at least one fight sorted by Skeffington but Godfrey went to bed, light-headed but remembering the good wishes of his friends.

The following day, it was business as usual with the first guests arriving. David was surprised to greet Olivia, apparently travelling alone apart from a servant.

"I know that you're busy with the wedding but Mother thinks that it's time that I bagged you," she said. "She doesn't want anyone else to be the next Duchess of Barabourne. She won't accept that you're tiring of me."

"But I'm not." David exclaimed, "It's just that after what happened in London, you would see me differently."

"Well of course, I do." she laughed, "Robin Hood who takes on the wicked rich to help the poor. Father and his friends talk of something bad that happened. It's all in whispers and they shut up in front of the ladies but I've heard enough of inverts and taking gelding shears to a policeman to guess. Some snicker that you probably enjoyed it but I know you. You may relax and be at ease in the company of boys but when I'm around your eyes cannot leave the assets that no boy should have."

She took in a deep unladylike breath, puffing out her chest to better display those assets.

"I'm right, aren't I?" she whispered.

David grinned then nodded, "It was so terribly humiliating. I'm embarrassed that you know anything about it."

"And another weekend will pass when we don't make mad passionate love. You have a wedding to worry about and I have to convince you that you're my hero. My friends would be so jealous if they read the social columns and saw us romantically connected. Now if there was also a photograph of me dancing with Skeffington, it would confirm me as the debutante of the year."

"So you don't love me. You just see me as a stepping stone along the social season."

"That's the strange thing. I can imagine us married with me waiting impatiently at home for you to return from your latest improbably wild adventure. You know, like the knights and their ladies of old. By the way, I'm in the Peacock Suite, I hate sleeping in a strange room so I'd have no objections to company."

~~~

At breakfast, the following morning, Jethro saw a light in David's eyes that had been missing for sometime. Maybe not a light but there was definitely something different, happier maybe. Jethro also noticed the smiles shared between David and Olivia and understood. As guardian, he should disapprove but it was good to see David so at ease with himself.

The stables were in a state of organised chaos preparing the vehicles. Wilson was in his element organising the house and the rector was in a state of panic when the dowager duchess descended on the church to check the arrangements there. David was uneasy, it was not so much the quest but the shadowy enemy behind it all. He knew nothing of its true powers except that it could make people do things; Lord Carlton and his cronies wanted control of Barabourne and the wedding seemed like an excellent opportunity.

At the Royal George, it was bemusement as transport to Barabourne arrived, a steam coach. It was Skeffington who jumped out to greet the landlady, Mary Styles.

"I must say, you look stunning." he said as he bowed politely before turning to the others, "My apologies, I'm guessing at Mr. and Mrs Lambert, Mrs Williams and Mr. Barton. I'm expecting a party of nine, including the lads so may I assume all is in order?"

No-one corrected him as they all got in the bus. A couple of ramblers stopped and stared as Mark gave a cheerful blast of the whistle and they chuffed away.

Danny and Darren giggled as Craig took off the windcheater that he had been wearing to put on his morning coat, obviously embarrassed.

"Your father didn't come then?" Danny's mother asked.

"Not when we told him that we were visiting a steam rally at a stately home." Mrs Williams explained.

"The clincher was, we said that we didn't know if there'd be a bar." Craig added, "We didn't mention that Wilson may have a private one in his pantry."

"Mr. Wilson." His mother corrected him, "You shouldn't be so rude."

"We do call him Wilson." Danny's mother explained, "Staff

call him Mr. He insists. Junior staff are called by their first names."

It was Mary who least understood, even though she had been expecting something strange. The youngsters, including Jerry were more concerned about the way they were dressed, while the Lamberts explained more about life at Barabourne to Mrs Williams.

Mary did not think so much about travelling to parallel worlds as travelling back to Victorian times. The village, Barabourne she assumed, was certainly old-fashioned, if not, quaint. As she saw the other guests, she reviewed her own clothes, relieved that she had gone for a vaguely fifties look which fitted in well. Many of the men sported sashes, medals and badges, including Malcolm who looked particularly resplendent as he accepted bows and curtseys from guests. As a pub landlady, she needed to read people's attitudes and many wanted to catch Malcolm's eye but they waited for him to notice them. The ladies then dutifully curtseyed but did not approach. Avid students of royalty were puzzled when Mary received her own nod of recognition and a cheerful wink. Everyone turned to her, wondering who she was as she attempted her own curtsey. Malcolm whispered to an aide who hurried over.

"His Royal Highness apologises. He forgot that you would not be prepared but he congratulates you on coping so well."

No-one else heard the message, but others were even more curious, jealous or simply trying to assess how much of a rival she was. However, it was time to enter the church and take their seats.

The service was familiar, but she was startled when Godfrey was referred to as Sir Godfrey and his bride as Lady Isabella. His Royal Highness, His Grace the duke, Sir Godfrey, and it was not an act. Everyone's body language fitted, they accepted it.

As always the bride and groom took precedence as they left the church though the congregation deferred to the distinguished lady escorted by Malcolm – Prince Malcolm, the lady could be his mother so that would make her ...

Her reeling mind was returned to the wedding by the sound of loud cheers. The happy couple were in a strange looking car. It could have been vintage, no, a replica built to modern standards. That was still not quite right but the cheers were because it had succeeded in driving off. Apparently to the rest of the crowd, it was an engineering marvel and they were surprised that it worked so well.

During the excited crush as the bride and groom drove off,

Mary found herself standing beside another very autocratic looking lady.

"Mrs Styles, I believe. I'm David's mother and I'm delighted to meet you." the dowager duchess said, "You've created quite a sensation amongst my circle and that includes Her Majesty. Irish coffee is the talk of the season."

The crowd surged again, this time heading for the vehicles and they were separated. Somehow Skeffington remained close and they were soon seated leaving Mary to wonder about the photographs. Godfrey and Isabella had paused for Danny who even managed a group shot of their immediate friends but too much else was going on, including her first sight of the hall.

"I'm lost. Where are we now?" she asked.

"Barabourne Hall." Skeffington replied, "The family has been associated with Braborn since the Crusades. Even when the dukedom was created, it never occurred to anyone to break the link but there's some mystery how it became Barabourne. Anyway, David is the Duke of Barabourne and the Earl of Braborn. Locals call the village Braborn, visitors; Barabourne so it's all a little confused."

"What about Chasebourne?"

"That's a village on Lord Dalton's estates. I know, it's a town on your world, isn't it? I've never been there."

"I'm surprised that there was not an official photographer." Mary said.

"They'll be taken later in a studio. I've seen Danny's efforts, he can snap away while one of ours would need us to freeze for ages."

Others were also trying to get their bearings. While his brother and sister-in-law chose to forget their station talking to the stable boy's cronies, Lord Carlton found himself isolated and ignored. Only Billy approached him as the less formal part of the proceedings began.

"Still angry with me?" he asked.

"No." Lord Carlton replied, "I can respect your loyalty to your master. It was well done but our business is concluded is it not?"

Billy shrugged and wandered off as the Queen suddenly made a break for freedom. Both her son, Malcolm and the dowager duchess had stayed close, protecting her from the less *predictable* elements of the guests. Nobody had a clear meaning of predictable but it included Jeremy, other likely drunks and Godfrey's friends. Grabbing a chance when her consorts were distracted she stepped backwards, turned and made a beeline for Danny's family.

Danny looked startled, straightened up as he tried to remember how to bow but Queen Anne winked and shook her head.

"It's very kind of you to remember our ways but I'd like to relax. My husband talks of your natural good manners and politeness so that will do." She turned to Mrs Lambert, "How do you like our world?"

"Well I only see the best parts of it and Danny does talk of the nastier parts but it's nice to be so welcome here."

"May I borrow your sons, please? My escorts are more like guards and it's not done for me to be completely alone. Beside I wish to enquire about that remarkable camera."

"I wish you luck." Mrs Lambert replied, "They're good lads but I don't know about their behaviour."

"Hmmph. You see that group over there. One of them is His Grace's cousin. They're probably drunk already and I'd have to hold them up. Come on lads, you can introduce me to Godfrey's friends."

By then, David was more relieved than anything. The wedding breakfast had gone well. The only room available to seat so many guests was the ballroom. Now, servants were desperately clearing it, ready for the dance. The orchestra was already preparing and Wilson almost scowled at him if he got too close to the activity. However, he was happy to spend time with Olivia but smiled as Mary approached them.

"What's the fascination with Irish Coffee?" she asked, "I keep getting asked about it."

"It's this year's fad." David replied, "Anything to do with my family can make the news, so when Mother offered it to guests, it took off. I gather that Harrods' and Selfridge's are inundated with orders but they've never heard of it or those bottles you send over."

"Good God."

"I heard something about it being invented for early transatlantic air passengers. Apparently they stopped over at Shannon airport and needed a reviving drink. None of that has happened over here, at least, not yet."

"Good God." Mary said again.

"This season, the most fashionable doors will be open to you. Next year, you will be ignored."

This time, Mary grinned, "I tried the smart set when I was younger and I understand. I'm happy with the Royal George, nowadays. I wish I could speak to Wilson, though."

"Even I'd get a clip around the ear if I distracted him too much." David laughed, "This is Barabourne on display to the world and it's Wilson's show."

"He's a lovely man." Mary said, "I wish he'd pop in more often."

David looked at her then glanced across to Wilson and wondered.

Chapter 9

As David's guardian, Jethro was nominally in charge, so he had also been worried that something might go wrong but instead, he was being complimented. As he pointed out, David had taken on most of the duties of the duke so he deserved the credit. Most had agreed but a worrying number whilst applauding his loyalty had pointed out that a boy, so willing to forget his station, could not possibly maintain order so effectively.

The surprise of the day was Isabella's father. Known as a bully, an inveterate snob and a tyrant, he spent a good deal of time socialising with Godfrey's friends and they all seemed relaxed and happy.

His wife, Sybil, joined Jethro.

"He hardly speaks to his brother, nowadays." she said, "Those scandals in London shocked him and Lord Carlton is linked to them. I hear that there's a couple of banking scandals about to break and Richard was being pressured into taking part. He refused but his brother is going broke and may already be under investigation. Carlton's hold on him is broken, Richard is more relaxed and sees what your people are doing for you.

"He still believes that he has the right to beat me, a servant or a horse in equal measure but that's God given. He now believes that he should try other methods first and I have to admit, it is a genuine effort."

"So are you happier?" Jethro asked.

"Oh yes. He still believes that women are incapable of understanding complex problems and is amazed when I make a telling point on some subject. He'll never change, except he wonders why your ideas work so well but he's so much calmer now that he's out of Carlton's shadow."

She paused before continuing, "He's no reader but he understands that Isabella's books are well-received. He also understands her struggle to prove that she can compete with male writers in her genre so he's more proud of her than I would have thought possible. All our married life, he only thought in terms of a son and heir but now … Let's just say that Jeremy has the trappings of a gentleman but there's no substance yet. Richard can see how

Godfrey works so hard to provide for Isabella. He's noticed that it's Godfrey and his friends who are behaving like gentlemen and he accepts that it's something Jeremy won't be doing for much longer."

More than anyone, Jeremy took after his Uncle, Lord Carlton, believing his stories that David was destroying the family, more importantly, it's wealth. Lord Carlton himself, no longer believed it but still hoped to find cracks in David's position that he could exploit. On the other hand, Jeremy was young and impressionable as well as jealous of Isabella's improving standing in his father's eyes.

There was a small group of cousins around Jeremy, all from that side of the family who Jeremy happily bullied when he could. Jeremy did not realise that even they considered him more of a drunk than a leader but so far, no-one had openly opposed him.

It was as Mark was passing that one of the group allowed his curiosity to get the better of him and exclaimed, "I say, you're one of Godfrey's friends aren't you? Do you know anything about that amazing carriage of his?"

As Mark began to answer, Jeremy interrupted, "Bloody Hell, Cuthbert, it's bad enough that we've got one in the family. You don't need to socialise with more of them."

"You're drunk, Jeremy." Cuthbert snapped, "I'll speak to whom I damn well please."

Jeremy was sober enough to realise that Cuthbert was challenging his authority, drunk enough to forget where he was and still in enough control to land an unexpected but hefty punch in Cuthbert's solar plexus.

Cuthbert doubled over and would have sunk to the floor if Mark had not grabbed him which Jeremy also saw as a challenge. He raised his arm for another assault but instead, it was grabbed and twisted up behind his back while a strong arm wrapped around his neck.

"Where I come from, we save brawls for the alley." Skeffington said quietly, "Shall we all calm down?"

Lord Carlton took in events with a degree of satisfaction, certain that guests would see drunken louts attacking respectable guests and he was right in that few had seen the initial assault and more were noticing Skeffington holding Jeremy. Fortunately others had seen the whole thing. Mary's pub instincts had warned her and she had spoken to Skeffington. Jethro knew of Jeremy's reputation and was keeping an eye on him while Jeremy's father was comparing his son's increasingly bad behaviour with other youngsters present. Lord Carlton's hopes of trouble were raised as both Jethro and Richard closed in. Probably less than half a minute elapsed before Richard stood in front of his son and Skeffington.

"I'm Sir Richard Darrow." He said, "And you are?"

"Skeffington Tamzon, sir."

"What! The Flying Horseman of London? It's a pleasure to meet you, sir. What do you intend doing with my son? Don't worry, I saw him strike Cuthbert and attack his rescuer but we're disturbing proceedings. Perhaps we should step out onto the balcony."

Jethro had seen many strange things over the last year or so but the change in Richard shook him the most. They were gone for some time but Skeffington and Richard returned laughing together at some joke.

"We decided that he should take a swim to cool off." Richard chuckled, "We'll apologise to the ducks in the morning. Now is it true that you leapt a costermonger's barrow on Holborn Viaduct?"

"I feel sorry for Skeffington." Sybil laughed, "Richard can now talk about the only subject that he's passionate about, horses."

Cuthbert, Mark and a couple of others had disappeared and Jethro guessed that they were at the stables looking at the latest thing in road transport.

~~~

The following morning many of the guests and household alike dozed, quietly reviewing the events of the previous day. The dowager duchess was particularly pleased. Godfrey and Isabella looked radiantly happy as they headed for their new home. Few had seen any disturbance even though many guests had spent a disappointing evening trying to spot Godfrey's friends through their social gaffes. David led the way in studying and listened carefully to Wilson on the running of the house. Godfrey's guests could hardly complain about receiving their own lessons with the result that they mixed comfortably with the *sneering* classes.

Guests heard how Jeremy had attacked his cousin, and how Skeffington had quietly dealt with it. Skeffington was something of a hero, protecting the family honour twice now. The dowager duchess was satisfied; her son, David chose his friends well. Her impression of pub landladies was of half drunk wenches, eyeing up likely customers for her nightly romp in bed. Mary Styles had amazed her. Firstly by dressing in a way that put many guests to shame, secondly by speaking in a confident but cultured manner, knowledgeable on many subjects. Mary had spotted Jeremy and by warning Skeffington had done much to avoid trouble. In the future, Mary would be a welcome guest for afternoon tea.

That Sunday morning, events were dictated by train timetables as guests took their leave. Church would be a muted affair. When she went down for breakfast, she found a number of unexpected guests still there including Cuthbert.

"Good Morning, Aunt. I hope I don't smell too horsey but I slept in the stables."

"I'm not sure I approve but I thought that our stable loft was particularly well-kept."

"They're better than the school dormitories but Nobby only agreed providing I helped with the mucking out."

"But you're a guest. That's no way to treat you. I'm so sorry."

"It's quite all right, Aunt." Cuthbert said, "My parents left last night and I want to learn more about these new carriages that you're developing here. I knew that you had other guests so there might not be room for me. Mark asked Nobby who said that the loft wasn't for passengers and I'd have to do my bit. I tell you what though, yesterday's clothes were taken away to be cleaned and I was supplied with work clothes. Afterwards I took a shower, a hot one, not like school, and there was a change of my own clothes. I hope that you don't mind me inviting Mark to breakfast."

"Surely you could have stayed with Mark?"

"That's because I also decided to stay on." Malcolm said, "Mark's parents only have one guest room and I must say, it's exceedingly comfortable."

The dowager duchess turned to Wilson, "It seems that Barabourne can manage very well without us. You and I shall take lunch at the Royal George. Arrange it, if you please."

Like everyone else, David found the event too big to take everything in. He had missed the disturbance with Jeremy, but heard the tales that circulated. However, much to his relief, he had not spotted anything amiss during the whole day and was content to spend as much time as possible with Olivia; he would catch up with his friends after she had left.

Jethro also spent the morning reviewing events. He was aware that many guests had gone home, disappointed that the only trouble had been caused by one of their own class. He was also aware that as the carriages and steamers were summoned, many offered a pleasant 'Good evening' to their own drivers and footmen. It was only a small thing but it was new. He was also aware that many had broken ranks and no longer followed Lord Carlton.

It seemed that Danny's real passion had earned him the role of royal photographer. All Jethro knew was that his *darkroom* consisted of odd boxes that produced marvellous colour images almost instantly and that Her Majesty wanted him to take pictures of her gardens. She had been fascinated as Danny had wandered around taking pictures and Danny had accompanied the royal party to London. Jethro assumed that it was another project that would help break social barriers so he was content. The day remained quiet and the necessary work continued. It might be Sunday but as Cuthbert had discovered, country life continued and livestock had to be looked after.

The Barabourne boys were lucky in that they had arranged a week's holiday. Danny, Darren and Craig were less lucky and returned home that evening, with Danny getting quite blasé about travelling on special trains as he returned from London. However, it was Mark who started to turn to other matters as he sought out David.

Petrol-head! That was Danny's description of anyone with a fascination for carriages - motor cars on the other world. He grinned, agreeing that Darren was definitely an airship-head, if there was such a word but Cuthbert was likely to be this world's first petrol-head.

"Cuthbert's seventeen." Mark said, "I'd like to take him to Jerry's place and look at this Defender. I know you don't want others to know about the portal but Jeremy talks about this ghostly pub that only appears every so often and he recognised Mrs Styles. He's also picked up on your phones and things and talked about them to Cuthbert and the others. The trouble is, is Cuthbert really interested? I don't know; he may be looking at the profit he could make or be thinking of blackmail but I think that he's curious."

"Is seventeen relevant because of driving permits over there?" David asked and Mark nodded as David continued, "Cuthbert's father is an extremely distant cousin of father. The family were invited partly because of that, partly because socially, they're acceptable and partly because they do business with Isabella's family and that last part puts me off a bit. What's your feeling about him?"

"I don't know, I shouldn't be speaking about your family like this, should I?"

David frowned, "Don't clam up on me now. If we do nothing, he'll keep digging around. If we send him away, he could team up with Jeremy and cause trouble but if we show him, will he fall in with us? You've spent time with him, what do you think?"

"I'm sorry, sir." Mark replied, "I know the rule of three so supposing he can only travel if there are two others with him all the time and not just as far as the portal?"

"Good thinking." David said, "How are you getting on with your Dad?"

Mark grinned, "Prince Malcolm joined us in the stables yesterday while we looked at the new vehicles. He was a bit tipsy but realised that he would cause problems if he stayed an extra night in the big house. I forgot who I was talking to and suggested he stay with me. Mum's always said that my friends should be as welcome as theirs. Anyway, he accepted, Dad was in bed, Mum always waits up for me and greeted Malcolm just like anyone else. We talked for a while, Mum got the spare bed ready and we went to bed. You should have seen Dad's face at breakfast though. He recognised Malcolm but couldn't understand why we hadn't."

David laughed, "I think that His Royal Highness likes it here."

"He and Cuthbert are maybe what you need for your quest."

"Don't forget yourself, then there's Skeffington and Jerry and before you say anything, you used your initiative concerning Cuthbert. It's made you a more likely contender."

~~~

At first Cuthbert was worried about going with them.

"I told Father I was staying and he wasn't too happy until Lord Carlton said that it was a good idea. He said that anything I learnt about Barabourne could be useful. He also told me that I should tell him all about it so that he could point out anything significant."

"Fair enough." David said, "Do you really want to tell all or shall we feed him what he wants to hear?"

"You trust me, after that?" Cuthbert exclaimed.

"That depends, are you telling me because you're concerned or because you think that I may trust you more so it'll be easier to spy? Since I already trust you, then telling me could have made me more cautious so it would have been a mistake. Of course, you might have realised that I would realise that telling me was a mistake therefore I would trust you more ... You see where it goes. You told me, we've got our own way of checking on people and so far, you're proving to be one of the good guys."

"We're using a steamer." Cuthbert said, disappointed.

"Motor cars are still in development and we're still geared up for steam." David explained, "Fuel is limited so we can't rely on it yet. Don't worry though, I think you'll enjoy this visit."

At first, it was Jerry who was most excited riding on the brake. He gave directions to a large house beside the railway line.

"It was built for the crossing keeper but they built a footbridge and closed the crossing. There're just paths for hikers on the other side and a long dirt track to a road. It's easier if we park on this side and use the footbridge."

The road they were on ran parallel to the track and Cuthbert stared as a high speed train roared past.

"Where's the engine?" he gasped then, "Electricity?"

Jerry nodded, then asked, "What's this about teaching you to drive?"

"Surely you need your own permit to do that, don't you?" David asked.

"I've got a car licence but I want to go for my LGV; that's lorries and it's expensive. We're here, turn into that gate."

Cuthbert and Mark stared at the vehicles parked there.

"The house was split into two so there's two families but the neighbours will be at work. The Fiesta is mine but I can't afford to tax or insure it, the Vestra is Mum's but she only uses it to drive into Chasebourne." He said pointing as he walked to a large off-road vehicle, "And that's the Defender."

He opened the driver's door and said, "In you get, Mark."

Mark's eyes grew large and round, "I can't drive that. It's a monster."

"It's smaller than your steamers, it's just different. Let's see what you can do. I'll be in the passenger seat and the other two can sit in the back."

Once they were settled, Jerry touched a stalk in front of the steering wheel and snapped, "What's this for?"

"Indicators and lights." Both Mark and Cuthbert snapped back.

Jerry looked at Cuthbert, surprised and said, "OK, while I was waiting, that portal thing stuck up a screen and talked to me. It can teach you languages and it gives information about a new world. It said it had taught you the basics and I was to give you this, Mark. It's a driving licence. It also said that it can't give experience. That's my job. It also said, U*nexpected candidate. Need time to establish presence.* Just relax and let's see what you do know."

To his surprise, Mark knew the procedure until he let out the clutch and promptly stalled it.

"That's something you need to feel," Jerry said, "Ease up on the clutch until you start to edge forward."

Mark tried again and almost yelled in triumph as they rolled forward.

"Right, at this speed, it's a lot smaller than that steam bus of yours so ease out onto the road. Do it for real as if you're already on a road and you're coming up to a T-junction."

Mark nodded, muttering 'Mirror, Indicate, Manoeuvre' as he turned into the lane.

"Be careful at junctions. I suppose that you do look around on your world but remember traffic's a lot faster here."

Mark nodded, recognising the sign for the junction at the end of the lane and braked to slow down. The Defender would have skidded to a complete stop if Mark had not eased on the brake in time.

"I understand what power-assistance means now." He said, "It's good."

He stared as a car roared past but the traffic was not that heavy. As Jerry had said, he had driven far larger vehicles so he could adapt some of his experiences. He had the knowledge implanted in his mind and Jerry was proving to be an excellent instructor giving him the confidence he needed.

They eased into heavier and heavier traffic until Mark found himself driving at about seventy miles an hour along a motorway.

The only thing that bothered David was that the Defender was an off-road vehicle but so far, they had only driven on roads but it was enough for Mark. He was exhausted as his body interpreted the flood of information that his brain had absorbed. Once back, they ate the picnic lunch that cook had prepared and discussed what to do next.

"How about you, Cuthbert, do you want a go?" David asked, "I won't explain computers so using our world, you need to carry all sorts of documents and they need to be properly registered."

"I've never driven. Father says that we've got grooms for that. There was something I heard once, 'A good master should never tell a servant to do something that he can't do'. His reply was, 'In that case, don't tell the hands to plough Lower Meadow'. Sorry, I'm going on a bit but beyond tending my own mount, I'm pretty clueless.

"My father had the same idea but he didn't mind if I could claim that it was mentally challenging." David said.

"You know our side of the family. The only question is whether a gentleman should do it and the answer was usually no."

"You're a right load of snobs over there, aren't you?" Jerry exclaimed.

"And we were at the wedding because David is challenging it." Mark interjected, "You've got to choose Cuthbert, are you going to be a gent to fit in with your side of the family or David's."

"You mean, do I put up with a stable hand talking to me like that?"

"If you like." Mark replied.

Cuthbert laughed, "I think it was Nobby that decided me. He was clear that I wouldn't be treated any differently and he made sure that I did my share of the mucking out. You know what though, he arranged for my change of clothes and he didn't let me go for breakfast until I was properly cleaned and dressed. He's what, in his twenties and he's a big lad. I didn't feel like arguing when he inspected me."

"He went a bit far." David said.

"That's the thing. Once he was satisfied, he knuckled his forehead and said, 'Good day to you sir' and he expected me to be the gentleman then."

"OK but do you want driving practice or not?" Jerry asked.

"Sorry, I have been blathering on. Lord Carlton says that Barabourne is descending into chaos. I know now that he's wrong because Nobby has his own sort of order and it works. I feel comfortable at Barabourne but I couldn't stay at Father's and just visit. If I stay then I'd have Nobby glaring at me if I didn't help out and that includes driving. Neither would I be able to report back."

"You're still waffling but it sounds good to me." Jerry said and David nodded.

The number of potential companions for the quest was definitely increasing and he was going to have to decide. The Creators wanted Craig involved because of his scientific knowledge. David could not imagine going anywhere new without Danny except Danny was finding his niche, and apparently they needed Miles' flying machines.

Most of the other candidates were only three or four years older than David. Godfrey had been part bodyguard and part adult looking out for trouble. Skeffington and Prince Malcolm were older but … David wasn't sure what he wanted to say; less enthusiastic, less flexible, more adult and in charge? He was not sure but they may not be the best choices.

David's musings were interrupted as Jerry said, "OK Mark. Time to go solo. Go and see if there're any papers for Cuthbert. While you're gone, David can teach me to drive a steam car."

David was not really involved in the proceedings but he watched the three lads sharing experiences and becoming friends, they could make a good team but there was another problem. He felt as though he should be doing something but he could not think what. He worried whether it was just part of his convalescence or whether he had forgotten something. All his projects were in hand and all he had to do was monitor them so maybe it was just concern about this mysterious enemy.

~~~

For a time, it was Danny who was least happy and felt as if he was just tolerated. Even his friend Craig had a sense of purpose. Craig enjoyed sport but had been pushed by his father to excel. There is nothing wrong with encouragement to do better but encouragement to win no matter what, and being taught that fouls or aggressive behaviour were only wrong when he was caught, put too much pressure on him. Now that he had a whole new life that even his mother actively hid from his father, Craig was far more relaxed and his sport improved even if his father did complain that he was getting soft.

Similarly, he had an incentive to go to the library and join clubs to expand his interest in science. It annoyed his father because increasingly he could not understand what Craig was studying and felt control slipping away.

It was not long after the wedding that his mother stopped Craig for a talk.

"How would you feel if I left your father?" she asked, "I still love him but I'm tired of being a doormat. It's the wedding that brought it to a head. You've got wonderful opportunities and running away aside, you could leave home far sooner than I expected and I want to do my own thing."

"And Dad won't let you." Craig said, "You're just good for doing his dinner parties and I'm okay providing I become an accountant. Do you want me to move to Barabourne like Todd?"

"No, I never told anyone but your Nan left me with a nice little inheritance. There's a two bedroom cottage for sale in Hartbury, not far from the Royal George. I'm not going to argue over custody but one of those bedrooms will be yours whenever you want it."

"It sounds as if the portal has been planning things again." Craig muttered.

"How do you mean?" his mother asked, "I've been bookkeeping since before you were born and I've been thinking about this since that first trip of yours. I said it was two bedroom, but the garage is properly insulated and I could fit it out as an office. Are you saying that the portal can plan all that?"

"Dunno but it bothers David."

"I see. The alternative idea is that it becomes a sonny flat."

"Huh?"

His mother grinned, "It was altered to be a granny flat. I was thinking that if my son took it over it would be a … Never mind. It's got two rooms so you could use one for all your science stuff. What worries me is that you'd think I was trying to push you to one side instead of making a home."

"And you'd use the spare bedroom as an office, while I work on a nuclear bomb in the garage. It sounds stupid, doesn't it. I don't know anything about them. Scientists spend years at university learning about them. How am I going to help?"

"Don't ask me. I'm still getting used to parallel worlds. There are a couple of houses that I like better but when all your stuff came up, I started thinking more about this place. Anyway, how do you feel about me leaving your dad?"

"It feels as if everything is changing." Craig said, "When I realised what was happening that first trip, I only thought about getting back here and being safe but you've got to do it. When are you going to tell Dad?"

"Are you going off with Danny, this weekend?"

"Dad wants me to watch the match with him Saturday afternoon but he'll be boozing all through it. It's not much fun when he's like that so I'd rather not. I'll see if Danny's visiting David's."

"Go Friday night if you can. I'll run you out to the gate."

Danny was happy to go with Craig and both boys chose to cycle to the portal straight from school. Instead of Craig having a chance to talk about his mother's plans, Danny was given a message requesting him to go to London. Since it was the King's request then he would fly there and would leave immediately.

"Ah, Danny, it's good to see you again." King Charles said, "I hope that I haven't spoilt any plans that you might have."

"Not really, I was going to show Craig around but we met Todd and Craig couldn't wait to see the laboratories."

The king chuckled, "And you visit me, definitely second best."

"No. I kinda like it." Danny replied.

"It is good of you to say so but I'm wondering what you know of scandals and bank collapses on your world."

"Not much." Danny replied, "They happen but I don't really know what goes on."

"That's the first piece of information. Your press feels free to publish the details. They're not served with notices by the Treasury."

"No." Danny said then grinned, "You've got a load of Sir Humphrey Applebys then."

"Who?"

"Sorry. It was an ancient TV programme called, *Yes Minister* and some were called, *Yes Prime Minister*. Sir Humphrey was the head of the Civil Service who wanted to protect its power rather than do anything while Jim Hacker was a bumbling politician who wanted to change things but never succeeded."

"It does sound as if our civil services are similar in make up;

you are referring to a moving picture play and you see me as this Jim Hacker."

"No, but it had stories about banks and it made them sound like a club. A member could be fired but it was a private matter. Jim Hacker wanted to do things but he was blocked by Sir Humphrey."

"And did you agree with either character?"

"Jim Hacker. At least he tried." Danny replied, "Like I said, I don't really follow this stuff except that I am more interested in politics because of coming here. A couple of countries arrested the bankers and sent them to prison. I do get the feeling that they recovered more quickly than countries that didn't."

King Charles nodded, "My instincts are the same as yours and yes, I also have my Sir Humphreys. There is a minor Treasury official who tried sending a story to the newspapers. He has been dismissed and faces charges of stealing Treasury materials namely pens, bottles of ink and blotting paper which were found in his home."

"A whistle-blower." Danny exclaimed, "And they have trumped-up charges to discredit him."

"What do you think I should do about him?"

"I don't know." Danny replied, "Give him a job? I could get a load of stuff from my world and he could turn it into something that you could use. Can you quash the charges against him?"

"Yes, I can but challenging the court's authority could be strongly opposed especially in the Lords."

"And they all belong to the bankers club."

"As do I." King Charles said, "I allow my money to be invested though I don't become personally involved."

"OK, it could be embarrassing for you so you'd cover it up. On the other hand, you could be furious that the Crown has been implicated in something shady and you cannot condone it. You could be furious that the banks think so little of the nation's reputation."

While the King again nodded, an idea occurred to Danny, "Try a *Sir Humphrey* solution. Don't oppose the whistle-blower's trial, if his crime is so serious, demand an audit and an enquiry into the extent of the thefts. Maybe they'll consider whether it's worth prosecuting him."

"I think that I would like to see these stories but we will see what we can do. You are right, the crown's reputation is affected so that was a royal *we*.

Danny grinned as the king continued, "By our standards, you are a dangerous radical wishing to weaken the monarchy and government. However, when *we* say something, it is almost treason to disagree so never argue with *us* in public. I shall send for my *Sir Humphrey*, Sir Sidney Lorre, the permanent secretary to the Treasury. He won't arrive until late tomorrow afternoon and I'd like you to be present. You're staying at His Grace's town house, I believe, so would you return at about 4 o'clock tomorrow, please? We do remember that you are a guest to our planet, and I'm still not used to saying it out loud. Be that as it may, allow us to entertain you. Is there anything that you wish to do?"

"Yes but it'll sound silly. I'd like to pack some sandwiches and some drink and just sit somewhere I can watch those great express trains of yours."

Later he described his trip to his friends, "They just can't do simple. An equerry took me to Euston Station in the morning and the manager of the railway company had arranged for a restaurant car and a locomotive. We travelled to some station where there was a load of kids and anoraks on the platform and they all watched as my train got shunted into a siding. They offered to clear the platform for me but I said no, I'd rather they make snacks and hand them around. That went down well especially when no-one stopped me taking a lad about my age beyond those signs saying we shouldn't. We ended up on an embankment and just sat. He was quiet unless a train went by and then he told me all he knew about it."

He paused, "I'm learning about steam and coal so a lot laughed when I put on coveralls, you know, the white disposable kind. I explained that I had to see His Majesty later and I shouldn't get all sooty, then it was OK. That station was near the top of an incline and the expresses were just reaching top speed. The ground shook, there was soot and steam everywhere and my overalls were black when I left but it was fun. The restaurant-car staff enjoyed themselves too. It was easier than being on an express and one or two of those anoraks were quite wealthy so they did well out of tips. I had a nice steak dinner on the way back."

Such a trip would be unthinkable on Danny's home world but it showed him the influence that the King had on this. It helped Danny prepare for the meeting with Sir Sidney who stared curiously at Danny when he arrived. There were papers on a desk showing that they had already been working.

"Is Donald Bergman's trial in hand?" King Charles asked.

"Yes, Your Majesty. We trust that he will get at least two years hard labour."

"Good. If the sentence matches the offence, then it concerns us that we were extremely lucky to stumble across his thefts. If he had not tried embarrassing the Treasury, then we would never have discovered it."

"That is so, Your Majesty. It is why we should make an example of him."

"What concerns us is that he might not be the only one. It would be embarrassing to discover that the whole department considers crown money to be at their disposal. I think that a full audit of Treasury affairs would be in order and all sharp practices rooted out. What do you think?"

"I think that a full audit is unnecessary, Your Majesty. I'm sure that most employees are completely honest."

"All the more reason for the audit. One rotten apple taints the whole barrel. The audit will vindicate the rest. Just what did Bergman steal?"

"I'm not sure, Your Majesty. The matter is very low level so I don't know the details, I just gave permission for a warrant to be issued. Since you're requesting an audit based on this case, I suggest that I review it personally and prepare a report."

"Thank you. I do not need a full investigation, a list of stolen materials and an opinion on whether it warranted a charge of theft will do. By tomorrow, if you please."

"Tomorrow? Yes Your Majesty."

Both men turned to Danny as he stifled a laugh but the King turned back and said, "Thank you, Sir Sidney. I'll not keep you any longer."

As Sir Sidney left, King Charles turned to Danny.

"I'm sorry for interrupting, sir." Danny explained, "But he sounded just like Sir Humphrey when he had been beaten. The programme always finished with him saying 'Yes Minister'."

"You know, sometimes, something is so obvious you wonder why you've never seen it before. Normally I would have demanded a report and assumed that I would have got it as soon possible. Like your stories, I suppose that I knew that the Civil Service took too much upon itself but I was vague about how. Would you say that I worried Sir Sidney?"

"I don't think so, sir but he did backtrack a little."

"Would you say that he used a *Sir Humphrey* reason?"

Danny grinned and nodded.

"Our royal knowledge and experience detected a moment's panic. We are back to His Grace and his Great Decline. Do you think that this is all part of it?"

"I would say so but even if you cleaned up this country, how would it affect the rest of the world?"

"What do you know of the political situation here?"

"Not much. It's taken all my time to get used to Barabourne and meeting you."

"Yes I understand. France, Spain and Holland support the German states as much as possible. They provide a barrier against the Russian Empire and the Austro-Hungarian empire. The Dutch royal family in particular are very much figureheads and real power lies with their parliament. Barabourne could transpose there or Scandinavia and fit in. France and Spain are possibly more extreme in their attitudes than we are. What you call America consists of a loose confederacy. Each state's politics is influenced by the homelands of its settlers and while they'd unite against an outside attack, they'd be concerned enough to turn on any state that broke the status-quo. However, states under British influence swing towards liberalism and might find His Grace's new attitudes very much to their liking."

"His Grace is obviously prospering by his ventures and new methods. That prosperity is influencing many peers so I notice a change in their attitudes here. I assume that the portal thinks in terms of years or even centuries so over time that same influence will work with countries that see our prosperity."

The King hesitated before making a decision, "This is for you and you alone. Do not repeat this to anyone, including His Grace. We are already upsetting the French. They cannot understand how they can be intercepted so easily and so quickly. If it was an airship then it remains on station and doesn't leave to report: they try to steer away but still our ships appear from nowhere. If they're spotted from land, ships appear from over the horizon or out of the mist. Our

Paris agents suggest that they may start arming their airships to attack ours. The French are getting very interested in what we're doing so I'd say that the process has begun."

"As long as you don't go to war." Danny said, "How bad are things with France?"

"Judge for yourself. As I just said, to the east of France are the German states but it's more complicated than that. Prussia in particular is backed by the Austro-Hungarian empire while France tries win more influence. However, France cultivates good relations with the czar of Russia. It also keeps the bulk of its army guarding its eastern border. To the west is us though I should include countries such as Spain, Denmark and the Low Countries. We both have colonies and protectorates around the world so we both need ocean trade routes. That makes the English Channel of vital importance to both of us. However if we went to war, there's no telling what political alliances would be formed. We're happy to hold back and allow France to keep its army in the east, while they don't want to split their defences either. We content ourselves with probing each other's channel defences looking for weaknesses. We were concerned about a build up of ships along their Atlantic coast but they appear to be dispersing again. We have more ships in port than usual waiting for radio to be fitted so they were testing our readiness. Do you play tennis?"

"I've played a bit on a hard court, but there's also lawn tennis and real tennis that dates back to Henry VIII. I'm not even sure what that is."

"Then it would be my pleasure to teach you while you tell me more of Sir Humphrey's tricks. You seem puzzled."

"I'm surprised that I've got anything new for you, sir."

"You question things. We had considered the Civil Service to be part of the club and never questioned it. Sir Sidney was definitely hiding something and now we're wondering what else is being kept from us."

As they stood to head for the tennis courts, a man in his mid-thirties arrived.

Danny stood uncertain what to do.

"Ah William. Allow me to introduce you to Mr. Danny Lambert. Mr. Lambert, this is my son Prince William. Many on their first visit attempt to kneel but a bow is sufficient for a prince."

Danny obliged, bending at the waist and Prince William seemed a little warmer in response though he said, "I hear that this boy is persuading you to interfere in that banking affair. Has the Treasury asked you to? Why was Sir Sidney here?"

"The treasury plan is to put a threepence in the pound increase on Purchase Tax." the King said, "They want the proceeds to go to their contingency fund. That's the third tax rise for the general population to rescue the banks."

"If banks go under, everyone suffers so it's only fair that everyone helps."

"Does Purchase Tax go down when the banks make a profit?" Danny asked.

"Be quiet, boy." William snapped, "I take it that you're one of Barabourne's brats that cause so much trouble."

"Danny shouldn't have interrupted, but the question has been asked so now we're curious to know the answer."

"Of course not. When the banks prosper, everyone prospers."

"How? Do wages go up?" Danny asked.

"Danny, please." the King murmured, "You're right, William. We are influenced by the new ideas evolving at Barabourne. However, agitators are active around coal mines and we may need to deploy troops to prevent strikes. The French are far more active so those same troops should be on coastal defence. Despite your opinion of the Duke, he has made the French more cautious so we have a breathing space. If we deploy the troops to the coal-mines, then the French will wait while civil unrest weakens us."

"Crush these damn agitators once and for all." Prince William snapped, "Then we'll be ready for the French."

"Your grandfather hung as many as he could. Now they're seen as martyrs for the people to rally around. Danny, would you return home, please? I'd like to know more of Sir Humphrey's ideas and anything else that may be relevant. Will you assist?"

"Of course, Sir. If you were willing to visit the Royal George, then I know adults who know a lot more than me."

"No. You'll do. Is it possible for you to return during the week? Once you're at Barabourne, transport will be arranged, either airship or, if the weather is bad, special train."

"Wednesday afternoons are sports. The school says that if students have to miss school then that's the best time. I've got an

167

idea but I'd need to fly over London and take some pictures."

"Even if you need the boy, just summon him." Prince William exclaimed, "Why this rigmarole?"

"When you become King, you will need to know Barabourne's secrets. However, for now, you oppose any reform so allow me my secrets. Whatever you need, Danny."

The story that Danny made up was simple. Through knowing Mr. Barton, he had become interested in history which his history teacher could confirm. Through an uncle he had an opportunity to gain work experience with a computer-graphics studio. Although too young for an official work-experience placement, the pictures he took showed impressive images of an alternative London.

"They seem almost real. How did you take them?"

"From a gantry, sir. It's a combination of 3D models and graphic overlays. The film is a steam punk story and I was flying over London in an airship. See, I've got a video clip."

"And it's all tied in with your passion for steam cars. I understand. It is unorthodox but you're obviously keen. I will excuse you sport for now but you must produce evidence to show that you continue to be involved."

For some time, Danny had worried that he was not really helping but just a hanger on. True, David always seemed happier when he was nearby especially at the start of some project but now he had his own and was getting insights into how stopping the Great Decline was working. He was beginning to understand the fundamental difference that radio made to the world and it all tied in with an adventure that Darren enjoyed.

Chapter 10

In Napoleonic times, even in Danny and Darren's world, boys as young as nine could serve in a warship as powder monkeys, fetching powder and shot while officers could start their training at twelve. Darren was eleven and had grown up in a world of smartphones and the internet. Radio communication was second nature to him, he loved flying, so there were definite advantages in allowing him flying time, teaching him to command an airship in exchange for his help in using radio. CPO Hammond preferred Darren to many commissioned officers because of his willingness to learn and it was now rare for him to countermand Darren's instructions. In his turn, CPO Hammond was beginning to *think radio.*

Even so, the navy would still have been cautious listening to Darren except that he had offered to demonstrate helium to the king. As Danny had discovered, when the king wanted something, then no-one offered anything less than five star service. For Darren, it was a matter of ordering some bottles of helium on-line while at home with his parents. For the Royal Artillery School of Gunnery at Shoeburyness, it meant a royal visit with all the pomp and circumstance that involved. For the senior gunnery officers, startled out of their routine existence, it meant paying heed to an eleven year-old boy and his peculiar bottles of gas. They patiently explained that lifting gas was highly inflammable and asked him if he had ever heard the word hydrogen.

Demonstrations were set up to prove their point and in the faint hope of getting him to admit defeat, allowed him to fire guns loaded with tracer.

Then Darren asked them to repeat the experiments using his gas. Smug complacency turned into consternation as tracer bullets, blow torches or any other ignition device failed to provide the expected flames.

"Yes I have heard of hydrogen but have you heard of helium?" Darren asked when they finally gave up and turned to him."

Major Dunhill drew himself up to attention and replied, "No sir, we have not. You have something that the War Office and the Admiralty will be very interested in. Is there anything else?"

Darren had tried to ignore the patronising comments and put

downs but now he had the advantage. He opened a tap and inhaled before offering the pipe to Major Dunhill.

"Try it." he said in a high squeaky voice that made many onlookers chuckle.

Reluctantly Major Dunhill complied as Darren asked, "How much gas will we need for the royal visit?"

"We should ..." Major Dunhill stopped, startled by his own high-pitched voice.

"Go on." Darren said, his voice returning to normal.

"What we've used today is ample." Major Dunhill tried again, relieved as his voice also returned to normal, "We should have the same amount in reserve though."

"As you can see it's not poisonous. How do we demonstrate that point to His Majesty?"

Major Dunhill was not used to military discipline being undermined by a cheeky schoolboy and was uncertain how to reply.

Finally, Darren relented, "I know I'm a kid but I know about hydrogen, helium and a load of other gases. You take me seriously and I'll get a couple of my mates to show how safe it is."

On the day, both Major Dunhill and Darren got what they wanted until Prince Malcolm decided that he wanted to test it for himself. Fortunately the parades were over because he insisted that others try. No-one on that world had ever heard of Donald Duck but for a long time, a good few soldiers would remember their feared Sergeant-Major sounding like him.

Afterwards, Darren was probably taken too seriously for he was asked about polystyrene panels faced with aluminium sheets, aluminium alloys and other materials used in airship construction.

"I don't know," he replied petulantly, "I want to fly the things not build them."

No-one risked challenging his presence on a naval airship again.

It was a calm but hazy day with visibility at least five miles otherwise Darren would not have been flying over the English channel but CPO Hammond was giving him a navigation exercise. He might have taken control when they spotted a French airship carrier escorted by destroyers, sailing towards the Isle of Wight. Just six months before, the only way of giving a warning would have been for them to fly to within signalling distance of a naval base or to search for ships at sea but French airships were already airborne. They would attempt to block the British airship and a dangerous game of cat-and-mouse would begin which was why CPO Hammond was ready to take over. However, Darren ordered a course away from the airships and showed CPO Hammond a copy of a message that he would send.

"Carry on, Mr. Lambert." CPO Hammond said formally, "They won't stop us following their ships if they don't think that we can make a report. What do you intend?"

Darren grinned, "They think that this haze gives them the advantage. If you can check on my dead reckoning, I'll give regular position reports and keep requesting assistance."

The French were surprised when two British airships suddenly appeared out of the haze heading directly for them. That a British cruiser and its destroyer escort arrived not long after might have been a coincidence, but when a destroyer group on the opposite heading arrived it was certain the French fleet was successfully intercepted. The Commodore aboard the British cruiser took over command.

Darren's airship was now irrelevant and it flew unopposed back to Barabourne.

On the surface it was a minor incident but it stunned two major naval powers. In France, it was the idea that so many units could converge on their fleet from beyond the horizon. Their plan had been to test the British ability to respond while claiming that they had been carrying out exercises in open waters. They fully expected to operate within sight of the British coast for several hours while the Royal Navy assembled a large enough force. Instead, the exercise was called off.

What jolted the British admiralty was Darren's chart. He had meticulously noted the position of any vessel that had contacted him as well as the time and it was then that the scale of the response became apparent. The British admiralty was startled that a boy could coordinate such a large operation without any vessel being in sight even if, in reality Darren had done little except ask for help and remain calm enough to transmit his position.

As Admiral Smythe said, "He did not issue a single order but he effectively commanded the entire Channel fleet because he was the only one who knew what was happening. Wireless is going to change the way that battles are fought."

With wireless so new, most naval officers still only saw it as an extension to other signalling methods but now it had proved its value. The new system meant that instead of ships kept in harbour waiting to respond to an alert, ships on patrol could be diverted. Years of planning were suddenly obsolete, on both sides of the channel.

For Darren, the hardest part was at school. After an adventure like that, how could he get excited over some game on a phone? If he used his phone then it was to learn more about signalling and navigation and his favourite app was the weather forecast.

~~~

When Danny reached the palace on the following Wednesday, King Charles was talking to the French ambassador. He waited until the king saw him and beckoned him over where, still a little self-conscious, he bowed.

"Allow me to introduce the French Ambassador, the Comte De Bras."

"Enchanté de faire votre connaissance, Votre Excellence."

"Vous parlez Francais?"

"Non. A little. I learn it at school and my family's had holidays in Provence but I hope you can speak English."

"My mother is English. It's easier to speak it than to have translators whispering in my ear."

Danny grinned.

"His Britannic Majesty seems to hold you and your friends at Barabourne in high esteem and Barabourne seems to be the key to your navy's success in detecting our ships. I am curious as to how boys your age can be so er, shall we say, significant."

"You need to speak to my brother about that, sir. I deal with another project."

"And you know how to speak cautiously. Forgive me, but Barabourne is something of a mystery and I hoped to learn more. His Grace the Duke, seems involved in so many projects. I'm surprised that one so young understands so much."

"I think that he understands people." Danny replied, "He can persuade a doctor to talk to a tramp to help produce new medicines."

"Yes, he encourages everyone to forget their station. Mon Roi, my King would never tolerate such behaviour."

"Behaviour that allows us to find your ships so easily."

"Touché. I'm also tasked with obtaining licences for electricity apparatus. I'm not sure that we'd just give it to the poor though."

"I don't know if Paris has a smog problem but we were told to reduce pollution and that means controlling coal burning. The poorer the people, the more crowded the homes to be heated are, so the more smoke there is."

"Interesting. I thank you, Your Majesty for your permission to speak with M. Lambert. It has been most instructive."

"I think that you've just nudged David's ideas across the Channel so well done." King Charles said, "Now I want you to meet Donald Bergman. What you call the whistle-blower and your idea worked. All of a sudden, the thefts were far more trivial than I had been led to believe. I'm now told that he used the materials to work from home. However, events have left Mr. Bergman a gibbering wreck in my presence. It's not all that uncommon with my subjects but time is pressing. Can you help?"

"Let me guess. Your staff will tell him how to bow and not to argue with you. How about that tennis lesson? Will it be okay if I'm not much of a courtier when I miss the ball?"

David was unaware of the furore that his friends were creating. None of them understood the King was preparing to take on the Civil Service on a scale that no-one had seen before but he was glad that Danny seemed happier now that he had his own project

Darren was thriving despite his problems at school so David still felt that he neglected Billy the most and was glad when Billy sought him out one day.

"They've got their new priest." Billy said, "Two for the price of one."

David looked suitably puzzled so Billy continued, "Who did Bran try to kill and who have we already saved twice? Who was Bran going to blame when she didn't get pregnant to order?

"Iain and Megan?" David asked.

"That ring is weirder than you know. Those other priests and priestesses do have something about them and it's stronger in the ring. Bran never had it but Iain and Megan do. The other thing is, people reckon that they talk sense and listen to them. I reckon my job's done over there."

Billy hesitated, "I said that I'd be a travelling servant for you but I like working with Mr. Wilson looking after your offices. I still can't believe all the stuff we do, so I want to ..." he trailed off, uncertain what he did want.

"Todd would say that you need time to get your head around it." David said.

Billy grinned as he nodded. "You don't mind?"

"No, of course I don't." David exclaimed, "When you're ready find yourself another project but make sure that it's right for you."

David had been brought up to believe that he was responsible for *his people*. Before his adventures, that responsibility did not go much beyond insisting that they did not embarrass the estate. Now he was far more concerned for their well-being and it had expanded to include those friends who had become involved in his activities.

He could not always do much. Danny, Darren and now Craig had problems at school keeping so much of what they did secret. Billy and Godfrey had stopped being employed but had some vague undefined status as did Todd. He included Miles and now Cuthbert on his 'responsible-for' list though they were guests. Jerry was becoming a dependent on the estate but his life was not there. It was with his family and for now, job prospects on his world.

However, David was satisfied that projects were in hand and *his people* were content so his thoughts were turning more and more to the quest. However, there was nothing he could do before he was given more information. Little was happening except that Mark had to drive a trailer down to the portal to collect Miles' flying machines.

As always, work faltered on Home Farm when a new marvel was about to be revealed so there was considerable disappointment when Mark appeared to unload beams and panels.

"Hangars." Miles explained, "Billy's friends are very generous; they're supplying me with everything. I should have asked first but I didn't expect buildings."

"There seems to be a lot of it." David said, "You can put it up beside the barn."

"There are four buildings. One each for the autogyros and the equipment and two spares. I mentioned your quest and apparently, they're their equivalent of tents. There are foundation pins you can use and then the buildings will resist a hurricane."

"Let's find Mark. On second thoughts, we'd better find Nobby and get his permission." David laughed.

Miles grinned, "He does take his work seriously, doesn't he?"

"He's the ideal foreman. He knows what's needed and gets on with it and expects everyone else to. He's got no imagination though and Godfrey deals with anything unexpected but since he's the manager, that's how it should be."

Neither David nor Miles were wearing ties when they found Nobby but he still straightened up and knuckled his forehead.

"We need to borrow Mark for a few days." David said.

"Yes Your Grace. Is there enough work for him to answer to you full time, Your Grace? I ask because there's a village lad, the family is struggling a bit and we could take him on. If he stayed in the loft and we fed him, together with his wages it would be a great help."

"And you'd have an extra hand on the mucking out." David smiled, "You don't allow passengers in the stable loft."

"With your approval, that is so, Your Grace. It's not the best of jobs so the quicker it's done, the better."

"Tell Godfrey, I approve. It's good thinking on your part. You can relax, you know."

"Thank you, Your Grace."

In one respect, David was relieved. Nobby would never be a contender for his inter-world activities.

By contrast, Mark greeted them with a cheery 'Hi' startling an older hand who was walking past. David grinned.

"Morning Thatcher." he said, "It's a fine day, is it not?"

The hand, pleased at being recognised, managed to reply, "Yes it is, Your Grace, but there could be rain this afternoon. Er, I don't rightly know if you're interested but I've heard from Sam. He's been made corporal."

"That's excellent news. Give him my congratulations and tell him that there'll be a couple of pints waiting for him in the pub. I'd join him but last time he was on leave, he just snapped to attention whenever he saw me."

Thatcher smiled, "You know the old army saying, *If it moves, salute it. If it doesn't move, paint it.* We're getting used to your ways but he's not here enough."

"At least he wouldn't moan about some hard work the way Mark's going to."

"At least I'm big enough to do some." Mark retorted, "Shouldn't you boys be at school?"

Even Thatcher managed a chuckle but gratefully continued on his way. Not so long ago, he would have been shocked at a hand speaking to their lord and master like that. Sam would still be shocked but Thatcher enjoyed the relaxed atmosphere even if he was still not comfortable enough to join in.

However, it was Miles who knew what was needed so David ended up as Mark's assistant.

"I'm not sure what carbon fibre is." Miles said, "I just know that it's strong and very light. The amazing thing is, it all slots together and you just lock the clips. It all stops being bendy and becomes rigid."

Miles was right, even the largest panels could easily be carried by Mark and David and the biggest problem was that they were so flexible. They had sloping roofs yet the side walls were over two metres high; seven foot on David's world. The floor space was approximately four metres by three metres yet both structures were built in less than hour.

"Right, all we do now is push the foundation pins through those eyes. You see how those spurs are sprung? When you push the pins in, the spurs are forced into the recesses. When you try to pull them out, the spurs spring out and dig into the soil. There's a hole for a locking bar on the top if you really want to pull them out. That's why the whole thing should withstand a hurricane."

There was more excitement as the autogyros arrived but David got a message that a Mr. Hardcastle wanted to see him. He was not clear on his feelings but somehow he sensed that his visitor was connected to his unfinished business but was he a threat sent by his mysterious enemy? Mr. Hardcastle turned out to be a middle-aged gentleman with a cheerful twinkle in his eye though at that moment though, David also detected intense sadness.

"I'm sorry to disturb you, Your Grace but it's about my son Gerald." As David looked puzzled, Mr. Hardcastle added, "I think you know him as Robin Cashman."

"Ah!" David exclaimed.

"May I explain. He stood trial for the murders of Ian Jarvis, another policeman and some reporter. The evidence was overwhelming and he pleaded guilty in the hopes of a lighter sentence but he was still sentenced to hang. I believe that there are a number of lesser charges, some of which involve you but there seemed little point in pursuing them. He's convicted of three murders, though two other charges were dropped through lack of evidence. He's in the condemned cell at Pentonville and contacted me for help. I know what he is but he's just a scared child now, wanting his father. He is my son so I'm duty-bound to help him."

"Yes, I see but there's nothing I can do. I understand your position but since the charges concerning me were dropped then I'm not even a witness."

"You're in the king's favour. Perhaps an appeal for clemency?"

"It would be considered interfering in affairs that don't concern me and would count against him."

"I see. You understand that I had to ask." Mr. Hardcastle said.

"Has a date for his execution been set?"

"The 15th of next month."

"You and your family are welcome to use the town house until then and I'll have a word with my Uncle Jethro." David said, "If I may be blunt, I'd rather put the effort into helping his victims and their families."

"Yes, Your Grace. I understand. I thank you for your time. To be equally blunt, I expected you to be far less welcoming, so I am grateful. Your offer of the town house is most generous."

"I can't imagine how you're feeling right now but I honestly don't think that I can save him. Is there anything else that I can help you with?"

"Yes, Your Grace. Under happier circumstances I'd be interested in your warehouse schemes that I've heard about. I'd like to know more about them. It's just that at the moment ..."

"Yes of course. You have more pressing matters. Write when you are ready and I'll see that someone looks after you."

David rang for Wilson and the meeting was over.

He was upset but with a range of conflicting emotions. The sense of unfinished business was considerably diminished. He remembered Robin's lost, scared look as he realised that there would be no help for him but David also felt relief that Robin would not ruin any more lives. The evidence against him for Ian Jarvis' murder alone was overwhelming. David had provided nothing that was usable in court so he was not responsible for Robin's death sentence but he was still involved. He was quiet for the rest of the day, but the following day he sought out Miles and told him of Mr. Hardcastle's visit.

"When I was at school, I'd have said 'Good riddance'." Miles said, "If he was one of Barabourne's crowd you'd fight tooth and nail to save him because you care so much about them but he's still manipulating people."

"How come?" David asked.

"How did his father know to come here?"

David nodded thoughtfully, "You're wrong about one thing. If Robin had been a Barabourne man, I still couldn't have done much more for him. I'm responsible for everyone, so imagine if I got him released and he killed someone else. I just don't like the idea that someone I know is going to die. I honestly don't think that I can do anything but should I try?"

"No, but you're going to feel bad if you don't try. How about delegating? Let me speak to Father and ask him to review the case."

"Why?" David asked, "Why do you care about him?"

"I don't. If you ask me they should have just strung him up and not wasted money on a trial. I do care about you though and you'll feel better if you're doing something."

"Thanks Miles." David replied, "I'm glad you're here."

"I'm glad you said that because Father is talking about me returning to school. The stone circle world have said that I can read aeronautics with them and they've promised to arrange a trip to their moon base." Miles paused, "I can't play the idiot any more and I don't want to be part of the in-crowd that thinks that the sun shines out of their arses. I don't want to go back to school, I want to stay here but Father isn't too happy."

"Couldn't you go as a day boy? It would only be a half hour flight in that autogiro of yours."

Miles' face lit up, "You wouldn't mind? What about secrecy and all that?"

"Call it a proof of concept machine. Explain that it ties in with work we're doing here and you got the idea from sycamore seeds. It's just a toy at the moment because it's so limited."

"It's pretty much the truth." Miles said, "They're amazing machines but the battery operated ones are limited in range and height compared to the hydrogen-converter-turbines."

"The what?"

"More technology and completely new to us. It's odd. Petroleum is a by-product from oil which the chemistry industry doesn't have much time for. Godfrey can get it cheap for his one car but demand is going to outstrip what the refineries can produce and the price will shoot up. I can use that example to explain my one and only autogyro."

"Good idea. Uncle Jethro deals with that side of our schemes so he'll help. You know, I think that we're ready for that quest now."

"Maybe not." Miles said looking unusually serious, "Father may be traditional enough to want me to have a proper education; his word and I think he means conventional because he's definitely on your side."

"Go on." David said.

"You don't have much to do with Lord Carlton but he's not been hibernating. Apparently he's one of Prince William's inner circle and according to father, the banks are turning to the prince for support against the king. Danny has made a good few enemies as some sort of adviser and Carlton would like you dead. A sizeable part of the court and a good few judges are going to lose money if the King blocks the Income Tax plan so there's a growing movement to make Lord Carlton your guardian."

Miles hesitated, "There's also a rumour that you're involved in sorcery. It explains your appearances and disappearances as well as your access to all your knowledge. Father's visited and says that the research labs should answer that part and youngsters do sneak off to find mischief. However, a judge nearing bankruptcy is likely to look for an escape route."

"I get the idea." David said, "Is your father trying to get you back to school to protect you?"

"Actually, he says that Barabourne is making me a son to be proud of. What school did you go to: Winchester, Harrow, Eton? No, I went to Barabourne village school. He worries that people will look down on that and he's probably right. Look, I've never denied that I'm still a snob and you still need the right schools and the right universities to get on. If I stay, then I'm committed and I'll make my way in aeronautics but that depends on me being welcome here for the next twenty years or more."

"It's a big step." David said, "I've committed Barabourne to scientific development for life so unless you become a mass murderer or something we'll need you. We helped Will Scarlet tell his tales, others have helped worlds as well as individuals and helping others is the price we pay for our own progress. You're welcome for as long as you can accept that."

"Definitely." Miles agreed, "I'd like to invite Father to show off the autogyro but could I take him to the Royal George? He's pretty sharp, he's impressed with electricity but he's concerned that too many ventures will prove to be impractical and drain your money. Before the warehouse projects, he complained about the down-and-outs demanding charity. After he visited Stable Row, he gave instructions to his factory managers that anyone living there not only gets a job but gets listed for training and apprenticeships. I don't think that he knew our boot-boy's name but he makes Billy welcome and he asked me whether he should send our boy to school."

"I don't see what you're getting at." David said.

"Dad's very conservative." Miles explained, "He would never have dealt with the lower classes if you hadn't involved him. He was shocked by what he learnt about his own class and he's open-minded enough to look at your methods. What you call domineering is what he calls not being half-hearted which is why Billy is always welcome but I'm not sure how it started. Equally, if he fully understood what goes on here, I'm sure that he'd support it. To him, the pompous bit is honour. He'd keep it confidential if he promised to do so and he also supports the King who supports you."

"What you're saying is that your father would make a powerful ally."

Miles nodded, "My brother wouldn't though."

"OK! I've avoided giving Sir Douglas the grand tour but if Lord Carlton is likely to cause problems then maybe he does need to understand. The problem is he doesn't understand a footman serving at dinner then settling down in the library to read when he's off-duty."

"Father's got an advantage over him. He discovered that one of his footmen worked in a wine shop and actually knows something about it."

"Billy's mentioned that. He reckons it's the butler who disapproves but he can't say anything."

Later, when David spoke to his uncle, Jethro replied, "I agree. Legal attacks will have to be dealt with in London. You need your own, fully briefed team up there and they should know what they are protecting. It's a pity that you can't ask the king to speak with them."

"No, *I* can't ask." David said, "Danny might, though. He's becoming more of a courtier than me."

That evening he managed to speak with Billy and Danny. Miles was also there as he explained then concluded, "Billy, could you handle them?"

"Yes but why me?"

"I'm hoping that you're ready for another project and you have a knack for fitting in anywhere. It always seems to come back to position on this world and you have none but on the stone circle world you're at the top."

Billy nodded but looked uncertain,"I get it. It's seeing people again and not rank but are you sure though? Being a traveller on the Divine Path is still a bit much to take in and it seemed more like a game. This is real life and I'm still the boot boy with no family."

"You nearly got killed in your game. Not even my mother thinks of you as a servant any more. You already get on with Lord Markham so I think he'll trust you and Sir Douglas will follow suit. I don't want to get all sentimental but you're the best in what Barabourne can achieve and I want others to see it."

"And I'm also one of the accusations that they'll have to respond to. Your cousin Jeremy should be getting jobs like this, shouldn't he. He's your class."

"That's what others will claim."

"What about me?" Danny asked. "You've taxed and insured Jerry's car and he lets Mark and Cuthbert practice. He's more useful than me."

"The king allows you to talk to him far more freely than anyone else around him. No-one will move against him but he is involved in all this. Your role is to keep him informed, unofficially but just so that no-one can spring an unfortunate surprise on him."

Danny nodded, "I know enough about the court to get what

you're saying. Quite a few would let him get into an awkward situation then *rescue* him – for a price. You're being upfront with him and he'll like that. Prince William is the biggest threat. He'll help his father out but expect a little bit of power to – in his own words – make sure it doesn't happen again."

David nodded, "I always assumed that I'd want you on my quest. Now I'm beginning to think that I'd like you to stay here and take charge or rather, help Uncle Jethro. He'll manage the day-to-day affairs but you'll understand our projects and the threats better. The trouble is, you'll think that I'm getting rid of you, won't you?"

"Part of me would but the other part would be relieved. I'm turning down offers to photograph other weddings but I can go anywhere I like as photographer to the Queen. Like you say, I'm interested in politics and talk with the king. I'm making a video to prove that I'm taking my day release from school seriously and I really would like to get into that so I've got plenty to do now."

"OK, how about Craig?"

"His parents have split up and his Dad is causing trouble. Craig stays with him during the week and hates it. When he's sober, he's just bad-tempered. When he's had a few, he just keeps going on about Craig's mother and trying to put Craig down. He wants full custody of Craig because having to travel from Hartbury is affecting his schoolwork."

"Is it?" David asked.

"If you ask me, it's his Dad. Others travel further without problems and it's only Friday evenings and Monday mornings. By the way, Craig's mother has hired Jerry to do some alterations and decorating. Apparently they swapped phone numbers at the wedding."

"That's good. I'm wondering whether the Creators still use Mr. Hemmings because if they do then they might be able to advise Craig."

"Good idea." Danny said, "I'll ask the portal or should you?"

"No, you." David replied, "When I first got back from your world, there was just a small group of us but it's all changed and grown. I'm just glad I don't keep a diary because I'd have to write a book a day and I'd still miss stuff out."

"I hear that Todd's got a girlfriend, a village girl." Danny said, "He keeps it quiet though, I gather he's worried about whether you'd approve."

"I'd heard that as well." David replied, "I've no problems with it except he's tying himself down to Barabourne. I should be pleased but he's got so many opportunities in two worlds."

"Don't worry. It's what he wants, to be part of something. He knows a hell of a lot about medicine. He came home with me the other weekend and a kid fell over and had a really deep nasty cut. Anyway, Todd's always got a first-aid kit with him and he treated it."

Danny paused as David waited, "Anyway, the Mother was upset that her precious child had been 'poked around' by a teen and took the kid to hospital. She came round later and apologised. According to the doctor, the wound was clean and sterile, and he wanted to know what antiseptic Todd had used. He could hardly say that it was one that he had helped develop from mouldy bread, could he?"

"Are you saying that Todd can only be himself here?"

"More or less. Anywhere else, he's just a kid who should leave it to his betters. And David, stop worrying about everyone, Barabourne's a good place."

"I didn't know that Todd went back to his world."

"He doesn't very often. Craig tries to make up for the way he treated Todd before, but others reckon he's still a loser because he doesn't know the latest stuff. He tends to wear suits instead of jeans which makes him weird and it doesn't make sense, how can you look like a well-off loser?"

"One of Todd's skills." David laughed, "And you're OK?"

"Oh for fuck's sake. Don't go on about it. We're fine except Darren may want to move here permanently."

"Why?"

"He had a maths test, and he finished early so he started fiddling with a problem of his own." Danny said, "It was something to do with air-speed and lift. Anyway, he'd finished his school test in half the time, was working on something at college level and the teacher accused him of using a phone to cheat. Apparently Darren had to answer extra questions to prove that he hadn't cheated but do you know what? He and the teacher spent the break sorting out his airship problem. He got away with it but he can't do it too many times."

"No, he can't." David agreed.

"Mum and Dad are worried that he's just a nuisance and getting in the way but he's really impressed your Admiralty."

David, nodded, "It was pushing things to promote Jimmy to lieutenant because of his age. Darren will only turn twelve next week yet he virtually commands the airship and understands radio. Darren has no authority yet the admiralty wants to send airships here to be fitted with radio, and him to teach them proper procedures"

"Oh Jimmy's sorted it. Do you remember Captain Povey at Dartmouth College."

David nodded so Danny continued, "He's arranged for a radio school to be opened at the college and it's available to all ranks. Darren's been watching war films at home and he's adapting those old Fighter Command centres. Coastguards and volunteer watchers are getting telegraph and Darren reckons all the data should go to a central command then back out to the relevant local centres. A lot of Admirals and whatsits don't like it; they don't understand that it happens in minutes rather than days."

As David nodded in approval, Danny continued, "Captain Povey really did hate the way that scholarship boys were held back and he can do something about it now. Remember the local lads that helped with the exercise for the king. He accepted some of them into the first intake. Some had already been practising so they had an advantage. It's all a rush, and the navy's introduced a formal rank of signals-midshipman. Anyone with the least bit of experience can be appointed and the best get promoted to lieutenant, pretty damn quick but Darren is still too young to qualify."

"OK." David said, "We're doing very nicely from the licences. Going back to that exercise, the army wants light-weight tractors equipped with radio for reconnaissance. Again we've got the licences for the design and they're looking at Godfrey's petrol engines as well. Uncle Jethro handles the business side and he seems happy enough so the only thing I have to worry about is Lord Carlton. And I'm not worried, just alert."

"Maybe Cuthbert could help." Danny said.

"No. He's too concerned about being used by Lord Carlton. He wouldn't like being used by us so don't put him in the middle."

Danny nodded.

"I'm going to talk to the portal." David said, "I need to know more about this quest. Then I'm going swimming. "

~~~

Quest is complex. The portal typed, *Creators have much to do. Plan involves subsidiary portal, and rocket fired through. Calculations and timing must be right. Craig must be given much information but rarely visits. Needs help. Lord Carlton is threat but not much progress yet. Has powerful friends though.*

"So we don't have to steal it then, as in carry it away." David said.

No. Impracticable. Missile weighs 60 tons. For comparison, Defender 2 tons. Suggestion, introduce metric system to your world. Missile, already in firing position, Craig's task, enter target coordinates, warn you of dangers. Maybe replace defective modules. As with Mark and Cuthbert learning to drive. We can supply knowledge, Craig can already implement more.

David nodded, "He knows what the buttons on a keyboard do. Danny prefers his phone and is less used to it."

As an example, yes. Another example, EMP, radiation, toxic fuel, are not just words to him. He will know when to run.

"That's comforting and it makes more sense to involve Craig."

Few survivors on chosen world. Submarine abandoned. Miles will be observer. Others adult strength. Subsidary portal unstable, must drive from here.

"Whoa! Why few survivors?"

Virus but of the computer kind. Launched during worst winter across Northern Hemisphere for many years. America, deep snow as far South as Florida, Europe and Russia record low temperatures. Transport badly disrupted. Virus attacked communications. Phones and computers died then services that depended on them. Heating, water failed. Population unsustainable. Breakdown became irreversible. What water was left, contaminated. Disease then biggest killer. Todd will explain inoculations.

"Yes. I do know about them." David exclaimed.

Biggest threat now, scavengers. Problem unresolved.

"I was going to ask about weapons." David said.

Would you take a militia force with you? How big would it need to be?

"No. Yes, I see. If we rely on force, then their forces could be even bigger."

Small groups of guerillas can erode more powerful force. Creators considering options.

David nodded thoughtfully then sought out Danny and Miles. The quest made more sense, was more feasible but the dangers were also clearer.

"Coming to your world is dangerous." Danny said, "Visiting the wrong parts of your London is dangerous, maybe mine is as well. Guys at school have had sports injuries, there're stories in the papers of kids being killed. Driving is dangerous. Mum worries all the time Dad's on the road. I reckon the safest way of doing it, would be to go by airship and around the coast. Three airships going, two full of supplies. Return in one but we'd need three adults."

David nodded, "You sound as if you're coming but don't forget the engine room crew."

"Yes, I had." Danny replied. "That's too many people, isn't it?"

"Miles, could those hydrogen-converter thingys be installed on an airship? Could they be electrically controlled from the forward gondola? Will you have a word with Billy, please? We're supposed to be in contact with all powerful gods. How much help could we ask for without raising questions?"

"Ah!" Miles replied, "The situation has changed. If the gods wish us to be children then so be it. I think that there is something about the gods dealing with supernatural enemies while we deal with the worldly ones. After Billy's adventures with Bran, they're impressed with how we deal with the worldly with a little help. I hope that's clear."

"How about, the gods trust us to get on with things without relying on them all the time?" David asked.

"God helps those who help themselves." Miles replied, "They're very spiritual. Cradawg would never have touched Billy if his spirit, soul if you like hadn't been ready. Billy reckons he was ready but nervous at first. I think that it was a bit like ancient Greece where a youth chose a mentor and he trusted Cradawg."

"How about you, over there?" Danny asked, "Any adventures of your own."

"They all know about what happened to me and they agree

that my soul is still unwilling. They warned me that I could be very confused and the confusion could include curiosity but I should wait for my soul. Look! I don't understand all this stuff so I probably do sound very confused but they live by it all and I'm trying to understand things they take for granted and never think about mentioning."

"It's cool." David said, "Still liaise with Billy and see what we can do with airships. If we can come up with a plan, I'll put it to the portal."

Chapter 11

Craig was beginning to hate his father who found fault in everything he did. The basic problem that Craig's father had; nothing was ever his fault. His wife had walked out on a perfectly good marriage and Craig was losing touch with the real world. His father's idea of the real world meant crushing underlings before they became a threat and getting noticed by the right people. By being less aggressive, Craig was sucking up to the wrong people which simply meant that Craig was making more friends. He was getting all nerdy and filling his head with rubbish at the library which meant not focussing on business studies. That Craig was steadily moving up in class did not fit in with his father's ideas, so it was a blip.

It all came to a head when Craig accompanied his father to a function. As usual, his father had not thought it through and assumed that the dutiful son would replace the dutiful wife. It was at an art gallery which his business had done work for.

Instead of waiting for his father's lead, Craig chose to stroll around the gallery looking at the work. He stood looking at a painting of modern art.

"Bloody Hell." he muttered, "A two-year old could do better."

Unfortunately, he was far louder than he intended.

"I suppose you prefer a biscuit tin with a nice twee picture of a cottage complete with roses around the door," a woman sneered.

"No." Craig replied, "Photos do a better job of that sort of thing. I like something that draws me in, has a message or brings out something only the artist has noticed. I just don't see anything in this."

"So you don't think that the bold strokes of red symbolise the frustration and anger of the modern world."

"Maybe it does but the artist would have to issue a code book if he wanted me to understand it." Craig replied.

The woman laughed delightedly, "An honest opinion at last. I'm Sonia Carlson, the artist and you see that guy coming across. I bet he either looks for the price tag or says that he prefers proper art."

The guy in question was Craig's father and Craig did not have a chance to reply.

"Hello Dad." Craig said, "This is Sonia Carlson, the artist. Mrs Carlson, my father."

"I'm sorry that Craig's been annoying you." Craig's father said, "He should stay close to me."

"Why?" Sonia asked, "Why do you assume that he's been annoying me?"

"Er, surely you have people that you need to speak to. It's an important night for you."

"My business manager invited most of the people here and most are more interested in tax breaks and investments which he can explain. I'll chat to the critics later. For now, Craig is a pleasant distraction so will you excuse us, please?"

Craig watched his father stomp angrily to the bar as Sonia said, "I'm sorry. I shouldn't have been so rude to him."

"You weren't rude but I'm more into science, I don't know much about art. This is art appreciation, isn't it? My art teacher is happy if I produce a few sketches but he does give me good marks."

"Let me guess, your Dad doesn't think it's proper schoolwork."

Craig laughed, "You've got it. I wish I hadn't moved back with him."

"Go on. Tell me about it."

"Mum and Dad split up and I wanted to stay with Mum. Dad said that the extra travelling was affecting my schoolwork and insisted I stay with him during the week. I'm not allowed out, I can't see my friends and I'm ungrateful because all I want to do at the weekend is get out. Mum and I only agreed because we didn't want the courts involved but I'm getting pissed off with it all."

Craig blushed, "Sorry, I shouldn't have said that."

"I asked. Oh you mean 'pissed'. Don't worry about that, I've heard worse. Have you put any of your sketches on your phone? I'd like to see them."

Craig nodded, pulling out his phone and finding the gallery. Shyly he handed it to her.

"They're good." she said after looking through a few images.

189

"It's a sort of under-stated steam punk, isn't it. I can't get on with the more extreme forms but these feel real."

Just then Craig's father joined them, "It's time to go, Craig. It's a school night and I need to see what sort of mess you've made of your homework."

"If his sketches are anything to go by, I doubt whether he's made a mess of anything." Sonia interjected, "If you wish to leave, I'll send Craig home in a taxi. I need to have a word with Mr. Munro before he leaves so please excuse us again. I'm sure that he'd like to meet Craig."

Mr. Munro owned the firm that Craig's father worked for. Mr. William's was high enough in management to be included in team building exercises which was why he and Craig were there. In their turn, as property managers who tolerated an erratic tenant whose rent was usually, nearly up-to-date but never quite making it, they rated invitations to opening nights and other events.

Mr. Williams left them without another word while Sonia sought out Mr. Munro and introduced Craig who was aware of his father glowering at them.

"An impressive turnout, Sonia." Mr. Munro smiled, "Does it mean we can expect some rent?"

"No, but we could discuss that commission more seriously." Sonia replied, "Craig here has an interesting idea for a theme. Will you show him your sketches please?"

Craig obliged but Mr. Munro looked puzzled, "Perhaps you'd better explain."

"Right, he's a little immature still but Craig does have an eye for detail. It's probably scientific observation and on its own, the stately home's a bit chocolate box but adding the airship and I can only assume a steam car turns it into something else. I'm not sure that it would work with your more modern buildings, maybe a futuristic setting. An alternative world theme, do you see?"

"You're suggesting that if there were parallel world's then Munro's would be thriving on all of them." Mr. Munro said, "I don't suppose you'd work with advertising for once, would you?"

"Maybe. I'm ready to explore new styles and this project could be a fun diversion while I experiment."

Mr. Munro swiped through the drawings again.

"I'm not sure about this one. It looks like a modern Stonehenge and I'm not happy about the nudes in it. I don't suppose you like the quaint little cottages do you, Sonia?"

"I do actually. Telephone poles and street lights set it in an interesting time of change."

Mr. Munro caught Mr. Williams eye and beckoned him over. Although Mr. Munro smiled, it seemed to Craig that there was a coldness that was lacking when he dealt with others.

"It seems that you're raising a budding artist." Mr. Munro said, "With your permission, I'd like to invite him to lunch on Saturday, that's assuming that I can persuade Sonia as well."

"I can't do weekends, sir." Craig said, "It's when I visit my mother and catch up with my friends."

"I see but you're at school during the week and I'd like to get Sonia started before she loses interest."

"I'm sure his mother would understand, Clive." Mr. Williams said, "We'd love to have lunch with you and Sonia."

"No." Craig said, "Last periods on Tuesday are art. I'll explain it all to Mr. Woods and I'm sure that he'll let me skip them. I'm not going to be that helpful though."

"Correct me if I'm wrong, Sonia, but Craig is to be your muse, to provide the inspiration to twist reality." As Sonia nodded, Mr. Munro continued, "I thought that we could visit likely buildings and throw around ideas."

"Could you message me the addresses, I'll get someone to drive me around over the weekend and you can buy me a burger and chips on Tuesday. My friend Danny is into video and photography and he may help."

"Burgers would suit Sonia's bohemian outlook on life as well." Mr. Munro laughed handing Craig his card, "Very well! My car will pick you and your friend from school and take you to my office. Let me know the time. Sonia will insist on walking. Let's see if we can save her a few months rent. Williams, your son is an impressive young man, you should be proud of him."

"Er, yes Clive." Craig's father stammered. Mr. Munro was astute enough to realise that Mr. Williams was furious. *Could he be as bad a father as he is a manager?* He wondered.

Mr. Williams contained his anger until they were nearly home.

"How could you be so rude to Mr. Munro?" he yelled, "How can you be that stupid?"

"I wasn't rude, Dad." Craig exclaimed, "It's Sonia's project. Danny and I will just produce some weird background pictures and that'll be it."

"That's another thing. Why on Earth did you mention that no-hoper? Use some sense, boy. You convince people like Clive that you're indispensable. Get him to dump that Sonia woman and take over."

"No. You use some sense, Dad." Craig yelled, "I'm not an artist and Sonia is a great one. I've given her an angle for a project and that's all. Danny and I will sketch a few background ideas and then I'll be done."

"Don't you yell at me, you little ..."

Craig's father had twisted round to slap Craig's head. He was drunk and pulled the steering wheel around as well. He saw what was happening just in time, pulled the wheel back to avoid the parked car and over corrected, swinging into the path of an oncoming car. Luckily the impact speed was low and the fronts of the cars absorbed the impacts as the airbags deployed. No-one was hurt but Craig was badly shaken.

His father, dulled by alcohol, was less affected.

"Now see what you made me do. When are you going to grow up?"

Doors were being pulled open and an anxious face peered at Craig.

"Are you hurt, son?" it asked.

Craig shook his head, he was recovering and the face turned into a kindly looking old man offering his hand.

"I'm OK! Thanks." Craig replied, "Lets see if I can manage."

On the other side of the car his father was struggling to close the door again so he could drive off. The occupants of the other car were also out of the car. Craig was taking in more of the scene and watched as the old man's wife beckoned everyone into the house and heard the sound of approaching sirens.

"Is that your Dad?" the old man asked and as Craig nodded, he continued, "I think that the police may keep him busy for a while, so is there someone I can call?"

"I could call Mum but I don't want her panicking. I'll call a friend."

He picked up his phone, aware that he could be overheard.

"Hello David. It's Craig. I've been in an accident. Can I come to your place please?"

"Thanks. I'll give it a bit then phone Mum. Could someone collect her?"

"Dad and I were arguing and he said the accident was my fault. It wasn't, he was trying to hit me but I don't want Mum driving tonight. Stupid, isn't it?"

Craig hung up, gratefully drinking the tea that was being passed around. His phone rang a few minutes later.

"It's Jerry. How about I come and collect you? I can take you straight to your Mum's."

"Thanks Jerry. I may be a while though. The paramedics want to look at me and I suppose the police will want to talk to me."

"No worrys, mate." What's the address?"

Craig handed the phone over to the old man, realising that he did not even know his name.

"Just call me, Joe," he replied when Craig asked. "Now is not a good time to take in a lot of introductions."

Craig smiled and sat back, quietly dozing. Once the paramedics were satisfied, and the police had questioned him, Jerry led him out to the car. Craig hesitated, staring between Jerry's car and the wreckage. He took a deep breath and got in.

~~~

The following morning, Craig slept until nearly midday and when he did wake up, the previous night was just a blur. He was decent so padded barefoot down to the kitchen where he found his mother with David, Jerry and Mary from the pub.

"Were you drinking at the pub last night, Jerry?" Craig asked sharply, "How come Mary's here?"

"I came with David because he needed directions." Mary said,

"I've got to go and open up."

"Thanks Mary. You too, Jerry. Dad was drunk last night and it just came out. Sorry."

"Don't worry about it." Mary said, "Just rest and get better."

As Mary took her leave, a police car drew up. Craig's mother brought two policemen through to the kitchen.

"This is just an informal chat but maybe your friends could leave us to it?" the senior policeman said before turning to David, "You're not Danny Lambert, are you?"

"No." David replied, "I'm David Pevensey. Come on Jerry, you can show me how to wire those sockets."

"No." Craig snapped, "They're my friends. I'd like them to stay."

"Very well. You said in your statement that you were returning from an art gallery, you were having an argument and your Dad swung around to hit you. He says that you were hysterical and disruptive during the event and he was worried that this Danny Lambert was supplying you with drugs. When he tried reasoning with you, you completely lost control and grabbed the wheel."

"But … But … That's not true." Craig stammered.

"Your Dad was well over the limit so he has been charged. However, we need to know what happened, there were no witnesses and the occupants of the other car couldn't see behind the headlights."

"Mum, I could say something but I could get Dad into trouble with his boss."

"Say it." his mother replied, angrily, "I could kill the son-of-a-bitch for implicating you like that."

"I was discussing an art project with Dad's boss, Mr. Munro, and Sonia Carlson. She's an artist. Dad thought that I was annoying them but I don't think he liked not being involved."

"Why does your Dad think that Danny deals in drugs.?"

"Danny's parents are foster parents. For other kids, I mean." Craig replied, "Mr. Lambert is a taxi driver and Dad doesn't think that they're good enough. You can test me for drugs if you like."

"Unfortunately, that would be against your civil rights. Don't worry, I've seen enough druggies and you're not showing any typical signs. We have to tie up lose ends and we'll speak to Mr. Munro and Ms Carlson but for now we'll leave you to it. I suggest that you and your mother stay well away from your father, especially in light of the threat she just made. Take out an injunction if you have to. Have the courts arranged custody?"

"No. We were trying to keep it friendly." Mrs Williams replied.

"We can only act on breaches of court orders." The policeman said, "Try to see a solicitor today, and get things moving as quickly as you can."

Back in the car, he said to his colleague, "I've heard about these boys. They're steam-car nuts. I reckon we're more likely to catch them joy-riding in a steam engine than doing drugs."

Back indoors, Craig was white-faced and trembling.

"If this was happening at Barabourne, I'd just give orders." David said, "They'd be on the lines that you should stay at the hall and Mark, Cuthbert and Jerry act as bodyguards whenever you come back to this world."

"I'm not going to be a prisoner." Craig exclaimed and his mother nodded.

"I felt the same way when the king ordered me to stay at Barabourne or use my hideaway as he called it." David said, "It's Thursday today. How about you stay at Barabourne until Sunday? Use the time to get organised."

"It makes sense." Jerry said, "I can knock out the power and really get on with the wiring, especially if Mark can help me."

David nodded, "Yes of course."

"Can we walk there?" Craig asked.

"It's not a good idea." His mother replied, "If you're nervous, could someone collect us in one of those steam-car things?"

"No problem." David said, "Once you're on the Barabourne side, Craig can drive it, himself."

Teenage moods can swing rapidly and Craig was definitely excited by the prospect, seeming more cheerful especially when Mark arrived in the steam brake. Jerry followed in his car to collect Mark once the rest were through the portal but it did not work out that way because it was Jerry's car that vanished. The rest waited, puzzled more than concerned until Mark reappeared.

"The portal wants to talk to Craig and David." he explained to Mrs Williams, "We're to take you and the luggage up to the hall then return."

David was not happy about Jerry's car being seen at Barabourne but on reflection, he decided that it was just an extension of Godfrey's work. Jerry called it an old heap but briefly it would be a grandiose 'proof of concept' machine. Mrs Williams was not happy either but since it was all normal to everyone else, she decided that it would upset Craig more to argue. Once the exchange had been made, Craig and David found themselves in a woodland glade, deserted except for a man that David recognised as social worker, John Hemmings.

"I brought you here once before." Mr. Hemmings said, "Last time I used John's body but my therapy has worked too well and now he can resist me. You're seeing a hologram. May we talk?"

Craig followed David's cautious nod.

"David, you're concerned that we're meddling and involved in Craig's accident."

David nodded again.

"Craig, your father was struggling to regain control of you. Every time you cooperated, it became harder to stand up to him. Sooner or later there would have been a crisis point where you either broke away or surrendered to him completely. We have tried influencing you to break away.

Craig nodded so John continued, "The crisis came last night and in the worst possible way. We would not create a situation where you could be killed or seriously injured. It might sound callous but it would not benefit anyone except our enemies. You have been injured in that you are now nervous of travel. Is that correct?"

"By car, yes." Craig replied.

"You have an eye for detail, good eye and hand coordination and could make excellent illustrations of scientific observations. Beyond that, you lack the imagination or inspiration to become an artist. However, your analytical skills make you an excellent critic.

"Sonia Carlson sees herself as a rebel, using art to express her contempt for the *capitalist fat-pigs* that rule the world. The usual phrase is fat-cat but fat-pig makes her an individualist. Do you understand?"

"Not completely." Craig said, "It's got nothing to do with her being a great artist."

"If she is a great artist and not a fraud." John, the hologram said, "Do you know the fable of the emperor's new clothes?"

"The emperor was conned into buying clothes that were invisible to idiots. The truth was, they did not exist." Craig replied.

"Consider her business manager who could have been one of the emperor's conmen."

"Surely she can't fool everyone like that?" Craig exclaimed.

"She doesn't. Top class galleries ignore her. She claims it's political but she is mediocre and only impresses mediocre art lovers."

"Like Mr Munro."

"Mr. Munro is a benefactor of art. He has a good eye but believes that he is just a business man. Despite his doubts about her, he lacks the confidence to openly defy the image of Sonia's talent."

"Excuse me." David said, "It's all very interesting but how does it affect me?"

"We, that is the creators, built a portal that can physically and mentally cross dimensions yet we were defeated. Have you never wondered how?"

"No, I suppose not." David replied, "I assumed that they tried invading through the portal."

"Let's say that you're thinking two dimensionally while they were thinking five. I'm not sure that I can explain more."

"OK, that doesn't help but how does this involve Craig?"

"There are cruder more dangerous ways of doing what the portal does. Ways that we would never consider. Let's say that an enemy which was willing to take appalling gambles took us by surprise by their stupidity. They are beginning to turn their attention to you and at this particular moment, Craig."

Both boys stared at the hologram.

"You're saying that they tried to kill me last night." Craig said.

"As I say they're stupid and that may have been their plan but deceit, scheming can also be done by idiots." John paused and smiled, "Explanations can be ruined by becoming too confused and I've introduced too many threads. Let me start again. This time though, consider how much effort it would take to influence the people involved to hurt you."

"It's scary but OK." Craig said.

"Your father wants to control you and pressured you into going to the exhibition. Sonia did not dismiss you as a child making a stupid comment. Instead, she took enough interest in you to realise that you were beginning to see through her facade. She couldn't risk that so decided to set you up for a fall. Between her inflating then crushing your ego, your Dad twisting your mind, by the time the quest began you would hate the universe. Imagine what you might do when you are in a submarine and in command of the computers."

"Whoa." Craig exclaimed, "They want to send me mad."

"In effect, yes. Influence is difficult to control. Your father was pushed too hard and resorted to physical assault, causing the accident. Feedback is just as unreliable so they're unaware of just how close you, Danny and David have become."

"I'll tell Sonia to fuck off." Craig said, "Sorry, I don't suppose you like language like that, do you."

"Don't be shocked, but she may have considered that word in its true meaning with you."

Craig grappled with what the hologram was suggesting before stammering, "You mean me and her … sex?"

"What better tool to crush the ego of a handsome young man than to get pleasure using him then abandoning him?"

Craig just stood, staring, before asking, "How do you handle it all, David?"

"By having a couple of breakdowns." David smiled, "Are you upset by their description of your artistic skills?"

"No. I liked the comments about observation and analysis. It's the idea that people want to hurt me, I don't like. I feel so helpless."

"We always tell David to find time to play but you may like a project to occupy you. You become manager to Danny and likely art students at school. You propose to Mr. Munro that he sponsors project encouraging young artists."

"Won't I get into trouble with Sonia?" Craig asked.

"I believe that you will be a capitalist lackey betraying the cause for money. Does it worry you?"

"No." Craig chuckled, "What do I do about Dad?"

"You must decide. Let your mother deal with the legal procedures then consider. Also consider project to help Mr. Munro spend his money more wisely. The damping field is closing in again. David present your ideas on using airships for your quest to the portal."

The hologram vanished leaving Craig and David alone.

"Can they all read minds?" Craig asked, "I get thoughts that I'd hate to share."

"I don't really understand it." David replied, "Split it into thoughts and ideas. Portal gets ideas because they spread across universes. Thoughts are your own and the portal can't read them. At least, that's the idea I got when I met Robin Hood."

"When you met who?"

"Actually it was William of Braborn. He introduced the tales of Robin Hood into this world. It all started in a glade like this one but I sort of remember it as hiding in the greenwood with Robin Hood. The portal thought that I needed to play."

"I wouldn't mind games like that but I'd like to go back now. I'd like everything to be normal for a while. Well, as normal as hiding on a parallel earth can be."

"I know what you mean." David laughed, "It's great being involved but it's scary too."

Craig was deep in thought as they left the glade and allowed David to guide him to the brake. It was not until they were seated that Craig realised that he was in the driver's seat.

"I've only driven it around the yard before. Are you sure?"

"Check the water level, then see that the coal feed isn't blocked and add a couple of shovelfuls yourself. That'll build the fire up and then you control the feed with your left foot. The rest is just the same."

"OK! Drain valve. Select forward. Brake. Whoops we're rolling backwards."

199

Craig reapplied the brake.

"It takes practice but let the pressure build up in the piston then slowly release the brake."

"The brake of the brake. Why can't they have different names?" Craig mumbled to himself, trying to ease the tension as he followed David's instructions, yelling in triumph as the brake rolled forwards.

"We don't have a Highway Code but we're supposed to drive on the left. Horses tend to pass that way but we shouldn't meet anything. Just slow down and stop if it's a horse."

For once, David had got it wrong. As they approached the first sharp bend, they heard an approaching car and Jerry's car careered into sight. As he took in the sight, David was worried to see Cuthbert driving. Two inexperienced drivers meeting head on, did not seem good.

Craig edged towards the side of the road, far too close to the ditch for David's liking, while he watched the car slide as Cuthbert braked too hard on the gravel. The car recovered and Cuthbert steered past the brake, coming to a stop as they passed. He lowered the window.

"Sorry about that." he said, "I can't get used to power-assisted brakes."

"No harm done." David said, then glanced at Craig who was white-faced and trembling.

David waved the other car on then sat, waiting for Craig.

"I saw us hitting the other car. I heard it, too." Craig whispered, "Did they try to kill us again?"

"No. Definitely not." David exclaimed, "You didn't drive us into the ditch and Cuthbert got back control. It's the first time that anyone's driven a car on this world. He wasn't used to driving on gravel, that's all."

Craig nodded, "I thought that I was a tough guy back home but I'm not, am I? I'm pretty useless when there's trouble."

"What did you do wrong?" David asked.

"How do you mean?"

"Last night, your Dad was driving. You were just sitting there. Who was pushing the argument, him or you? Who should have left the argument until you were home? Just now, who pulled us up beside the road? I'm still not sure who the enemy is but if they are involved, then they're trying to destroy your confidence. Are you going to let them?"

Craig got back a little colour as he sat quietly for a moment or two before shaking his head. Muttering the procedure to himself, he turned to the controls and soon they were bowling along the lanes with the wind in their faces. They did not head straight for the hall as David guided him around the lanes, watching him relax. They even drove though a village or two, and Craig confidently dealt with the traffic: pedestrians with no concept of giving way to motor vehicles and children who saw the road as their playground. Craig managed some cheery blasts on the whistle and even managed to release clouds of steam to the delight of the children and they were both cheerful when they reached the hall.

With most of his friends at school or working, David spent the rest of the day on his own assignments and going over estate business with his uncle. It was not until the evening that everyone began to gather in the library.

Wilson had long ago given up the idea that the library was a place for his masters to sit, contemplating the arts, philosophy and other intellectual matters. He conceded that it was still used for the pursuit of knowledge, but village children doing their homework and off-duty staff quietly reading did not fit the image.

Wilson had dismissed one footman who should have been working but claimed that David had given him permission. Two stable hands were barred because Wilson had caught them playing cards but on the whole, those that used it guarded their privilege. Wilson never saw a speck of dust on a table or a crumb on the floor; the indoor staff who used it took pride in *their* library.

When David used it to talk to his friends, Wilson was as adept at stepping with a tray in his hands over sprawled bodies as serving tea to the dowager duchess. He might breathe a sigh of relief when he returned to the sanity of his pantry but he agreed that the library was the right place to discuss the sort of problems that David dealt with.

That evening, Wilson happily served lemonade, teas and coffee to the assorted ranks assembled. It was enough that they would glance nervously at him if they thought that were misbehaving, David included.

However, that evening they were all too intrigued by the information David had about the quest. During all the recent events, it had been there, in the background but now it was coming to the fore.

"First of all, the portal thinks that everyone here could take part. Does anyone want to back out?"

No-one spoke until Mark said, "What about Prince Malcolm and Skeffington?"

"Wilson, I believe that you have something to contribute."

"Yes Your Grace. Although it is Billy's project, there are a number of adults involved. Billy believes that I can speak more authoritatively than him and I'm well-enough acquainted with the Royal George to host visits there. The plan is that I escort Lord Markham and Sir Douglas Mayhew there and generally introduce them to the less usual tasks and responsibilities that you have. His Royal Highness and Skeffington are both willing to help you in threats from Lord Carlton and the like."

"They don't want an adventure then." Danny chuckled.

"I would suggest that Prince Malcolm finds enough adventure exploring his father's capital incognito. Skeffington is finding a world away from brawls, fights and scrapes with the law."

"Sorry." Danny said, "I do know what you mean. Craig could have had enough adventure over the last two days."

"Very well. Billy, are you happy with things?" David asked.

"Yeah. I spend time in London. There are pubs and places where servants meet and I listen to the gossip and there's a lot about you. You're helping us teach the Frogs a lesson which is good. Electricity is good. You help the poor folk, also good, well good providing you don't push up lower class wages. You're breaking up society and undermining the established order. That's bad and it could wreck the good things you're doing. I'd say the consensus is that you're too young and someone needs to slow you down. That's when Lord Carlton's name comes up and most reckon he's a down-to-earth, no-nonsense sort of bloke. I'd say that a lot follow their master's opinions and Carlton's got a lot of support."

"So it's worth involving Lord Markham and Sir Douglas." David asked.

"Definitely especially now that Danny's stirring up so much shit."

"Explain."

"Everyone hates him because the king vetoed bailing out the banks again." Billy said, "It's odd but it's where servants and masters disagree the most and it's the servants that support the king. One other bit of gossip. Why haven't you helped Robin Cashman? Most reckon he should hang, because of the girls not because of the murders. A few try to put it about that it's because Cashman's got something on you and you want him out the way. That seems to come from Carlton's mates."

"Who's Robin Cashman?" Jerry asked.

"You heard, a murderer and someone who cheerfully raped and tortured young girls to entertain his bosses." Billy snapped, "David got the lot of them but don't push it. It was a nasty business."

"Enough." David snapped, "I can't help Robin and I'm not going to try. I'm not a variety act trying to make a name for myself so let's forget the gossip. Or rather, let my London team deal with it. Wilson, Billy, do you agree?"

Billy nodded as Wilson replied, "Yes Your Grace. We shall see that they're properly briefed."

"Carlton just doesn't go away." David said, "We'll have to deal with him at some stage but I wanted to talk about the quest tonight. Miles, any thoughts on using airships?"

"The stone circle world will help but there are boundaries." Miles said, "It's all based on what the gods would approve of. Billy is well favoured by the gods so it goes a long way if he approves. Apparently, he sorted their problems with a little help from this world so now they should repay the favour."

Miles paused, "That's a long-winded way of saying that they'll give us all the help we want. They would withdraw it if it was for our personal profit or something."

"OK. What do they offer?" David asked.

"They're not hot on airships and offered one of their big

transport aircraft but I turned it down. Assuming the portal could handle it, we'd have to build a runway at this end and hope that we could land at the other. We'd also need a trained flight crew."

"That's right." Billy interjected, "It wouldn't take much on a runway to block it."

"I also turned down helicopters." Miles continued, "I might be able to do a conversion course but it would mean others learning from scratch. They accept that the gods expect us to work within the limits they set; children who have to learn everything and asked to see our airship designs. They're not secret so I took plans across."

Miles paused, "You know, their technology really is impressive. They scanned the plans into a computer which turned them into a holographic model. So far as I can tell they've got it all spot on including the flight characteristics but I think that Jimmy and Darren should visit and check."

"That makes sense." David said, "I need a better idea of what or who is opposing us so I'll work on that. In the meantime, we're getting an idea of how dangerous this quest could be. You'd all better decide whether you want to commit yourself and I know that look Danny. I repeat, someone or something is willing to kill us to stop us. That's not what you expected so think about it."

The following morning, David visited the portal again repeating his conversations with the others.

Damping field fluctuates. Creators can weaken it further when it is at low levels but it takes energy. Energy drains Creator's resources. Next low level expected during school holidays. Airships must be ready in three weeks. Original plan, you drive, subsidiary portal provide defensive screen. High demand on resources and less certainty of success. Creators pleased that you ready in time to come up with plan.

"Why didn't the Creators think of airships?" David asked.

Lack of certainty. You may not have been ready, too few friends willing to crew. Travel to coast, find boat, also possibility. Final plans have to be yours.

"So you're not forcing us to do this." David asked.

No. Creators do not take your destiny.

"But their enemies will take it."

Yes but they are weak. Creators encourage strong minds. Enemies like weak minds to control. Cannot control yours or your friends'.

"How do I tell which is which?" David asked.

Cannot answer. Remember, starving man has weakness, craving for food. Easily persuaded to steal.

"How about Lord Carlton?" David asked, "Would you call him weak?"

You know answer. He has craving for power. Now is good time to distract you, divert you from quest.

David was thoughtful as he strolled back to the hall and was startled when Wilson intercepted him.

"Sir Douglas Mayhew is in the library, Your Grace. I believe the matter is urgent."

Once David and Sir Douglas had exchanged formalities, Sir Douglas looked pointedly at Wilson and asked if he could speak alone with David.

"Wilson is one of my advisors." David explained, "Uncle Jethro is visiting our other estates and I have a feeling that I'm going to need adult advice."

"That is very astute of you." Sir Douglas smiled, "Lord Carlton has requested an order removing Lord Westerham as your guardian. He cites bad financial management in that your capital is greatly reduced and that you indulge in witchcraft or sorcery which is sending you mad. In both cases, he relies on the extraordinary and impractical patents that you apply for."

"I don't suppose that the hearing is set for about three weeks time is it?" David asked.

"How on Earth did you know that?" Sir Douglas asked.

"School holidays and it ties in with one of my projects. Wilson, where's Billy?"

"I believe that he's on his way to London to visit Lord Markham. He's planning on asking him to visit and agree a time with Sir Douglas. I believe that Mr. Danny is keeping Mr. Craig company. May I suggest that he communicates with Lt. Worthington at Buckingham Palace, who in turn will send on a message to Lord Markham's?"

"You mean radio." David smiled, "See that a copy goes to Prince Malcolm. Sir Douglas, I know that you will find this most irregular but would you allow Wilson to take you to lunch. Wilson, ask Mark to drive you. It's too early to eat, Sir Douglas but you may find a morning understanding the source of our knowledge useful."

Sir Douglas looked at David with a mixture of anger and puzzlement. In his world servants did not eat with guests and he wondered why he was being insulted but he looked on startled as Wilson took a flat box from his pocket, poked it then held it to his ear.

"Hello Mark. I require the brake to be at the front entrance as soon as possible. We are going to the Royal George. Sir Douglas and I will be wearing ties."

Puzzlement now dominated as David said, "One of our more impractical and extraordinary projects. I didn't know you had one, Wilson."

"Your friends convinced me of the wisdom of having one, David."

Sir Douglas looked startled again.

"My apologies, Sir Douglas but the purpose of our luncheon is to demonstrate to you that the work done at Barabourne is based on solid foundations." Wilson said, "Trouble with Lord Carlton is not entirely unexpected and David has other projects that may be affected and they will need dealing with. He may wish to inform the airship team."

David nodded, "I was going to do that because of other information I got this morning."

"Very well. I'll radio the message to Billy then change. Will fifteen minutes be convenient, Sir Douglas?"

Sir Douglas was impressed. Wilson obviously had more extensive duties than a butler usually had and was certainly one of His Grace's confidantes but still something bothered him.

Once they were alone, Sir Douglas asked David, "Should he be calling you by your first name?"

"If I'm not wearing a tie then everyone forgets that I'm the duke. He was cautious when you first arrived but since you're going to learn Barabourne's secrets then he's being a mentor and not a butler."

"Ah yes. Lord Carlton did mention that the servants were running wild."

"Uncle Jethro knows that I plan to tell you and Lord Markham about Barabourne's secrets. Do you know of Wilson's private cellar?"

"Yes I do."

"You're about to discover his source so will you go along with our plans for now?"

Sir Douglas smiled, "Providing he can provide a case of that 13 year old Scotch he produced at the wedding."

Once he was alone, David sought out Danny and Craig. He found them in his office, quietly reading though Danny kept glancing at the radio. They listened carefully as David brought them up to date.

"How come you're so calm?" Craig asked.

"I'm not really." David replied, "Danny will tell you, there's been times when I've just about had enough but this time, I'm not going to be raped or killed. I was kind of expecting it and I've got my own plans ready and there's something else, I was born to be duke; I have duties and obligations because of it and somehow, it helps. The portal is giving me new duties and I have accepted them. Nothing in your life has prepared you for any of this; even Danny has had time to get used to it all, so are you still willing to help?"

"I'll be the wimp if I don't."

"Definitely not, no." Danny exclaimed, "You've got bad stuff to deal with. You can't do everything and no-one expects you to."

Craig smiled, "Thanks, Danny. I'll do what I can."

The conversation might have gone on but Danny recognised a call sign and leapt to the radio. Morse code had been clicking away in the background as traffic, mainly naval operators used the frequency that they used. It was the equivalent of his name being called across a noisy room. Danny instinctively reacted to the call sign, replied, wrote down the message then referred to a small leather book as he wrote some more, looking increasingly surprised. Finally he read it out to the others.

"The King has sent for Lord Markham and Billy and they are

flying to Barabourne. Officially, the King is watching a demonstration of radio but he wishes to arrive incognito and visit the Royal George so as few people as possible know of his visit."

"Like I said, Craig, my problems are not life or death but dealing with royal visits does add to my stress. Danny, this Morse code, I take it every ship in the navy received the message."

"No. It's the next stage of development, making communications secure. It's the first time I've needed the code book though."

"Don't tell me, Darren has watched films on your world and using the ideas in them."

"No, Todd did. You have typewriters over here but he found an old electric one on our world. He's also found a lot of stuff about teleprinters and codes. Oh and he now wants to be a signals-midshipman if he can specialise in cryptography."

David laughed, "I wonder what he'll want to be tomorrow. I'd better get this trip organised. Listen out for any messages will you and bring them to me. I'm going to see what Cuthbert's up to."

Chapter 12

Jerry was driving the steam bus with Cuthbert acting as fireman. Cuthbert looked embarrassed when he saw David and David knew why. Gentlemen do not act as firemen and they could both imagine the fuss if anyone on Cuthbert's side of the family caught him.

When he saw David, Jerry gave a cheery toot on the whistle as he brought the bus to a stop.

"Have you left the yard yet?" David asked.

"I've taken it down the drive to the lane but that's all. I was wondering though. Could I use some of your vehicles on my world? You know, hire them out for weddings and the like."

"It's a thought. We'll talk about it but not now, we're having visitors today." Feeling like a parrot repeating the same thing over again, he brought the others up-to-date before concluding, "You know as much as I do now. I'll understand if anyone wants to back out but I need a couple of chauffeurs to drive His Majesty to the Royal George. Mark's already over there, driving Sir Douglas and Wilson. Jerry, this is a tie event and I know that you don't like me being the duke."

"I get it now and I'm not backing out either." Jerry replied, "You need me to be a good little serf, knuckling my forehead and saying Yes, Your Grace; No, Your Grace; May I lick your arse, Your Grace."

David laughed, "That's Nobby's style and he still ends up doing it his way. The original plan was to tell Sir Douglas and Lord Markham what was going on here but it's all moving faster than I expected. Having the king visit like this can only mean more trouble and I'd still like to give Sir Douglas and Lord Markham time and space to adapt."

"It makes sense except that today's Saturday and the Royal George will be packed, at least until three. What time do they get here?"

"Let's see, I was back from the portal at about nine, and Danny sent the message at nine thirty. I'd say that they could be here after midday, probably after one."

"Right! I'll phone Mary and see if I can book a table." Jerry said, "I bet you forgot that you're not a duke over there. Then I'll go and fetch my car and park it by the portal."

Jerry paused, "No! Why don't you use the bus. Let's be a group of steam nuts over there. It'll explain who you are. Who's going to drive it though?"

Everyone looked at Jerry.

"What me? No way. I've only started driving it today."

"No, but it's a good idea." David said, "Nobody will expect the King to be collected by a bus. Telephones. You take them for granted. Phone Mark. Arrange for him to bring Wilson back at the same time and we'll swap drivers at the portal. Godfrey can come as far as the portal and drive Wilson, the rest of the way."

"OK!" Jerry replied, "Or should it be, Yes, Your Grace."

"Don't make a big deal of it until we figure how the King wants to handle things."

King Charles VII was actually excited at the prospect of travelling in the bus that was waiting for the airship to land. David was more concerned because it had arrived just after eleven o'clock, far earlier than he expected.

"Such a sociable way to travel. I haven't been on one since I was your age, David." he said, "Let's have your friends on board."

Once they were all seated, the King said, "Now I learned of these legal proceedings yesterday, probably before Sir Douglas Mayhew. Young Danny keeps me informed so I knew of your plans and I took the liberty of arranging this trip. That's how come Malcolm and Skeffington are also here. I've arranged for Billy to be met at Victoria and put on the first train back."

He paused before continuing, "I've convinced Lord Markham, that it is in order to sit beside me, he struggles to make do with a simple 'sir' but is learning. I do know that it would not do for Sir Douglas to bow in the Royal George so this omnibus may be a better idea than you thought. We'll use it as a travelling palace. Now I believe you use phones to communicate. Can we arrange to meet Sir Douglas at the portal, please?"

Godfrey drove the bus and Jerry followed in a brake. At the King's insistence Mark and Wilson got on the bus as well as Sir

Douglas.

"Very well. I understand that David cannot discharge all of his responsibilities without help and you are all part of the team that supports him. I think that stopped by the portal on our side is secure enough though perhaps we could arrange something if the need arrives."

David nodded, "Yes sir."

"Good. Prince William is behind these legal proceedings and it's part of his plot to take power."

The king paused, pleased at the shocked surprise that his announcement created.

"He has the support of the City, the top financiers, mine owners and a sizeable part of the Lords so if it came to open conflict between us, he could bring the country to an economic standstill. I have the support of the Commons and their supporters, the army and navy with exceptions. From his point of view, the Duke of Barabourne is just a boy, with little influence and has been in enough trouble to scare allies off."

David grinned and the King continued, "From my point of view, he is instrumental in making the French more cautious of us which the armed services like. He has the support of the Commons which has been filling with radicals and reformers for years and now Prince Malcolm is also their darling for being so involved in the changes that are already happening. There are also enough in the Lords who see the Great Decline even if they were unwilling to act on their fears.

"Now Lord Carlton was involved in Sir Cloudsley's activities. Young Robin Cashman knew of him but not much else. However, that particular unpleasantness is more far-reaching than anyone realised and my investigators are overwhelmed. More so, as they turned their attention to William. However, Lord Carlton was involved enough to be tainted by his associations and much of society is closed to him. He should be bankrupt but someone is bailing him out."

The King paused again, "Now if Lord Carlton gains control of Barabourne then the balance of power will shift to Prince William's favour. The warehouse housing schemes will close, control of electricity will pass to the city. Anyone with radical ideas will be

211

liable to arrest. Now would anyone like to comment so far."

"Would a lot of waverers realign with Prince William?" Jerry asked, "You know, rats deserting a sinking ship."

"Probably. I did not speak very kindly about David earlier but many do see how his ideas are working. Those at the wedding were impressed that different classes could mingle so well. Barabourne's greatest strength is that it gets on with things without fuss. People see that and see how their own estates could prosper."

"So you see Barabourne as an example of what can be done." Jerry said then hesitated, "I'm not from your world, should I call you Your Majesty or something?"

"The occasional 'sir' will do. I travelled incognito to avoid a fuss but I fear that it's not working. Please continue."

"It's OK and I get the idea. David is important because he tells your allies what can be done. He knows what's solid ground and what's quicksand."

"I like the analogy and it's one reason why I wish to visit the Royal George. Stuck in London, I'm forgetting what the solid ground looks like."

"OK but hang on. How about David's take on all this." Jerry glanced around, seeing the startled and disapproving looks, "I know, I'm forgetting my place."

"Yes you are." King Charles smiled, "I suggest you never come to court but what's on your mind? Despite my teasing, David still tries to be a good courtier so it may difficult for him to speak up in front of so many."

"OK, I take it that you know about his quest. One of his mates had an accident but maybe it wasn't and the court date clashes with the quest and maybe it's not a coincidence."

"I see. Two maybes. Are you suggesting that Prince William is in league with some greater force who can arrange these things? David, what do you say."

"I don't know, sir. I was hesitating about mentioning anything because it is against court etiquette to speak against the Prince without evidence. On the other hand, someone could be persuading him to take power but only if it's what he wants to do anyway."

"Tell me about this accident and what you else you have learned."

David complied and then waited as the king considered it all.

Finally he said, "So both this mystery force and Prince William profit by your removal. If you defeat this force, Prince William loses an ally. Would you agree?"

David nodded thoughtfully, "Yes I do. I was only thinking about wild gossip at court, sir."

Looking at your two other visitors, they seem completely baffled. I suggest lunch and then a visit to the Chasebourne on that world. Ah! Jerry, your frown suggests yet another problem."

"I only managed to book a table for four, er, sir. Er, you're not the king over there, er, I'm worried about er, etiquette again."

"Lord Markham, Sir Douglas Mayhew, Wilson and myself shall eat lunch there. Could the rest manage as best they can?"

King Charles glanced around the group, mostly liking what he saw. The previous evening, Lord Markham believed that today would be as calm as any other. Summonses to the King, unexpected airship flights and discovering all sorts of plots had jolted him but he was adapting even if he did not understand references to other worlds. Sir Douglas Mayhew, had visited the Royal George so he was beginning to accept the reality of them but clandestine meetings with his sovereign and again, learning of plots and rebellion was way beyond his usual remit. Both men glanced at Wilson who sat back, unperturbed and looking as if it was all part of his usual routine.

It probably is at Barabourne, the king thought to himself, and then smiled to himself as he thought of one of Danny's expressions. *That takes care of the oldies.*

Cuthbert and Mark had been shocked as they learned of Prince William's involvement but otherwise seemed at ease with the rest.

Jerry intrigued the King. He was not of this world and on the surface, thoroughly disrespectful of his betters. However, every so often, he glanced at David for support and again, his questions were very much to the point. His remark earlier that his incognito was not working had been because none of the others seemed ready to offer a comment, not even Malcolm or Skeffington.

David was also quiet, but he was just absorbing the extent of his enemies. It was enough to jolt anyone let alone a young teen. To the King's surprise, it was Wilson who spoke first.

"With respect sir, David and Lord Markham should find

Miles. He, Lt. Clark and Darren are working on a related project, and it will introduce Lord Markham to the portal as effectively as visiting the Royal George. He may also be interested in Billy's role over there.

"I can easily visit another day so that reduces the Royal George party to five. Sir Douglas and I called in for morning coffee and then I was considering ordering us a taxi for a brief visit to Chasebourne or finding some way of explaining the electrical features of the place before luncheon. However, I suggest that Sir Douglas has already taken in more information than is good for him.

"If Sir Douglas, Prince Malcolm and Skeffington make up the Royal George party. On second thoughts, Jerry knows the other world and so could guide Lord Markham instead. Mark could drive the rest of us home because David should speak to his friends at the hall."

With Wilson organising the day, it became considerably less chaotic than it might have been. With the smaller group, Sir Douglas relaxed more. Malcolm and Skeffington knew to speak freely and gradually Sir Douglas joined in, asking about the marvels of electricity.

Lord Markham's arrival on the stone circle caused shock and consternation but mainly because they were dressed. Jerry had briefed Lord Markham and they hurried to the exit then stood, waiting for a local to speak to them. Lord Markham was highly embarrassed, trying to avoid looking at so much naked flesh and it was Kendal who approached them, waiting respectfully.

"Hi Kendal. Do you spend all your time here?"

"As much as I can." Kendal replied, "It's a good place to study."

"This trip is urgent otherwise we would not have been so disrespectful to your Gods. This is Miles' father and we need to find Miles."

"Bear with me. I'll go and explain then take you to the airfield. Is it urgent enough to send for a taxi and bring it so close to the ring?"

"We'll start walking and it can find us along the path away from here."

"That would be better." Kendal said bowing his head, "I'll see to it, Divine Travellers."

As they walked, Lord Markham looked back then around at the open countryside.

"You're saying that this is a different world."

Jerry nodded, "Yes sir."

"And Miles is here?"

"Yes sir." Jerry said again.

"Working on a flying project?"

"Yes sir."

"Dammit, call me Bernard. I assume I'm not a Lord here."

"No, and not on my world, either. Billy is some sort of high priest and when he speaks, their whole world listens."

"You're just making it worse. You're saying that Billy has become a pagan priest."

"No. They respect that he's a Christian but some funny things have happened."

"Funnier than walking through to another world?"

"How about funnier than a flying taxi?" He pointed to an approaching helicopter, "I think it's coming this way."

Bernard watched it land, staring in shocked disbelief. He hesitated when Jerry tried to guide him on board.

"It's OK. Miles is learning to fly and loves it." Jerry shouted above the noise.

That remark startled Bernard more than anything else had and he climbed aboard without any more hesitation. The flight to the airfield was short and Lord Markham was beginning to enjoy himself, almost regretting it when they landed. Almost! He breathed a sigh of relief when he was back on solid ground only to see Miles waiting for them.

"Hello Father." Miles said, "I didn't expect you to visit. Billy certainly arranged your trip in a rush."

"Hello Miles." Lord Markham replied, "There's some sort of emergency that I don't fully understand and I came down with His Majesty. Do I understand correctly? He's taking lunch at some place called the Royal George and introducing Sir Douglas Mayhew to Barabourne's secrets while Jerry has brought me here."

"Emergency?" Miles asked, "What emergency?"

"My dear boy, how on Earth would I know? Well I do know a bit about the legal proceedings, but malevolent powers, saving worlds? Please don't ask me to explain."

"I'm not used to hobnobbing with kings and lords so I'm not too clear what's going on either." Jerry said, "The airship project is more urgent and Bern, er, Lord Markham needed briefing. Can we leave it at that for now?"

Miles nodded, "Yes of course. You're on first name terms?"

"While he's in shock, yes."

While Miles grinned at Jerry's reply, Jimmy Clark approached them, "Your slot on the simulator's coming up. Ready?"

"Yes of course. Father, do you want to see me make an ass of myself?"

It was not the technology that surprised Lord Markham as much as his son's involvement and obvious abilities. There was no doubt that he was on a different world, holograms turning an ordinary looking room into the flight deck of a futuristic airship was amazing. Watching Miles take control and deal with a simulated emergency, calmly and without fuss was a revelation. He understood that a propeller snapping off and ripping through a gasbag would be catastrophic but Miles taking over from the computer and balancing the remaining engines against gas and ballast releases, to land the airship was impressive.

Neither did Lord Markham understand much of Miles' conversation with his instructor afterwards. Miles listened attentively, made his own points and the instructor often nodded in agreement.

Miles gasped a sigh of relief as he joined his father.

"I'm glad I didn't kill you, even in a simulation. It would have been so embarrassing." he chuckled.

Lord Markham also laughed, glad for something familiar; the old Miles' humour as Miles added. "Not crashing airships gives me an appetite, shall we eat though I'm afraid they don't have the Savoy over here but the food is good."

They found a table by a window and sat, watching the activity on the airfield.

"I wasn't expecting you today." Miles said, "I know that David wants to brief you because you've agreed to help us deal with Lord Carlton."

"Lord Carlton has started legal proceedings at the behest of Prince William. There's more and the King wished to inform the Duke. Most of your friends have also been informed but it's all something of a rush. I'm surprised that so many people are involved."

"It's difficult to take in what David is doing until you meet everyone involved. You've met Jimmy and Darren. Together we make up the flying team. Prince Malcolm and Skeffington are working on social reform, you and Sir Douglas are taking on Lord Carlton, David has some sort of quest which involves Craig and Danny. Mark, Cuthbert and Jerry are organising road transport. Then there's Wilson and I've never met anyone like him. He's just a servant but he makes me nervous if I misbehave but whatever is going on, I bet the duchess's afternoon tea guests never have any idea."

"Tell me about this world and what Billy gets up to."

Miles complied and Lord Markham listened, enthralled.

"Billy's not given a hint of all this." Lord Markham said, "I'm surprised that His Grace allows his relationship with Cradawg, though."

"It's the only world where it can happen but you know Billy, do you think that Cradawg could just use him?"

"What about you, Miles?" Lord Markham asked, "This is why you don't want to go back to school. Is it just the flying?"

"Kendal has offered, but Cradawg doesn't think that I'm over that court business yet. When I am, it'll be one of his daughters and she is ravishing or one of the girls who visit the stone circle to attract boys and ... "

Lord Markham put up his hand, "Enough. So this place does have other attractions. I understand. Now while we're alone, what about your brother? I'm afraid that I saw you as a fop and was glad that he would succeed me because he understands his station in life. He sings Prince William's praises enough and civil wars tend to split families. I'm also aware that His Grace does not have a high opinion of us. If we're to be kept on the sidelines, maybe we should stay neutral."

"Father, we're on a different world. How many even know that they exist. Surely that says something about our standing."

"I suppose so and you have no doubts."

"No." Miles replied firmly, "David didn't think about us until he needed our help, and then his true thoughts surfaced."

"I see. It makes sense which brings us back to a rift with your brother."

"I keep saying that all I'm doing is finding new fashions to follow. From what you've said, we're just following the new royal one."

Lord Markham grinned, before relaxing completely and bursting into a deep laugh that pushed up from his diaphragm.

"Very well. You and I commit to the King and His Grace. If relations with your brother become too strained, I shall insist that he moves to our country estate. I can see that there's no question of you returning to school and you have my blessing to stay at Barabourne. In case I didn't make myself clear, it's you who I'm proud of. Christian is a good son but he doesn't always make good choices."

By late afternoon, Lord Markham was completely at home on another world with one exception, returning home through the stone circle. However, he had watched Miles fly an autogyro around the airfield, watched a news account of his arrival at the circle on a holographic news display and marvelled at the variety of uses for electricity.

Discovering about electricity and fully understanding the implications of TV broadcasting was too big a step. Spotting the reporter who had commentated on his arrival he strode angrily over.

"Young Man, when I woke up this morning, travelling to other worlds, being a traveller on a divine path was the stuff of foolish romance. Visiting a holy place, in my case church, meant dressing respectfully to show the importance of the event. I thank this world for what it is doing for my son, I have no objections to him following your customs but please do not ask me to change the habits of a lifetime in less than a day."

"Divine traveller ..." the commentator began but Lord Markham cut him off.

"If anything, I am a baffled or an accidental traveller. The powers that let me travel may well be divine but I am not. When you speak on that incredible machine of yours again, please convey my deep gratitude for turning my son into an impressive young man. I have no wish to offend or insult your religious beliefs but I now wish to return home without embarrassing myself or going against my beliefs."

"I was trying to say that we are on air." the commentator said, "You are speaking to the world."

"Oh! So I have embarrassed myself." Uncertain what to say Lord Markham stood waiting for a response. Cradawg hurried over.

"You did honour to the circle by letting people see what was in your heart." he said, "We are also learning about parallel worlds. We never questioned the divine path before and assumed that it led directly to the gods. We should have realised that their domain would be bigger than we imagined. Make your journey today and please, feel free to return whenever you wish. Like you, I am set in my ways so I will not dress for your beliefs and we will agree to differ."

Lord Markham held out his hand and Cradawg clasped it.

"Billy has taught me this custom and I like it." Cradawg said.

As he approached the entrance to the circle, Lord Markham removed his trilby and held it to his heart, then walked, head bowed to the portal.

That evening, it was Darren who raised the subject of Lord Markham's departure.

"You're a hero." he said, "Until you spoke, no-one realised how lost you were. They saw you make an effort as you crossed the circle and they liked your thanks for looking after Miles. By the time I left there was a debate starting on how to handle divine travellers."

Everyone had gathered in the library including Billy who had returned from London though the king had left.

"Bran and his predecessors had been trying grab all the power." Billy said, "Now he's dead they have to work out what the gods truly want. They're pleased that the gods have revealed more of the universe to them and they have to learn how to use their new knowledge wisely. Oh yes, they reckon that Bran was defying the gods by trying to keep it hidden. I'd leave it at that."

"And it's quite enough." Sir Douglas said, "It seems quite trivial now but if I may refer to the case against His Grace. Licences for electrical products are returning an increasing income. Providing His Grace can show that he is not making himself destitute or harming his estates then there is no problem.

"Failing to control staff is harder to disprove. I am sure that there are plenty of witness statements citing examples. However, the stable hands are developing carriages and farm vehicles that also raise income for the estate and many who oppose you are installing the central heating systems also developed by them. It is His Grace's right to encourage initiative amongst his people even if it is at the expense of proper decorum.

"Under normal circumstances, I would find their arguments extremely weak and a judge may even find them vexatious; that is, a ploy to harass or inconvenience you rather than a genuine grievance. However you have suggested that there may be considerable bias against you.

"With what I have learnt today, it is the witchcraft and sorcery allegations that I find most worrying. From your point of view, the obvious defence is the least desirable; revealing the existence of the portal.

"I could request further and better particulars of the case especially specific cases of His Grace's mental instability. So far, there is only one real incident mentioned. You have a cousin, Jeremy Darrow. He claims that you took him to a public house and he was subsequently unable to find it. The suggestion is, you used witchcraft to confuse him. Would I be right in thinking that he's referring to the Royal George?"

David nodded, "I was trying to confuse him. I didn't explain anything."

"I know the young man in question and would doubt that under normal circumstances that he would make a very reliable witness."

Sir Douglas hesitated, "I would suggest that the case is indeed vexatious but a judge would need to be cautious. He may well order a more detailed investigation or something that would give the plaintiffs a toehold in your affairs and you would find that most undesirable."

"Indeed we would." Jethro said, "What do you suggest?"

"Bringing the case forward if possible. Cite the developments that are being made here. Indicate that it would impede the defence of the realm to divulge work being done for the Navy and further indicate that a degree of obfuscation in your affairs is necessary to disguise your work."

"What is ofer … overscation?" Darren asked.

"Obfuscation? Confusing the issue, making it unclear, confused or unintelligible; apparently, as I did when I used the word.

Darren grinned and nodded as Sir Douglas continued, "It is Lord Westerham who is the respondent and I await his instructions.

It means that it is unlikely that he would be called as a witness. However His Grace could well be called, if only to ensure that he remains in London. If you agree to my stratagem, then I shall petition the King to bring the case forward."

As David nodded, he glanced around the room. Whatever other doubts he had, he had chosen good friends. An idea was forming but he would have to discuss it with the portal but later that evening, he sought out Danny and Skeffington.

"I need Danny to go to London and photograph the poverty there but he'll need protection." David said, "Oh and try to be followed, let slip something about it being for the court case."

Both Danny and Skeffington looked puzzled but nodded.

"What about me?" Prince Malcolm asked.

"I can't involve the royal family in my affairs." David replied, "However, if someone were to prepare a report on our efforts in improving matters ..."

Prince Malcolm grinned, "And you want me to be just as indiscreet?"

"Yes please." David smiled, "Nothing may come of it but if you could get started in case I need it, I'd be grateful.

"I understand Danny needs protection. We'll just make the last train tonight, he can see what he can do tomorrow and I'll see that he's back in time for school on Monday. How's that?"

"Thank you, Sir. It would be most useful."

~~~

David managed to have his conversation with the portal before church the next day so as soon as he could, he spoke with his Uncle Jethro and Sir Douglas.

"Sir Douglas," David began, "Forget about bringing the case forwards and the further details. Do you know of an incompetent private investigator who could investigate Lord Carlton for us?"

"You said incompetent." Sir Douglas said, "You mean competent."

"No, I mean useless, bad at his job and easily bribed. I also need the best and most discreet detective you can find to investigate Jeremy. Oh and we need an aggressive barrister."

"Perhaps, you'd better explain."

"It's quite simple. The Creators want to tackle their enemies. Lord Carlton needs to be stopped once and for all, and they're expecting me to be torn between the two attacks. I want them to think that I'm concentrating on the court and intend going in with all guns blazing."

"Yes I see. You understand the situation better than me so I must defer to your judgement but such a plan could allow the hearings to drag on for longer."

David nearly said that he was counting on it but refrained just in time.

Next he spoke to Todd.

"How are electric torches doing?" he asked.

"Not bad. We've extended battery life to forty-five minutes so we're getting there."

"Good, I'll need some for the court case. Could you work with our patent people, I need a patent for some obscure and trivial detail that's not really worth bothering with."

Todd responded with a puzzled OK but David was happy. It was part of his upbringing to learn about large scale planning so that he could run his estates. The portal was training him further and he had a real adventure to look forward to. He chuckled as he thought about Jerry. He was still expected to seek work on his world but would being an airship pilot help all that much?

Chapter 13

As the three weeks passed, Prince William was well-pleased with David's decision to fight the case. Doubts niggled him that it was a mistake to challenge his father but the idea dominated that the country was being ruined by the King's softness and his reliance on anarchists and trouble-makers. Destroy them and the King would be alone.

Control of Barabourne would allow electricity to be exploited by the right people and Barabourne's disrespect for *God's Order* could be crushed.

Did they not realise that they were being watched? The report on Lord Carlton would disappoint them. A patent for a hook for a flash-light, whatever that was. What a waste of time when Barabourne should be preparing for the case. Pandering to the masses in the East-End. There were enough witness statements to show that it was Prince Malcolm who was fostering rebellion and not himself. Prince William smiled, the hearing would show that.

Wireless would be worth investigating but funny little clicks from a box did not warrant dispensing with years of naval strategy. More importantly, it would no longer be used to turn any low class riff-raff into officers. Only officers of the best breeding would be in charge. That was the correct order of society.

~~~

David stayed with Danny's family. The rumours suggested that he was in a sanatorium. As school holidays began, his friends began to assemble ready for the tasks in hand and David could gather them together. Sir Douglas was also present, uncomfortable in the presence of so many low-class teens but he tried fit in as David outlined his plans.

"The airships are ready and enough of you are qualified to fly them. Jimmy is organising everything, no-one seems to mind so he will take command officially. We'll call his airship, the flagship and Jerry will crew. Mark and Darren will fly the second ship while Cuthbert and Miles will make up the third."

"What about you, me and Craig?" Danny asked.

"Craig will travel in the flagship." David said, "We're not going. We'll be waiting for the summons in London."

There was a stunned silence before Craig exclaimed, "You've got to go. It all depends on you."

"No it doesn't. It's what the portal has been teaching me. I can't do it all so I choose the people who can help. Think about it. Mark, Jerry and Cuthbert will provide the muscle that I'm too young to give, Craig will deal with the computers which I know nothing about. Jimmy, Miles and Darren will navigate which they have trained to do. I'd just be extra weight."

"I've been doing what I can by throwing up a smokescreen. I haven't mentioned everything that I've done but it should be enough to convince them that I'm panicking, ready to go into court to fling all sorts of wild counter accusations."

"Is that why Robin Cashman's execution was delayed." Sir Douglas asked.

"According to the rumours that Billy spread, he's got something on Lord Carlton."

"I wondered why the King agreed to the petition." Sir Douglas said.

"When it's over, perhaps you could argue that it was cruel and inhuman to use him like that. He'll serve life but it's still a better option and it's all I can do for his family."

Sir Douglas nodded, "I've heard comments in town that you're almost hysterical with the strain and on the point of folding completely. Billy again?"

"No. Friends who happen to say the wrong things in the wrong pubs in front of the wrong people or is it, the right things in the right pubs in front of the right people? Either way, it's reached the people we intended it for and it may be better if you didn't pry further. It would be your professional ethics that would fold under the strain."

Sir Douglas smiled, "Indeed they might. Just to be clear. You have been preparing your friends to be ready to undertake the quest alone, and I assume, you are preparing to fight the case in a different manner. I await new instructions from Lord Westerham."

"You intended calling me as a witness. Will you remove me from the list at the last minute."

"It's most irregular. May I ask why?"

"They'll sense blood and call me instead; hopefully, first."

"The courts are not fond of games." Sir Douglas said, "I agree that you have unique problems but our barrister will not be able to help you. It will be theirs that can speak with you."

"I know. Neither will ours be in trouble if I play some games in court."

"True. Just don't end up in contempt."

"No, but I've got to protect the portal. The witchcraft allegations are the most serious and I need to admit that they're true. I'm sorry. I have to do this alone. The more I rehearse, the phonier I'll sound. For now, I'd like to speak to Danny."

Once they were alone, David said, "If all goes well, I will be going with the others. Remember, the case is vexatious, the opposition is a bit too eager and hopefully not too bright so they tend to believe their own lies."

"OK!" Danny said cautiously, "They think that you're on a wild scheme to destroy Lord Carlton but they know about it and plan to stop you."

"OK, you have to remember that the opposition is being pushed by this dark force. It doesn't care who wins the case, it cares about keeping me away from the quest. I don't suppose that anyone really believes that I've had a breakdown but like Craig's father, the force is overdoing the pressure. It may understand Carlton's lust for power, but maybe it doesn't realise that I've defeated him twice before and he wants revenge. I don't know. If a fraction of the gossip that Billy and the others are spreading was true then the judge could doubt Uncle Jethro's competency."

Danny nodded as David continued, "According to the portal, the force would not understand me not controlling everything. It only understands obedience and authority so it sees me under pressure to defend myself in court and running the quest at the same time. Our goal is to let the hearing collapse in a day and the portal has been coaching me."

"I get it. They call you first, put pressure on you and you collapse. The judge rules that you are not getting enough support from Uncle Jethro and appoints someone else as your guardian. Whatever dirt you've dredged up doesn't get heard but just in case, you've got bad information... Oh yes, your best witness is a murderer escaping the noose by testifying. In reality, they've only got Jeremy and our lawyers are ready for him."

David grinned, "The portal doesn't lie but somehow, it

reminded folk at the wedding of the moments that I've had."

"The wedding? How long have you been planning all this?"

"All the portal talks about is *possibilities*. It may have picked up on schemes but I'm not sure."

"So what are you planning?" Danny asked.

"Nothing. The portal mentioned the possibilities and I'll be ready for them, but apart from that nothing."

Danny frowned, "You're a kid and they're experts and adults."

"Normally I prefer people to forget that I'm the Duke of Barabourne."

"OK but it sounds risky to me."

"I could lose everything and so could the Creators and the King. I am the duke and it is my duty to fight when necessary."

"Sorry, Your Grace. I didn't mean to offend you."

"You didn't but does it sound so risky?"

Danny grinned and shook his head.

Although it centred around control of David, the actual case was against Jethro and his guardianship so all the paperwork was directed to him. David was just a witness, in theory with no control of the case. As he sat, waiting to be called, events really were completely out of his control and he was nervous but he breathed a sigh of relief when he was first to be called. Danny watched impressed because David had looked liked a frightened child close to tears. It had been so convincing that Danny was becoming concerned. As he stood so he became the Duke of Barabourne, a nervous teen still, but confident and ready.

He took the stand, took the oath and waited for the preliminaries to be completed then Lord Carlton's barrister stood up to begin questioning.

"Please do not worry. You are not on trial, David."

"Excuse me," David interrupted. "This is a formal hearing and I am wearing a tie. I would prefer to be addressed properly, as 'Your Grace'.

"I'm unaware of the expression 'wearing a tie' in this context," the Judge said, "Please explain."

"My apologies, My Lord." David replied, "A slip of the tongue. At Barabourne if I'm not wearing a tie, anyone may speak to me as an equal. I'm still learning about our estates and the other projects we have, and I find my people can tell me when I'm wrong more easily."

"I see and you see this hearing as worthy of a tie with the proper respect due to it," the judge said.

"Yes, My Lord." David replied.

"Very well. Mr. Gardiner?"

The barrister stood up again, "I also offer my apologies. My instructions said that you disliked formality. Since I understand that you are unwell, I was trying to put you at ease. How would you say that your health affects you?"

"I'm not unwell."

"I see. My instructions are that you are, shall we say, highly strung. Is there anything you need to help you through this ordeal?"

"It's not an ordeal so far. I've had to deal with some difficult problems over the last year which drained me at the time but I am perfectly fit and healthy now so please, can we get on?"

"I share that sentiment, Mr. Gardiner," the Judge interjected.

"Yes My Lord. My instructions are that His Grace's mind has been damaged by indulging in black arts. May I explore that possibility?"

"I see no evidence that His Grace's mind has been damaged," the Judge retorted. "However please proceed."

"I'm obliged, My Lord. Your Grace, you seem to have acquired a great deal of scientific knowledge. Could you explain its source."

"My Lord, I can explain but the explanation would be clearer if I could demonstrate. A friend of mine is waiting outside with information on patents but now seems like a good time to use it."

"I see no problem, what do you require?"

"Could the usher go and get the torches from Danny Lambert who's waiting outside the court?"

"Torches?" the Judge queried and David nodded.

All anyone saw was three silver tubes in the usher's hand when he returned. David took them, putting two down beside him, holding the other up.

David pushed the switch, and a gasp followed the beam as it shone around the court. He breathed a sigh of relief that the first one worked and he did not need either back-up.

"My people tend to call our latest innovations magic and I must admit, I do enjoy playing the magician. This torch is no

227

exception but once I've explained, it'll seem quite ordinary."

David switched the torch off and dismantled it, before holding up the bulb and reflector.

"Electric bulbs were originally developed by my stable manager for carriages. They now provide lighting in many homes, make roads safer at night and small versions like these offer other opportunities."

He picked up the battery.

"This cell supplies electricity. My knowledge is not that great because I have no idea how it works but I have a research team that does. I do understand how the switch works and we have patents for the different components. I wonder if we take out too many patents on the smaller details but it is all new territory so I insist on caution. There are fewer projects and less knowledge than you might imagine but different elements can be used in a variety of ways."

"It's an interesting toy." Mr. Gardiner said, "You mention research which must be expensive but who would want such a thing?"

"You must speak to Uncle Jethro about that." David replied.

"Uncle Jethro?" The Judge asked.

"My guardian, Lord Westerham."

"Very well. I assume that we are still examining your state of mind. Perhaps you would attempt to answer, Your Grace." The Judge said.

"Mine owners have expressed an interest, My Lord." David replied, "It gives off very little heat and it can be sealed completely so it can be used underwater. Once sealed, there's no spark to ignite gas. It could replace oil lamps and candles in almost any situation. Every home could have one stored away in a drawer ready for an emergency."

"So it's far more than a toy."

"Not at the moment, My Lord." David replied, "The life of a cell is measured in minutes. We aim to be able measure it in hours before long and then we expect to see considerable demand."

"Thank you, Your Grace" the Judge said. "Mr. Gardiner, I apologise for interrupting your examination but I was intrigued by the device. Do you have any more concerns about His Grace's health or can we move on?"

"Your Grace, do you practice witchcraft?"

228

"No, I most certainly do not. All the work we do is based on research and development."

"Then how does electricity work? What is it?"

David smiled, "I don't know and I'm not sure that anyone does. I know that lightning is natural uncontrolled electricity and that tall buildings are protected by copper conductors. Oh and copper conductors are a feature of the torch. Do you wish to see?"

"That won't be necessary but you seem to have a mystical faith in an unknown force. Are you sure that you don't summon it up from some dark source?"

"Has everyone here been taught not to stand under a tree in a thunderstorm? Electricity passes through copper very easily." David picked up the bulb, "Like a tree this bulb resists the flow and the resistance generates heat and light. It's not magic, it's learning about a natural force. We show the plans to engineers and artisans so that they can reproduce our work. Meanwhile, we're learning more about electricity every day."

"Mr. Gardiner." The judge said, "Much as I find the subject of electricity fascinating and would like to hear more, I'm afraid that we need to move on. Do you intend to introduce any medical evidence to support your concerns over His Graces health?"

"If I may have a few moments, My Lord."

David did not think that Mr. Gardiner was too happy as he wrote a note and passed it back to his instructing solicitor. When he rose again, he said, "My Lord, I have one more question for His Grace. I have a witness that claims you took him to a public house and it subsequently disappeared. The suggestion is that you confused his mind in some way to hide your secrets. Would you deny that you used witchcraft?"

"I believe that you're referring to cousin Jeremy. The village pub in Braborn was the first to be fitted with electric light, visitors come from all over to see them and it now supplies meals to cater for them. Jeremy and I went riding and we ended up having a pub lunch. I don't wish to speak unkindly of Cousin Jeremy but there's a saying, 'as sober as a judge' and I'm not sure that he's very judicial."

"You're accusing him of being a drunk."

As Jethro's barrister rose, the judge said, "Yes I know what you are going to say. Mr. Gardiner. He is your witness and you are not cross-examining His Grace yet you are encouraging him to undermine another of your witnesses. I have yet to hear you produce any solid evidence and you have had your chance to examine His Grace's state of mind. Again, can we move on?"

"My Lord, I request an adjournment."

"I think that is an excellent idea. I trust you will have time to build a more substantial case if we rise until 2.30. Your Grace, you are still giving evidence so please do not communicate with your uncle or his legal representatives."

David hurried out to find Danny.

"How's it going?" Danny asked.

"The adjournment's a good sign, I think." David replied, glancing around, "There's a better sign. Take a look down the corridor."

Danny looked and saw Lord Carlton and his solicitor arguing with Mr. Gardiner.

"What going on?" Danny asked.

"The barrister realises that his instructions are wrong. He expected a seriously disturbed boy but got the Duke of Barabourne. We're coming back to a vexatious case and reputable lawyers won't get involved in one."

"What about the Judge?"

"The King can't interfere except, this particular Judge has got some secrets. Now, imagine if the King tried to swing the case in my favour, there'd be hell to pay. However, if the judge was warned that he would be investigated if he was not scrupulously fair and beyond reproach then who could complain?"

Danny grinned then frowned, "Watch it. Enemy in sight."

Mr. Gardiner the barrister was approaching them.

"Your Grace, may I offer you lunch? I wish to speak to you alone." Mr. Gardiner looked pointedly at Danny as he spoke.

"Should I be speaking to you?" David asked.

Mr. Gardiner grinned, "You are our star witness and it should be with our solicitor in attendance but perhaps we can stretch a point."

"We have nearly four hours and I feel like being the Duke today." David said, "Mr. Lambert is a close friend and confidante. Allow me to offer you lunch instead."

"Lambert? The young man who speaks to the king?" Mr. Gardiner asked, "I accept."

They hailed a cab to be taken to the Palace of Westminster. As they alighted, David hesitated but spotted a policeman, strode over to him, presenting his card then beckoned the others over.

"It's the first time that I've eaten in the Peers' Dining Room," David explained. "I don't even know the way. Shall we go?"

Although Danny was getting used to life on David's world, this was something special. He had visited the Parliament buildings on his own world on a school trip and was surprised that it was so similar in design. However, statues and paintings were of a different great and famous; people and names that Danny did not recognise. What he remembered most was the policeman leading them past *No Admittance To The Public* signs until he found himself in a plush restaurant.

The portraits decorating the wall reminded him that he was in the heart of government but then it occurred to him that it was not. The King played a much bigger part on this world but Danny was not interested in politics just then, just experiencing a thrill as he settled in the leather back chair embossed with the portcullis motif.

"I have been badly briefed and I regret taking the case," Mr. Gardiner said once they were alone. "I believe that you are playing games as well so perhaps you would explain."

"Would you normally be a junior for a silk?" David asked then glancing at Danny added, "A KC, King's Counsel."

Mr. Gardiner nodded.

"So it was an opportunity that you couldn't turn down, even if you had misgivings." David said, "Were you told that the instructing solicitor was highly experienced and could guide you?"

"More or less." Mr. Gardiner replied, "As I understood it, my clients fully expected the case to go to the Lords of Appeal no matter what the outcome today and then of course both sides would need a KC."

"The present hearing is to establish my lack of abilities but why did they settle on a junior?"

"I've only been at the bar for a short time so I suppose that I accepted Mr. Smith's notion that you were mentally unstable more easily than I should have done."

"Mr. Smith?"

"The solicitor." Mr. Gardiner replied.

"Why did you say that I was playing games?" David asked.

"Lord Westerham's solicitor should have requested an adjournment while he got details of the evidence we planned to offer. Instead, you undermined my case by using that torch to mention and dismiss our allegations almost as asides. However, once the court saw how calm and confident you were, the case was over. Did you really forget that you weren't at Barabourne when you mentioned your tie?"

David grinned, "Not entirely. We are engaged on secret work for the Admiralty and that is for you alone. It must not be mentioned in open court. Supposing that someone is using Lord Carlton to slow our work and allow another power to catch up?"

"It's tenuous but it explains presenting such a weak case. My instructions were to show that you are mentally unstable and being used by Prince Malcolm. He is using your popularity with the masses to foment rebellion."

"And I would say that it is Prince William using Lord Carlton."

"And I am caught in the middle. I wish I knew what side the King is on."

"I'm the Mr. Lambert who speaks to him." Danny said quietly, "Do you suppose that's a clue?"

Mr. Gardiner looked at him and laughed, "Yes I suppose it is."

"Going back to the ties," David said, "I have been preparing for this case for some time, I've been coached and I have to protect the secret work we do. Let's say, agents fed Lord Carlton information that he passed on, to set you up."

"I see. What about a disappearing pub? You weren't being completely honest. What really happened?"

"Are you sure that you want to call Jeremy as a witness? If you do, I suggest you call him early morning before he's drunk too much."

Mr. Gardiner nodded slowly, "You're evading the question but I agree he would make a bad witness though he might not be as bad as Lord Westerham's witness, Robin Cashman."

"We're not calling him. We're relying on showing the case to be vexatious. Both sides want to establish my mental condition and proceed from there. Unfortunately for you, your side believed what they wanted to believe. Our side fed false information."

They finished lunch in silence before returning to the court where they took their places though briefly Danny and David were alone.

"On my world, a silk would be a Queen's Counsel, wouldn't he?" Danny asked and David nodded.

When Mr. Gardiner was invited to resume his questioning he stood and began, "My Lord, I wish to withdraw. Although I do not have to give a reason, I have to say that my instructions were not only wrong but malicious. I accordingly feel obliged to apologise for wasting the court's time."

"Thank you, Mr. Gardiner." the Judge said, "I was coming to the same conclusions. I mean you no disrespect but this court is best served by a king's counsel and you lack the necessary experience. However, in fairness to the plaintiffs, I shall adjourn sine-die but strongly urge that they find evidence to substantiate their claims before it is listed again and I further suggest they take advice from a KC."

David hurried over to his uncle who was talking to Sir Douglas and their barrister, Sir Algernon Verlan KC.

After being introduced, the KC looked disdainfully at David and said, "You get into far too many scrapes and the time will come when the grown-ups can't help you."

With that, he left and although startled, David glanced around and beckoned Mr. Gardiner over but Sir Douglas held up his hand for him to wait.

"Very quickly, Your Grace. Sir Algernon likes an ordered life which you are disrupting. He is also as straight as a die." With that he beckoned Mr. Gardiner.

"Yes, Your Grace?"

"Sorry to drag you over but do you find the law as corrupt as it was a year ago?"

"I could not possibly suggest that my colleagues at the bar or those on the bench were corrupt but if I suspected any corruption a year ago, Your Grace, then I would probably be less suspicious, today."

"Would Lord Carlton have noticed any change, do you think?"

"I would think that he would find change difficult to accept."

"Sir Douglas, should I ever need another barrister then I think that I would prefer Mr. Gardiner and if necessary, I'd follow his recommendation for a silk. I wouldn't normally question your choices, but I think Mr. Gardiner found my affairs easier to deal with than Mr. Verlan. One last thing; I think I know what sine die means but will someone confirm that it's just an adjournment."

"It's an adjournment until a time to be decided." Sir Douglas explained, "Given the judge's other remarks, I doubt that it will be relisted unless they can produce a far stronger case against you. It is not done to speak against a judge but I'm surprised that he was so impartial, possibly even favouring you. If I did speak against him, then I'd suggest that adjourning sine-die was the only way of keeping the case open which helps the plaintiffs who I would expect him to support."

They might have said more but Danny joined them and to David's surprise, he had Miles in tow.

"You're right." Miles said, "We are managing without you and the airships are ready to fly but we need to be airborne before dark. I've got an autogyro, fitted with floats sitting on the Thames and I've got my hours in. Are you joining us on your quest or are you planning a career in law?"

David glanced at Jethro who shrugged.

"Let's go." David exclaimed, almost running for the door.

With Thanks

I would like to thank James Apps for his help in editing. After spending so much time writing it, it becomes a case of not seeing the wood for the trees. James spots the trees that need pruning.

A number of people help me when I'm writing though they don't realise it. Chatting in the pub, sometimes on Facebook or at the Sheppey Writers' Group I gain insights on topics that I touch upon. I can't name everyone so in fairness I won't name anyone but I am grateful.

I also use images from the Internet. So far as possible I try to ascertain that they are public domain and copyright free but it is not always possible to track the artist. I do appreciate your efforts and would like to acknowledge you but all I can say is, where the hell are you?

Peter Apps

Peter Apps lives in England, and The Long Way Round was his first novel to be followed by Time Askew and Deja Vu To The Nth.

He was born in 1948 and has lived in Sheerness, Kent for most of his life. The Isle of Sheppey where Sheerness is situated has a long, rich history has always fascinated Peter. History might seem a far cry from Science Fiction but imagining life in a Roman settlement is imagining a world just as alien as a distant planet.

Although he worked in a series of routine jobs, he likes to do his own thing when he can. For example, all his computers are Microsoft free zones and prefers to use Linux. He has always had an interest in science, especially Astronomy. Now that planets have been discovered around other suns, he feels that the time is coming when we could discover intelligent life out there.

Other interests include classical music and jazz. He also likes to settle down in the evening watching a good film and enjoying a nice glass of bitter or occasionally visit his local for a chat over a friendly drink.

The author is just a click away by email, peter@sjtales.uk.

Science Fiction
By
Peter Apps

The Stuart Johnson Chronicles

The Long Way Round
Time Askew
Deja Vu To The Nth
Earth Against Earth
Across The Continuum Sea

Worlds Beyond

The Growing Universe
Consolidation

Other Science Fiction

Disastrous Science (Short Stories)
Meanwhile In Time (Novel, late 2018)

~~~

Non Science Fiction

Contributions to
Quirky Humans And Others
Flash Fiction
(Anthologies by the
Sheppey Writers Group)